Ch...

THE CASE OF THE PLATINUM BLONDE

CHRISTOPHER BUSH was born Charlie Christmas Bush in Norfolk in 1885. His father was a farm labourer and his mother a milliner. In the early years of his childhood he lived with his aunt and uncle in London before returning to Norfolk aged seven, later winning a scholarship to Thetford Grammar School.

As an adult, Bush worked as a schoolmaster for 27 years, pausing only to fight in World War One, until retiring aged 46 in 1931 to be a full-time novelist. His first novel featuring the eccentric Ludovic Travers was published in 1926, and was followed by 62 additional Travers mysteries. These are all to be republished by Dean Street Press.

Christopher Bush fought again in World War Two, and was elected a member of the prestigious Detection Club. He died in 1973.

CHRISTOPHER BUSH

THE CASE OF THE PLATINUM BLONDE

With an introduction
by Curtis Evans

DEAN STREET PRESS

INTRODUCTION

WINDING DOWN THE WAR AND TAKING A NEW TURN

CHRISTOPHER BUSH'S LUDOVIC TRAVERS MYSTERIES, 1943 TO 1946

HAVING SENT his series sleuth Ludovic "Ludo" Travers, in the third and fourth years of the Second World War, around England to meet murder at a variety of newly-created army installations—a prisoner-of-war camp (*The Case of the Murdered Major*, 1941), a guard base (*The Case of the Kidnapped Colonel*, 1942) and an instructor school (*The Case of the Fighting Soldier*, 1942)--Christopher Bush finally released Travers from military engagements in *The Case of the Magic Mirror* (1943), a unique retrospective affair which takes place before the outbreak of the Second World War. In the remaining four Travers wartime mysteries--*The Case of the Running Mouse* (1944), *The Case of the Platinum Blonde* (1944), *The Case of the Corporal's Leave* (1945) and *The Case of the Missing Men* (1946)--Bush frees his sleuth to investigate private criminal problems. Although the war is mentioned in these novels, it plays far less of a role in events, doubtlessly giving contemporary readers a sense that the world conflagration which at one point had threatened to consume the British Empire was winding down for good. Yet even without the "novelty" of the war as a major plot element, these Christopher Bush mysteries offer readers some of the most intriguing conundrums in the Ludo Travers detection canon.

The Case of the Platinum Blonde (1944)

"I suppose you haven't heard our local sensation?" I said.

"No," she said, and, "I didn't know there could be a sensation in Cleavesham. What was it? An air raid?"

"Only a murder," I told her.

--The Case of the Platinum Blonde (1944)

AFTER HAVING HAD his series detective, Ludovic "Ludo" Travers, become involved in a couple of investigations concerning highly nefarious activities in wartime London, *The Case of the Magic Mirror* (1943) and *The Case of the Running Mouse* (1944), Christopher Bush in *The Case of the Platinum Blonde* sends Travers vainly for a break to the lovely and seemingly placid little village of Cleavesham, Sussex. There Ludo learns that there is something of the truth in Sherlock Holmes's famous declaration (in the short story "The Adventure of the Copper Beeches") that "the lowest and vilest alleys in London do not present a more dreadful record of sin than does the smiling and beautiful countryside."

Travers has come to Cleavesham to rest and to visit his charming younger sister, Helen Thornley, who for the duration of the war has let Pulvery, her and her husband Tom's Sussex country house (familiar to devoted Bush readers), and with her "old maid" Annie taken Ringlands, "what she calls a cottage," while Tom is in military service in the Middle East. Soon Ludo encounters in Cleavesham a number of inhabitants who will play parts in the upcoming murder drama that afflicts the village, including Major Chevalle, the chief constable; his wife, Thora, young daughter, Flora, and Thora's poor relation, Mary; village warden Bernard Temple; Lieut.-Commander Santon, wounded in the knee at Crete and now retired, and Tom Dewball, his manservant; Herbert Maddon, "quite a superior old man," and his daily, Mrs. Beaney; and odd duck "Augustus Porle," a devout believer in harnessing the power of the Great Pyramid.

Like any amateur sleuth worth his salt, Travers has not been long in Cleavesham when he runs across a dead body, in this case that of the seemingly inoffensive Mr. Maddon, who has been shot to death at his cottage, Five Oaks. Evidence points overwhelmingly to the suspicious presence that day at Five Oaks cottage of a headily-scented, chain-smoking platinum blonde— and the seeming identity of this blonde proves most problematic indeed for Ludo Travers and Superintendent George Wharton, whom Scotland Yard has sent to investigate the case at the behest of Major Chevalle. This is but the intriguing opening to one of the most ingenious mysteries Christopher Bush ever penned, one that in the final pages will leave the reader facing the same moral dilemma as Ludovic Travers (who finds himself increasingly playing his own hand in the series, in the independent manner of an American private eye): now that I know the truth, just what do I do about it?

Reviewing *The Case of the Platinum Blonde* in the *Times Literary Supplement*, author and expert on Victorian melodrama Maurice Willson Disher commented on the "exasperating" tendency of amateur detectives in crime fiction to conceal "incriminating evidence from the police." Yet Disher concluded that in this case Ludovic Travers so thoroughly justified his fancy for obstructive behavior "that in future amateur detectives will be able to continue the bad habit [of obstruction] without objection. Readers who have asked 'Why?' impatiently at the beginning of this book will be twice shy." Will modern readers react to the outcome of *The Case of the Platinum Blonde* as Disher predicted? You, dear reader, will have to read on for yourself and see.

Curtis Evans

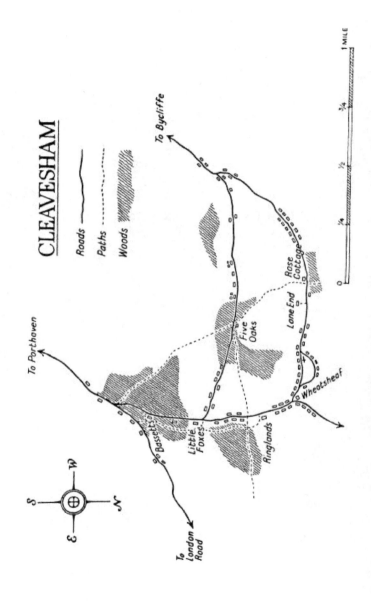

CLEAVESHAM

Roads ——————
Paths ------------
Woods ▨

To Bycliffe

To Porthaven

To London Road

Bassetts
Little Foxes
Five Oaks
Ringlands
Lane End
Rose Cottage
Wheatsheaf

N · S · E · W

0 ¼ ½ ¾ 1 MILE

Part One
FIND THE LADY

CHAPTER I
A JOB FOR WHARTON

I HAVE GOT to write this book more quickly than I ever wrote one in my life. A highly efficient stenographer whom I implicitly trust is to take it straight on the machine at my dictation, and I have bargained with myself that the job shall take a fortnight, and no more.

In order to run no risks whatever, I am disguising the names of places and people; except three of the people—George (Superintendent) Wharton, my sister Helen, and myself. And I'm also writing this foreword myself and am incorporating it in this first chapter unknown to the stenographer. She will think that everything is just fiction, but when the book is finished, and if I think she has been intrigued, I may ask her what she thinks, for that may help me to make the vital decision.

But all this must be mystifying you. What decision, you may ask, and why all the hurry to get the book finished? To that I would say that it isn't a question of hurry for hurry's sake. I am certainly not looking forward to the end of the fortnight and the making of that vital decision, for there is little real satisfaction in putting off an evil day when that day is inevitable. Conscience insists even now that a decision could be made before I dictate a single word, but one cannot reconcile divided loyalties as easily as that. As for the decision, it will affect someone's life; perhaps I should say death, and a death by hanging at that.

In writing the book, then—setting down the facts of the case, if you prefer it—I am throwing out a kind of challenge to myself. I am keeping conscience at arm's length by solemnly swearing that after a fortnight's respite the decision shall definitely be made. In other words I have a fortnight in which to make up my mind.

When you get to the end of this book, you may find yourself in something of the same dilemma. But you will not have a decision to make. All you may have are sympathies and hostilities, but I have got to make up my mind. I shall have to act or not act, and either way it's going to be tough. Maybe at the last moment I shall choose the coward's way, and the one to be let down will be myself. And that's that, and all that remains is to get on with the story.

That story begins on a June morning of 1943, when I called at the Yard and asked if Wharton was in. They told me he was in his room, so I went straight up. They know me well enough at the Yard—possibly as either George's shadow or his stooge—and my six-foot three and horn-rims are recognisable enough and proof against impersonation.

George was sitting at his desk, poring over some papers, and he stared at me over the tops of his antiquated spectacles as if I were a ghost. Maybe he thought I was one, for the last time he had seen me was in hospital, after an operation which had found me remarkably near the pearly gates.

Then his wrinkled old face beamed and he was getting to his feet, hand held out.

"Well, well, well. This is a surprise. And you're not looking too bad, either."

"I'm pretty well all right now," I told him. "A fortnight in the country will put me clean on my pins again."

He fussed round me and actually put a cushion on my chair.

"Well, it's good to see you," he said, and I think he meant it. George and I spar like fighting cocks when we aren't pulling each other's legs, and yet I suppose that somehow our fifteen years' association has become a something which we should be horrified to disrupt.

"And what's it feel like to be out of the Army?" he wanted to know.

"I don't know yet," I told him. "But after four years of red tape and routine I think it's going to be pretty good."

"Maybe," George said dubiously, and then I switched the conversation to what he himself was doing, and then we got to talking about old times. Then I said I'd have to be going, for my train left in an hour.

"Give my best wishes to your sister," George said, "and to her husband. Some time I'd like to go down to Pulvery again myself."

"It isn't Pulvery," I said. "My brother-in-law's been in the Middle East for the last couple of years, so Helen let the Pulvery place and has taken what she calls a cottage, at Cleavesham. That's about two miles from Porthaven."

"Porthaven," he said, and pursed his lips till that walrus moustache of his looked like the half of a fringed sunshade. "I know the Chief Constable there, if you'd like to meet him. A very nice fellow indeed. Chevalle's his name. Major Chevalle, D.S.O., M.C., and gawd knows what else. I think you'll like him. He's a really good chap."

The upshot was that he sat down there and then, and wrote me a letter of introduction!

"Mind you," he warned me as he tucked in the flap of the envelope, "I'm not giving you this so that you can go poking that nose of yours into his office. This is what you might call social. He knows everybody there is to know."

"Very good of you, George," I said. "As soon as I get settled in I'll look him up. But what about your running down for a day or so? There'd be tons of room for you, and a holiday'd do you good."

"Impossible," he said, but I knew he was wavering. "They tell me that country round Cleavesham is some of the loveliest in Sussex," I went on. And then something peculiar happened. He had been replacing the spectacles in their battered case, and then all at once he was goggling at me and thrusting the spectacles under my nose.

"Cleavesham," he said. "I didn't catch it at first. About two miles north of Porthaven."

"But not on the London road," I said. "The main road is a bit more east."

"I know," he told me impatiently. "But it's a good road, though, and you can dodge the traffic if you know the lanes. That's what I was doing."

"What *is* this, George?" I said. "Some lurid episode from your past?"

"It's something you can do for me," he said. "Did you ever know me forget a face?"

"I wouldn't go so far as that," I said, "but I will admit you have a staggering memory."

"Well, I saw a face at Cleavesham that I ought to have remembered," he told me. "Sit down again. You're not in all that hurry for a minute."

This was his story. He had been to Porthaven on business, and as the main road was full of military traffic, Chevalle advised him to take the Cleavesham route. George was driving his own car and just as he was approaching Cleavesham his near hind tyre went flat. So he drew in on the wide grass verge and prepared to put on the spare. There was a stile in the hedge right against where he was working, and as he was manipulating the spare into place he saw a man getting over the stile, and had a first-class view of him.

"You know how I am," he said. "I collect faces, the same as you collect china and all that rubbish you fill your place up with. And this cove's face was one I ought to have known. I tell you I knew it as if it was my own, and yet I couldn't put a name to it. That was about a year ago and if I've thought of it once I've thought of it fifty times. It worries me. It's a face I know and yet I can't place it."

"Describe the cove and I'll see what I can do," I told him. "Mind you, he mayn't be a local inhabitant."

"Then that'll be bad luck," George told me philosophically. "But he was an elderly man. Between sixty and seventy, we'll say. He'd a grizzled sort of beard and a face with those purple markings on it as if he suffered from blood pressure. He was about five foot eight and thinnish. Not that we all aren't these days. And he limped the slightest bit, as if he had arthritis in his knee."

"And his social class?"

"Oh, a retired sort of cove. Quite neatly dressed, I remembered. Might have been a retired anything. School-master or bank cashier for example."

"And his voice?"

"There you've got me," George said, and grimaced. "I spotted him before he saw me and as soon as I knew I knew him—so to speak—I kept my head down. He didn't speak and neither did I. He kept on walking towards Porthaven once he was over the stile. That's when I noticed his lameness."

"Well, I'll do what I can for you, George," I said as I got to my feet again. "But just one little thing. The sort of faces you pride yourself on remembering are criminal faces. Those you've seen on trial or had up yourself. So tell me. Did you place this particular man in that category?"

"Damned if I know," he told me bluntly. "It was a sort of intuition, if you know what I mean. I said to myself, I know that fellow!' Just as quick as that. Then I started puzzling my wits. I tell you it worried me. It's gone on worrying me. Once when I was down that way I nearly went a few miles off the road to make some inquiries for myself. I shouldn't have felt like that if it hadn't been something important."

It *was* important to him and I'll tell you how I knew. George calls me the world's prize theorist. Throughout our long association he's been living on and profiting by my theories, though he has never stopped pouring scorn on them at their initial propounding. I admit frankly that my average is one theory right in every three, and I claim that that average is remarkably good. George forgets the happy one, or annexes it as his own, and instances the other two. But now when I began to theorise, all he did was to listen attentively.

"An old criminal," I said. "And with a beard. That's why you can't place him, George. You knew him years ago when he hadn't that beard, or that limp, and maybe he wasn't thin then, either. Think of all that when you search your memory again."

"I reckon you're right," he said. "All the same I'd very much like to know just who he is."

"Right," I said. "When I run him to earth I'll send you his finger-prints."

"My God!" George said, and tried to look horrified. "They'd have the coat off my back if they found out that."

"You're a damned old humbug," I told him. "But you leave it to me. Tell you what. I'll bet you a new hat we know inside a week who he is."

"No you don't," he said, and gave what was meant to be a look of infinite wiliness. "But I will bet you a couple of drinks."

And on that amusing note we left it. Amusing because it was generally I who paid in any case unless George saw a way clear to wangling the expenses account.

It was half-past three when I arrived at Ringlands, which was the name of my sister's Cleavesham cottage. And on the eve of all the happenings I want to make something clear. Throughout this book I am aiming to be direct to the point of terseness. You don't want to wade through descriptions of scenery or listen to local chit-chat, and I have no wish either to live the one again or listen to the other. Everything then that I relate will be very relevant to the story. The rough map will help you to get Cleavesham clearly in your mind, and if a particular piece of scenery happens to be mentioned, then prick your ears at once, for it will be mentioned for a purpose and not for padding. And of the nine hundred inhabitants of the village, you will hear perhaps a half-dozen talking, and what they say will be very relevant too.

To begin with Ringlands, then. Unexpectedly it turned out to be a cottage and no more, with three bedrooms and two so-called reception rooms, one of which Helen was proposing to set aside for my sole use. She had brought her old maid with her, and a man—an octogenarian whose dialect I do not propose to imitate—came on three days a week to see to the rather large garden.

Helen is as far removed from me as it's possible for a brother and sister to be, and by that I don't mean that we haven't a considerable affection for each other. But I'm inquisitive—largely as a result of association with George Wharton—flippant, restless, and mercurially minded. I'm certainly not a man's man, though there are the devil of a lot of men with whom I get on remarkably well. But Helen is a man's woman: even-tempered, hating fussiness, broad-minded and always on the spot when most needed and well away from it when not. Perhaps that may explain why she comes very little into this story.

Tea was on within ten minutes of my arrival, and as we gossiped I didn't ask her about George's forgotten face.

Most of the talk was about the village, which was considered a suburb, and a highly refined one at that, of Porthaven. She knew the Chevalles, for instance, who lived well out of the village on the Porthaven side. Him she liked very much but for his wife she had very little use. Helen, I regret to say, is the least bit of a snob, though only where unpleasant people are concerned, and so I don't think she disliked Thora Chevalle solely because she was the somewhat promiscuously educated daughter of a wealthy jerry-builder; what she disliked was the particular brand of unpleasantness. What that was I didn't learn till later. There was a daughter—Clarice, aged just over four—so Helen told me, and a delightful child she was. There was also a poor cousin of Thora Chevalle's—Mary Carter—who acted as nurse-companion, and I gathered that Helen rather liked her.

"How do you come to know the Chevalles so well?" I wanted to know.

It turned out that although Helen had been in Cleavesham only four months she had already been roped in for war work as responsible for the war savings of a third of the village. Mrs. Chevalle did another third, and the people's warden, a man named Bernard Temple, did the rest. In charge of the whole district, including Porthaven, was a Lieut.-Commander Santon, who had been wounded in the knee at Crete and was now retired. I gathered that not only did the three local savings people have conferences with each other but also once a week with Commander Santon, who luckily lived in Cleavesham too, though on the Porthaven side.

It was typical of Helen that she didn't take me round the garden but left me to wander about alone. The octogenarian was weeding an onion bed. He was a sturdy old boy with a beautiful crop of white whiskers, and I told him that I hoped when I was eighty I'd be as hearty as he.

"It's quite a pleasure to see a beard again," I told him. "Reminds me of my young days."

"There's still a few about," he said, but as if his own was a rarity of which to be proud.

"How many can you think of?" I asked him.

He frowned for a bit and then began his short list. I recognised only one name, the Mr. Temple whom Helen had mentioned as a colleague on the war savings committee, so I had to resort to subterfuge. Names would have meant little to me in any case.

"Who was the man with a beard I passed just now?" I said. "A thinnish, elderly man with a limp."

"Ah! that'd be Mr. Maddon," he said. "Him that lives at Five Oaks. Been here about nine years or so now."

"Five Oaks," I said. "That's an interesting name. Where is it exactly?"

He said it was very simple. If I went two hundred yards towards Porthaven I'd see a stile on the right-hand side of the road, and a path that would take me straight to it. Used to be a large house there once, hundreds of years ago, but now there was only Mr. Maddon's cottage. Or I could go a bit farther on and there was a lane that led the same way.

I thought it best not to ask any more questions. What I did do was to go back to the house and ask Helen if she happened to have a large-scale map of the district. She did have one. It had been the one necessary thing when she arrived in the village, and indispensable for finding her way across field-paths and tracks to collect war savings. Thanks to that experience she knew every short cut in her area, and, what was more, she knew every householder and his family in the whole district north of Ringlands and along the Bycliffe road to the fork.

While I was having a good look at that map she told me a thing or two that might be useful. Bassetts was the Chevalle house, but if I wanted to see both the Chevalles, then I'd better wait a day or two as Mrs. Chevalle was away on a short holiday in town. Her father was a builder in North London.

"Didn't you say that a bit spitefully?" I asked.

"Not at all, my dear," she told me, and rather amusedly. "I don't mind who her father is. Some of the best friends I've made in the village are just the ordinary people."

"Then what's the snag about her?"

"Just her," she said. "For one thing she simply doesn't know nowadays what an honest job of work is. She over-dresses and decorates perfectly abominably, and under the veneer she's just sheer vulgarity. He must have been mad to marry her."

"Good-looking?"

"Well—yes. She'd be better-looking if she made up a trifle less artificially. And, my dear, simply seething with sex. But on very bad terms with him, so they say. And the way she bullies and drives that wretched Mary Carter simply makes me see red."

She clicked her tongue and then said we'd better talk about something else. Thora Chevalle was the one person in the village who brought out her worst instincts. Little Foxes, now, just opposite the cross road to Bycliffe, was where Commander Santon lived. One of the most charming men she'd ever met, but a bit of a philanderer.

"What's this Five Oaks place?" I asked her.

"Just a large cottage," she said. "It comes in Mrs. Chevalle's area. A man named Maddon lives there. Quite a superior old man I believe, but I've never met him."

"It looks to me as if you and Mrs. Chevalle share the war saving between you," I pointed out. "What does the other man, Temple, do?"

"He does all the outlying places off the main roads, and he's a sort of reserve if we're away or go sick." She smiled a bit spitefully. "That's pretty often for Mrs. Chevalle."

She told me a lot more. That there was an hourly service of buses to and from Porthaven, for instance, and that Bycliffe church was well worth a visit. Bycliffe was six miles from Porthaven and two and a half from Cleavesham. The Wheatsheaf was quite a good pub, she told me, and there were three shops in the village—a post office general stores, another general stores and a butcher's. And that reminded her. She ought to go along at once before the shop closed and see if she could get anything useful for some of her points.

I said I'd go with her, and I enjoyed that first glimpse of the village, for I'd arrived via Porthaven. It was a superb afternoon with the scent of hay in the air and the incredible sweetness of a late beanfield. There were hop gardens with the green already well up the poles, and chestnut woods with vistas of valleys between them. Helen said that from Little Foxes one could see the sea, but everywhere else the hills that sheltered Porthaven cut off the sea view.

There were lovely tile-hung houses and one or two half-timbered larger ones that made my mouth water. Farther along the Bycliffe road, Helen said, there was a bungalow colony, but the main part of the village was not disfigured. The spacious village green was lovely too, even if the cricket pitch was a hayfield, and the grey church stood perfectly placed in the far corner.

By the church was the post office for which we were bound. As we approached it a man came out, and when he saw Helen he came across. He was about six foot and rather thin, and with a closely cropped brown beard. His manners were far too effusive for my liking.

Helen introduced him as Temple, and at once he showed me all his teeth in a smile that was perilous for his upper set. But he didn't hang round our necks. A word or two with Helen about war savings and he said he would be going. A high-pitched voice he had, as if by some special dispensation of providence he had eunuch blood in him.

"I hope you will like our little village, Major Travers," he said. "We're humble people but I'm hoping you'll like us."

"We'll probably be humble all together," I told him, and he didn't quite know what to make of that. But he smiled again in farewell and then bent over Helen's hand like a shopwalker.

"Delighted to see you again. Don't forget next Tuesday's meeting."

He turned back along the Bycliffe road.

"Where's he live?" I asked.

"You can just see his cottage on the left," Helen told me. "That one with the rose arch in front. Rose Cottage. It's just beyond the stile."

I didn't go into the shop as there was a seat—erected to celebrate the coronation—under an oak just in front, and I sat there and enjoyed the view. A tractor passed with a load of split-pale fencing, and through the gap between two cottages I could see men haying. Then there was the faint sound of planes and soon I could see a whole packet of ours heading across the Channel. Then Helen came out and we walked round the green for a change of route, and so towards home again.

"My dear," she suddenly said, "weren't you just a bit superior with that poor Mr. Temple?"

"*I* know," I said. "I apologise. I'm sorry, but I just didn't like him."

"He's rather amusing," she said. "He does try so hard to make an impression, and he really does do quite a lot in the village besides war savings and being people's warden. How old would you think he was?"

"Don't know," I said. "Very near fifty perhaps. Beards are always deceptive."

On the rest of the way she told me about other people in the village, the moneyed sort principally. Most of the men were away and the few left did Home Guard jobs or worked in Town and came down only at week-ends. I said she ought to be doing well with war savings with all that dormitory class about, but it appeared that they subscribed on big occasions in big amounts to Santon direct. There wouldn't be any necessity for me to meet any of them, she said, and that was good hearing. I loathe polite teas and local discourse. I may be public school and Cambridge but neither is very likely to apologise for disowning me, and I loathe particularly those cast in the same mould—the soft-voiced and discreet, the strong silent men whose taciturnity conceals inanity and whose information is a poor re-hash of the correspondence columns of *The Times*.

I've got to say this some time, for it's highly important if we are to understand each other, and so I'll say it here and now. If Wharton boasted of collecting faces, then I collect characters. Work at the Yard may have got me into the habit and made me a student of humanity, but for me a railway compartment or a tram or a pub has all the excitement that some people find in the theatre. I like to look at people and listen to them and lure them into talk, and so deduce their circumstances, their general make-up and even their counties from their speech. If they are uninteresting or hackneyed types, then they can be discarded at will, and if not, then they can be savoured and enjoyed. It doesn't matter from what walk of life they come. One of my best discoveries was a chimney sweep and another a Cabinet Minister. And look at George Wharton, a man whom most would pass in the street without a second look. What a rich and fruity personality! No age can wither his infinite—if home-made—variety.

Well, we reached Ringlands again and I lounged about till the evening meal, which was at seven prompt. We had strawberries, I remember, though very little sugar, and altogether it was just the meal for a sultry evening. Thunder was in the air and Helen thought we should be lucky if we missed a storm.

"If you don't mind I think I'll go for a very short stroll," I said. "Just enough not to tire me."

She suggested just what I wanted, the field-path to Five Oaks, and home by Rose Cottage, which would be just about a couple of miles. I asked if she'd come too, but she said she hadn't better. When she walked it was always at a furious pace, whereas I would have to go steady and not tire myself. I said we'd compromise but she laughed and said she knew what compromises were, so I set off leisurely and alone. Perhaps of all the walks I've ever taken, it was to be the most amazing.

CHAPTER II
THE PRIZE SPECIMEN

I SOON CAME to the stile and guessed it was the one against which Wharton had put on his spare tyre and had caught a glimpse of a face that had so intrigued him. I also did a quiet chuckle. Already I knew the man's name and it looked a thousand to one as if within a week Wharton would have his mind at rest and I'd be entitled to claim a drink, though whether or not I'd ever get that drink was a vastly different matter.

The country was undulating and in a few minutes I could catch that glimpse of the sea about which Helen had told me. Much of the land was arable now and the crops looked in fine heart. Then I halted as I came to the first woods and watched men loading hop-poles, and then lighted a second pipe and strolled on again. Almost at once I caught sight of a man coming towards me along the path, and at once I knew him for Maddon.

Wharton's memory had been good and his description apt and I will add little to what he told me. But as I neared the man I knew by how he carried himself that he was of some breeding, and when I gave him a good evening he answered in quite a pleasant, cultured voice that it looked as if we were in for a storm.

"Then aren't we both rather risking it?" I asked.

He smiled and I thought I discerned an irony. "What would life be worth if there were no risks?"

"True enough," I said, and then tritely: "But that's no reason for going to meet them."

"Well, let's hope we both get back without a soaking," he said. "But this is my regular evening walk and no storm's going to stop me. You're staying here?"

The question had been fired a bit suddenly and I rather stammered over what I thought the minimum of information. But it did seem to me that he was very interested in even the little I told him, though at the end he merely nodded and said we had both better be pushing on.

So on we went and that was that. I began reviewing what I'd noticed about him. His clothes, for instance, were old but well cut. The arthritis was worse, for the knee now had a decided bend in it, but the purple colouring of the face was far less prominent than I'd gathered from Wharton. The grey beard was fairly compact but untrimmed, and the face reminded me rather of the doctor in Luke Fildes's picture. The full sensual lips were the worst part about it, and the whole expression, I thought, had been the least bit supercilious, except at that moment when I had been telling him about myself. As for my deductions, frankly they were very sketchy. I thought him a man who had once wielded a considerable authority and had come to regard life with a certain cynicism or amused indifference. And that was about all, and a pretty bad effort for one who claimed to be a student of humanity. Then I knew I should soon be seeing that cottage of his. Know where a man lives and you'll know the man himself, I could tell myself consolingly.

But Five Oaks was to be a surprise. Perhaps I can best describe it to you by saying that it reminded me of the scene of Hardy's *Woodlanders*. All round it were the chestnut woods, interspersed with oaks, and before it was a meadow of mown hay. It had the same atmosphere of cool, remote shadow, and a serene and aloof antiquity. It was rather larger than a cottage, with a garden in good order and its front hedge neatly clipped, and its long, low roof of ancient tile was incredibly colourful in that evening sun. A lovely place, I thought, for an author or poet, or any man who wished to keep himself to himself and emerge from that peaceful solitude only when the mood took him.

Now I guessed that Maddon would be taking the walk that avoided the village—the triangle to the stile, then to the fork and so back by the field-path—and so I sat down on an old oak stump and ran my eye over the house again at some leisure, a something which the absence of its owner permitted me to do. But no sooner did I sit than I heard a noise as of hammering. It seemed quite near—coming from the back of the house, in fact—and with that insatiable curiosity which is an ineradicable part of my make-up, I decided to explore.

So I retraced my steps for a few yards to where I remembered having seen a back gate. Young chestnut, trimmed back to make a shady avenue, hid the rear of the house from me, but the noise was very near. So I opened the little gate and made a cautious way along the dry path. The path turned sharply right and it was as suddenly that the back of the house came into view. What I had rather expected to see was a gardener working overtime and hammering at something or other, but at what I did see I drew back behind a thick holly clump.

A man was nailing something to the door and I was in time to see him put the last nail to the corner of some sort of a white placard and drive it home with a tiny hammer. Then he drew back and surveyed his effort, nodded at it with apparent satisfaction, replaced the hammer in his pocket and then turned my way. All I could think was that Five Oaks must be up for auction and that the man was an auctioneer, or a clerk, affixing notice of the sale. And that put me in a state of immediate alarm, for it would mean that Maddon was going away.

With my right hand I drew aside the thick holly leaves and had a look at the man as he neared me, and I saw him as clearly as if he had been sitting for his portrait. He was a big man but flabby-looking, and with shoulders somewhat hunched. As for his face, it was remarkably like Churchill's, but a roguish, impish Churchill, and with cheeks even fatter and far more richly red. He wore no hat, and his thin, white hair straggled across his bald skull and over his ears, and on his face was a look of blandest satisfaction.

The very moment he was out of sight in the bend of the path I took a chance and sprinted for that back door. As I neared it I saw that the notice, if an announcement of a sale, was a most unusual one, for it was hand-printed and there seemed very few words on it. Then when I got to it I saw it was a piece of white cardboard, evidently cut from a box, and the four corners were held down by tin-tacks. As for what was printed on it, here it is, and you can judge if I was staggered.

WOE TO THEM THAT DEVOUR WIDOWS' HOUSES AND REGARD NOT THE FATHER-LESS AND THE ORPHAN!

THE DAY OF VENGEANCE IS AT HAND. THUS SAITH THE LORD.

TO-MORROW MAY BE TOO LATE! REMEMBER—THIS NIGHT SHALL THY SOUL BE REQUIRED OF THEE.

So much for the large print. Then in smaller print below came the following

ABSOLUTELY FINAL WARNING!
TO-NIGHT, 11.00 P.M., SAME PLACE.

Frankly all I could do was to gape. Then I had an idea, and on an old envelope-back took a hasty copy of the words. Then as I glanced up I saw that the house had a telephone, for the wire was connected to the back of the kitchen chimney. At the same moment I heard the sound of an approaching lorry, and again I was in a fright, thinking that the man would be away before I could question him. Then I saw the lorry go by on the road which I had forgotten, and it was a military one and full of men.

I sprinted back along the path to where the three paths met, and there was my man making for the village. Something must have delayed him for he was only about fifty yards away, so at once I put my best foot forward and in under five minutes I had overhauled him. The path was wide and there was ample room for us to proceed abreast.

"Still no storm?" I remarked pleasantly. That the man was either a crank or a lunatic was very evident and it was policy to humour him.

He had given me a quick look as I came up, but now his smile was quite genial. What to say of his manner I hardly know, and you must judge it for yourself, but it had a rich urbanity and a certain dignified subservience, as of an old family butler.

"Still no storm, sir," was his echoed and rather pontifical reply. "You are taking your evening exercise?"

"Yes," I said. "I only arrived this evening and my sister, Mrs. Thornley—perhaps you know her—told me this was a most attractive walk."

"Mrs. Thornley—yes," he said. "A most charming lady, sir. You'll pardon me, sir, but you have the look of an Army officer. Would it be impertinent to ask if you are on leave?"

I told him my circumstances and he was most interested. What comments he made gave no signs of lunacy, far from it. But the mentally unstable are queer people at times, with the instabilities matters of mere moments in days or even months.

"I take it you have travelled considerably, sir," he remarked, and that deferential way of addressing me, I should say, struck me as simply a kind of old-fashioned courtesy; and his somewhat spacious gestures and perfect control of the conversation showed that he had his own well-founded opinion of himself.

I begged the question for a moment while I handed him one of my cards. He halted, produced pince-nez from his waistcoat pocket and then read aloud.

"Major L. Travers. The L. is for?"

"Ludovic."

"A fine old name, sir," he told me majestically, and pocketed both card and pince-nez. "German in origin undoubtedly. And with an historical military significance. But about your travels, sir. You have seen the world?"

Luckily for me we came to a row of craters where a stick of bombs had fallen some fifty yards from the path, and that gave me time to ease off the question and think of an answer. Then I said I'd travelled very little except in Europe and the Middle East.

"Egypt, sir?"

"Egypt I know very well," I said.

"Ah!" he said, and his fat face beamed. "There was a time, sir, when I could have gone to Egypt but I deferred the moment and then it was too late. The Pyramids, sir? You have been over them?"

"No more than the usual tourist does," I admitted. But now I thought I knew the particular kind of crank he was—a believer in certain prophetic qualities inherent in the Great Pyramid.

"After this war, sir, I hope to visit them myself," he said, and in a queerly matter-of-fact way. "I have certain projects in hand which ought to materialise."

A storm-cloud had been coming over at a good pace and just then there were a few great drops of rain. In the far distance was a rumble of thunder.

"Looks as if we shall have to run for it," I said, and we quickened our pace. Luckily we were now no more than a couple of hundred yards from the village stile, and as we came by it I saw Bernard Temple in the garden of Rose Cottage hastily dismantling a garden hammock. A second later, as we were almost at the stile, my friend grasped my arm. He nodded back.

"That man, sir." His voice was a hoarse whisper. "A scoundrel, sir. And a friend of scoundrels. Be on your guard, sir. Be on your guard."

"I will," I said. "And thanks for the tip."

As he mounted the stile the rain fell in earnest. We sprinted the few yards to his lodgings, a cottage called Lane End, which was at the end of a little pightle. There was a rose-covered porch, and there we stood and panted for a minute.

"We were just in time, sir," my friend said and opened the front door. "But only a storm. Perhaps you will honour me by waiting in my room till it is over."

Just inside the door were stairs and he led the way up to a large bed-sitting-room. Below us I could hear a woman busy with pots and pans in the kitchen.

"You have a lovely view here," I said, for the room faced south.

"Yes, sir," he said. "Things might be worse. The woman of the house is an excellent cook and I have a modicum of peace and quiet."

"You're an astronomer too," I said, pointing to the telescope that stood on a table by the window. On that table I saw, too, various books and pamphlets. There was *Ezekiel or The True Witness*, *The Great Pyramid and Its Message for Today*, and what looked like a weekly—*Daydawn, the Journal of the Sons of Light*. They were all the titles I could read, for he was telling me about his own special attitude towards the stars. I won't bother you with the ten minutes' discourse, but the gist of it was that the stars were our companions in space and friends for millenniums of years. From one's friends one learns much of one's self and by long watching and meditating one can achieve a sort of *yogi* state and be an apt vessel for revelation.

I said it was a sound enough argument, and asked what he'd received in the way of revelation.

"Ah!" he said, and on his face was part wiliness and part pride. "Believe it or not, my dear sir, but it was the stars that brought me here."

"And those projects you said you had on hand; do the stars promise success for them?"

He made as if to answer, then thought better of it. He merely shook his head and gave a dry smile in which was something of the same wiliness.

"Never count your chickens, sir, before they are hatched. Nevertheless I have hopes. Great hopes."

The sun was suddenly flooding the room and I said I would have to be going. Then he gave me that book on the Great Pyramid and told me he was sure it would be of interest. I could return it at my leisure.

"Or Mrs. Thornley might bring it," he added. "She calls for war savings, you know." He shook his head regretfully. "I'm afraid I have hitherto been a poor subscriber. In the near future, sir, I hope to astonish her."

At the foot of the stairs he shook hands with me warmly. "Porle is the name, sir," and he spelt it for me. "Augustus Porle. My compliments, sir, to your sister. And I trust you and I will meet again, if not here, on our walks."

As I made my way back to Ringlands I could congratulate myself on the discovery of one of the finest specimens of my career. A crank he might be, but a many-sided one and gifted with a singular clarity of exposition, even if his fundamentals had been somewhat cock-eyed. A man of some past affluence I gathered too, and certainly of some education. What he was up to with Maddon was beyond my powers of guessing. The only thing that was certain was that he knew Maddon's habit of taking an evening stroll or else he would not have tacked up that notice so brazenly.

One thing that did puzzle me was the use of Biblical phraseology in that notice. And, above all, what a colossal anti-climax had been that reminder at the end about a final warning and a meeting at eleven o'clock that night. If I hadn't felt damnably tired I'd have stayed up that night and tracked him down to the meeting-place, for the whole thing was profoundly intriguing to one as curious as myself, with whom any unsolved mystery, however trivial, will gnaw away like an unfilled tooth.

Mind you, I could find theories enough for everything. Porle suffered from a persecution complex, for instance, as witness his remarks—gratifying though they had been to me—about Bernard Temple's being a dangerous man, and consorting with rascals. Perhaps Maddon had found him trespassing and had been high-handed. Maybe Maddon owed him money for something, and he was out to recover it in his own way. From what I had seen of Maddon he was in for a remarkably long quest. Or maybe the stars were behind it all.

"Enjoyed your walk?" Helen asked.

"I've rarely enjoyed one more," I told her. "I met that man Maddon near Five Oaks, by the way. He looks quite a superior kind of person."

"The village doesn't like him a great deal," she said. "I think he likes keeping himself to himself and he has rather a caustic tongue."

"He does everything for himself?"

"I think so," she said. "There is a woman, I believe, who comes in to clean up in the afternoons. Mrs. Chevalle would know. He's on her beat."

Then I told her about meeting Porle, with not a word, of course, about that notice tacked on Maddon's door. She laughed as soon as I mentioned his name.

"He's a perfectly dear old soul," she said. "The most delightful manners. Like someone out of *Our Village*."

"A bit of a crank, isn't he?"

Her eyes opened wide. "Whatever made you think that?"

"What made you think he wasn't?" I countered.

"He never struck me as anything like it," she said. "Just old-fashioned. And very learned, so Mrs. Bray says. She's the widow where he lodges. I expect she means studious."

"He sent you his compliments," I said, "And he admitted he was a poor subscriber."

She laughed again. "It's just too funny. Every week he gives me a shilling. Has it all ready. Then about a fortnight ago he told me, most secretly, that he was going to astonish me in the near future."

"When did he mean? At your Wings for Victory week?"

"Oh, we've had that," she said. "I think he's expecting a windfall."

It was then about nine o'clock and I was made to drink a cup of hot milk and eat a slab of fruit cake which she had achieved by hoarding the butter rations.

"I thought it would be nice for you to meet Commander Santon," she told me, "so while you were out I slipped along to Little Foxes. But he wasn't in. Tom Dewball—that's his man—said he was away on some war savings conference or other at Southampton, but he'd be back tomorrow. You'll like Commander Santon. He's an awfully good sort."

"Married, is he?"

"Oh, yes," she said. "His wife's frightfully well off. I don't think he has anything besides his pension. Awfully hard luck about his wife. When he was serving out East she went out there to do nursing. Most capable she is, so everyone says. Now, of course, she's got to stay there."

"That reminds me," I said. "I must write a note to Bernice so that I can post it in the morning."

My wife is also nursing, but up in Yorkshire, and as her leave is scanty it was useless for me to go up there too. But we were hoping to have seven days together at the middle of July. I got the letter finished just before ten, and then Helen was wanting to know if I felt like bed. I said I certainly did. That pleased her, for she and Annie always turned in at ten so as not to have to put up the black-out. "You'll do all the locking-up?" I asked.

She said she would, and most carefully. During the last week or two there'd been no less than five burglaries in the district. People said it was the troops, for there are bad eggs in most batches. Whoever it was had only taken small things but valuable—old silver, bric-a-brac and miniatures, for instance. Helen was kind enough to add also, that it was good to have a man in the house, and rather spoilt it by adding further, "since there wasn't a dog."

I took much longer than I'd anticipated to get off to sleep, and I only did so when I'd thought up a plan to get Maddon's finger-prints for Wharton. What I would do in the morning would be to go that way again, and wearing gloves and carrying a stick. I'd call on Maddon and be very surprised to find he lived there, and then I'd show him a hand-drawn map and ask him if such and such a path would bring me out where. On that sheet of paper I'd have his prints.

After breakfast, then, I drew my rough map from Helen's large-scale one, being careful to wear gloves and to omit a certain field-path. Then I announced that the doctor had told me to take a two-mile walk every morning and gradually increase the distance, so I proposed to do again the walk I had done the previous night. Helen said if I was coming by the stores, would I hand in a list of things she was getting with my ration card.

It was getting on the way for half-past nine when I set out, and as soon as I glanced up at the sky I didn't like the look of things a bit. White fluffy clouds were floating across a grey-ey-black sky to the west of Porthaven, and before I'd gone a couple of hundred yards I heard the distant rumble of thunder. Just as I thought of turning back to fetch a raincoat I thought it might be better not to have one. If there was to be a storm it certainly would not break before I got to Five Oaks, and if the rain came down then, and while I was talking to Maddon, he couldn't very well do anything but ask me to step indoors till it was over.

An admirable opportunity, so it seemed to me, of seeing him at close quarters.

Quite near the path when I reached the first woods, an old man was splitting chestnut lengths for fencing.

"We're going to get the storm?" I asked him.

He told me that the storms nearly always went up the Channel, catching Porthaven and giving it a good soaking but rarely giving Cleavesham more than a splash. Which was a pity, he said, for his onions could do with a thorough soaker.

The storm was certainly getting much nearer, so I mended my pace. When I drew near the house I wondered if I ought to go to the front door, much as I should have liked to inspect the back and find out what had happened to Porle's notice. Curiosity got the better of me and I took the twisted path to the back door. The notice, I was not surprised to see, had gone, and it had been wrenched away as if in a rage, for two of the cardboard corners were still there. I also noticed quite an array of tintacks. That notice certainly wasn't the first that Porle had fastened to that back door.

I lifted my hand to knock, but just as my knuckles met the wood I saw that the door was just ajar. That put me in a quandary, but curiosity got the better of me again and I opened the door and put my head inside.

"Anybody there?"

I listened. My call reverberated through an empty house, so I called again for luck.

"Anybody at home?"

There was never a sound, so I had a quick look round the kitchen. It was stone-floored and scrupulously clean but I couldn't see beyond it, for the door to the room beyond was closed, though only with an old-fashioned wooden snack fastened with a string. So I put the door back as near to ajar as I had found it and then made my way to the front of the house. Maybe Maddon was working in the garden and had not heard my call, but when I had spent five minutes looking round and had found no trace of him, I knew my walk had been wasted.

A curiosity positively shameless got the better of me before I left, for as I came to the front path the window caught my eye and I thought I'd take a peep at the contents of the rooms. The first I looked at was a dining-room, sparsely furnished, but I couldn't see a lot, for the lattice panes were too dusty. The other room looked more interesting. The first thing I noticed, for it was placed quite near the window where the light would fall across the left shoulder of a user, was a roll-top desk. It was open and looked most damnably untidy, with papers strewn over its flap. Maybe some were on the floor too, and as I looked down I saw something that made my eyes pop out of my head.

Another moment and I was fairly sprinting for that back door again.

CHAPTER III
A GRAND-STAND VIEW

As I MOVED OFF I felt a spatter of rain, and by the time I had reached the back door the downpour had begun in earnest. So fast had I sprinted that when I got in the kitchen I felt a bit faint, and as soon as I was in that living-room I had to hold myself steady for a minute, for my head was swimming and my legs decidedly tottery.

Suddenly I smelt something. I sniffed, and there was no mistaking what it was—a perfume of some sort and rather subtle, like the distant scent from a bed of stocks or pinks. But there were no flowers in the room and the two windows were closed, and then as I moved forward the scent became stronger. It was so strong, in fact, that I located it. Some-one—a woman probably—had been sitting in a winged easy chair on the near side of the fireplace. I felt the cushion, but it had no suspicion of warmth but when I sniffed close against the arms and back the scent was there all right.

But that was of comparative unimportance. Maddon was what mattered. He lay on the wood floor with his head against the swivel chair, and a hole had been neatly plugged through his right temple. I judged the bullet to have been a small calibre one, for the hole was neat and there had been little bleeding—only a trickle of blood along the nose. As for the range at which the shot had been fired, I judged it to be a couple of foot or just less. On the one hand the shot had been remarkably close end on the other there were no flash marks on hair or beard. He was fully dressed except for collar and tie, and slippers for shoes, and he had not shaved.

I straightened myself, for my head was swimming again, and as I did so it dawned on me that somebody might come —a tradesman for instance—and find me there, so it might be as well if I had a couple of bolt-holes. So I undid the front door. It had a Yale lock, so I put on the catch and left the door virtually unfastened. Behind me, in the narrow passage into which the door opened, was a flight of stairs. Outside, the rain was now coming down in sheets and as I moved back for another look at Maddon there was a terrific clap of thunder and then a lightning flash that lit up the room.

But in spite of the storm there was plenty of light for me to see all I wanted. First I moved Maddon's head with my gloved hand and had a close look at him. The full lips seemed set in a sneer, and at close quarters he looked altogether a far less presentable specimen than the man I had met on his walk that previous night. In death his face was decidedly unpleasant. Then, as I let the head droop again I thought of something. "This night shall thy soul be required of thee." Well, if Pyramid Porle had done the shooting, there'd be plenty of time to rope him in.

Next, I gently insinuated my hand into his breast pocket, and with two fingers drew out a wallet. I didn't count the notes that were in it, but I guessed there was best part of a hundred pounds in the wad. There were about a dozen visiting cards—Herbert S. Maddon, Five Oaks, Cleavesham, Porthaven, Sussex—and two or three receipts, and that was all, so I pushed the wallet back and then had a quick look out of a window. But in that downpour I knew that nobody would be coming, so I turned back to the room again.

Once more I sniffed the scent that lingered on the chair. It was subtle, as I said, and very attractive, but I couldn't even begin to give it a name, for my knowledge of scent is limited to buying, as a present, a bottle of Coty or Houbigant. But I did have an idea about the woman who had been there. If it were she who had shot Maddon, and the small calibre of the gun was some added evidence, then she couldn't have gone out by the front door, for it had been bolted as well as locked. It was she, then, who had left the back door ajar when she had hurried away, and if so, then there might be the print of a heel where the bricks by the back door ended and the earth path began.

I had a look at once. Luckily the rain was not coming down so fast, but I don't think it would have deterred me if it had been a cloud-burst, for as soon as I was across the bricks I saw the deep print of the heel of a woman's shoe. Beyond it was a second, rather more faint, and then a third which was only just visible. That discovery was lucky, for I might have spun the yarn that it was the front door by which I had entered the house.

I didn't mind then about the damp marks that my feet left on the kitchen floor. The other room didn't matter either, for it was practically covered with a green cord carpet. But there was still plenty to see in that room. The side-table, for instance, that stood well within reach of the scented chair. On it was an ash-tray in which were stubs of cigarettes and dead matches. With a match-end I gently stirred them. Five of the stubs were of Players cigarettes and three were a far more expensive kind with filter tips, and on each of them was lipstick.

You may wonder why I was having the nerve to make that extensive survey instead of ringing up the police, and I think the reason was the dead man himself: the fact that he was someone who had intrigued Wharton, and that Wharton would want to know all I could tell him about his death. For when the police did arrive there would be little chance of my making an inspection such as was being presented to me now, and the last use I intended making of Wharton's letter of introduction to Chevalle was to thrust my nose into what would be Chevalle's business. Everything I knew should certainly be placed at Chevalle's disposal—or wouldn't it? That, I was telling myself, would have to depend.

But things were already fairly clear. The lady had knocked at the front door and Maddon had admitted her. The two had talked and smoked. He had sat on that other easy chair and later had gone to his desk to write or fetch something. Then she had shot him. Next she had ransacked the desk. There wasn't a doubt of that, and she had done it hurriedly; so hurriedly that not a single drawer had been properly closed and papers that had been looked through had not been put back. Also it seemed to me that if she had done the job so thoroughly, then there was no point in my searching the desk or looking through the papers.

I had another quick look through the window and then did some more thinking. Where did Porle come into all this? Had he been watching the house and was it he who had done the shooting after he had seen the lady leave? To that, as you will see, there was one clear objection. If the lady had not done the shooting or ransacked the drawers, then Maddon would have let her out by the front door. As it was, she had bolted through the back door and it was perfectly obvious why. From the front door and its brick path to the front gate the country lay open and she might have been seen, even from the back road, but once she was out by the back, then the woods concealed her.

Perhaps it was thinking about the lady that made me have another look at the chair. As I did so the sun came peering in and it glinted on something. It was a hair, a long, golden hair. Then I saw another, where the head had rested, and I had a sudden idea. On the desk were 32 scattered envelopes. In one of them I put a hair and then added one of the lip-sticked cigarette-ends. Maybe there would be a print, and if so Wharton would get it developed for me.

I glanced at my watch and judged that I had been in the house no more than a quarter of an hour. Plenty of time, then, to ring the police, and no doctor was needed for Maddon. He was deader than mutton and a quarter of an hour either way would make no difference to the doctor's opinion as to time of death. So I had a quick look round the room and found little of importance. On the mantelpiece, behind an ornament, was a packet of Players with two cigarettes remaining. In the grate was a tiny pile of ash, but not of a coal or wood fire. The weather had been too sultry for that, and as I gently stirred the ash I saw a piece of dirty white and knew that Maddon had burnt that notice which Pyramid Porle had affixed so brazenly to the back door. The only other thing I noticed was the telephone, standing on the desk top and almost concealed by a couple of old newspapers. Perhaps, I thought, I had better ring the Porthaven police.

But first I took a precautionary look out and it was phenomenally lucky for me that I did so. For just entering the front gate was a man. His back was to me as he shut the gate and he was carrying an umbrella and wearing a waterproof. It didn't strike me for a moment that I, a stranger in Cleavesham, might know him. All I had was a hunch that the sooner I was out of the back door, the better for me. So I grabbed my stick and in a flash was in the kitchen. Then as I lifted the wooden snack I saw two things. Below the snack was a hole through which I could have put a couple of fingers and it gave a clear view of the room. Lower down the door was a bolt, and that I pressed quietly home.

I heard steps before the front door and only a few moments later did it strike me that it was curious that there was no knock. But the caller must have opened the door, for I heard him calling as soon as the steps had ceased:

"Maddon! Are you there?"

He listened for only a moment or two and then I heard the handle of the living-room door. A man looked in.

Why I hadn't bolted out by the back I never shall know, but I was glad afterwards that I'd stayed where I was, eye at the hole. For the man was Bernard Temple.

His eyes fell on Maddon, and never did a man look more startled. He drew back a pace towards the door, then gave a cautious look round and stood intently listening. Then he shook his head as if he knew there could be no one in the house, and next he took a step forward. He leaned over and very gingerly his fingers touched the dead man's face. Then he drew himself up and across his face there flashed a look of the intensest satisfaction. It wasn't gloating; just a nod to himself and a sort of congratulatory smile.

Then he thought of something, for his eyes opened wide. His head went sideways and I guessed his breath was held as he listened. Then his hands were busy at the dead man's pockets. Even from my grand-stand I couldn't see all I would have liked, for by bad luck he had his back to me as he knelt. But I knew he was examining this and that, and everything seemed to be replaced. Then out came the wallet and by chance he turned sideways. Into his pocket went most of the wad of notes, and then he was examining the rest of its contents. The wallet was replaced and he was motionless for a good minute, shaking his head now and again as if in a dilemma.

Then he made up his mind. He had a quick look through the window and then went out by the side door. I heard the click of the bolt and at once he was back again, and feverishly searching that already ransacked desk. It was strange, I thought, that it didn't occur to him that the desk had been gone through, but maybe his wits were a bit muddled after the shock of finding Maddon dead. But whatever he was looking for he didn't find, for he was scowling and shaking his head as if he was now in the devil of a mess. Then he did something that made me stare, for he scowled down at Maddon and then suddenly swung his leg and kicked him viciously in the ribs.

I knew that the time had come for me to tiptoe out of that door behind me, but so personal was the drama beneath my eyes that I stayed on till it might be too late. But Temple was now standing in thought again, fingers nervously at his beard. A few moments and he fairly darted to the window. He nodded to himself as if reassured, and then there happened the strangest thing of all. He took a step towards me and straightened himself. Up went his head as if he were assuming some deliberate pose and then out of his mouth came the queerest squeak!

He squeaked again, then the noise became words.

"This is Miss Smith speaking. Yes, I'm a stranger here."

Then I tumbled to what he was doing, and my guess was confirmed. He nodded to himself and then his hand went out towards the telephone. Then it went back and he produced a handkerchief from his trouser pocket, wrapped it round the receiver and then did some dialling.

"Cleavesham two two nine," he said, in that high-pitched feminine voice. "I want the Porthaven police station. . . . I don't know the number. I'm a stranger here. . . . Yes, thank you."

His back was to me, for he was keeping a wary eye on the window and the front path. In under half a minute he had his number.

"May I speak to the Chief Constable, please? . . . It's a Miss Smith speaking, and it's urgent. . . . Then I must talk to somebody else. . . . Oh, I see."

There his voice went back on him for the falsetto dropped too low. But he covered it by a spell of coughing.

"I'm very sorry. My cough's bad this morning.... What's that? . . . Oh, I'm sorry. It's about a murder. . . . Here. Five Oaks, they call it. . . . A man, he's murdered. . . . Oh, no, it isn't a joke. I wish it was. . . . I said I wished it was. . . . You'll send someone at once? . . . I can't promise that. I have a bus to catch. . . . Yes, it's my aunt who's very ill. . . . No, no, no . . . I can't promise. Good-bye."

He hung up then and stood for a long minute, frowning away and nervously sucking at his lower lip. Then, before I was ready for him, he was on the move. A quick look round and he had gone. I heard the bolt click and then the slam of the door and at once I was through my own door and making for the window. I was in time to see him at the front gate. But he didn't turn towards the village or the path by which I had come. A few yards to the left and he slipped into the chestnut undergrowth and was gone from sight. All I remember is one incongruity—when he drew the closed umbrella in after him.

I let out a breath and then wondered what next. To Porthaven was just over two miles and the police would arrive in under ten minutes—if they'd really taken the message seriously, and they couldn't afford to do less. And what about myself? Oughtn't

I to be making for the same undergrowth? And if I didn't, then what was to be my yarn?

Then it struck me that as far as I was concerned, not only was my position impregnable, but that if I disappeared I should miss quite a lot of interesting things. With Wharton's letter in my pocket I could hardly be held as a suspect, though I very genuinely hated the idea of thrusting myself forward. But I did want to see the reactions of Chevalle and his men, and, above all, to the missing Miss Smith.

And that makes a good moment to reveal a little more about myself, though maybe you have already guessed it. Even my wife says that at times I can be the most exasperating person in the world, for I seem to go deliberately out of my way to put people's backs up. Perhaps I do, and because I love ironic situations and even creating them. And the matter of Miss Smith seemed very definitely such an irony. Could I not swear on a stack of Bibles that I'd never seen the lady? True I might have added the white lie that she must have gone before my arrival, but that wouldn't make a pennorth of difference to the case. Later, of course, I'd reveal by a fake telephone call or anonymous letter just who Miss Smith had been. For the bearded Bernard wouldn't bolt. Why should he? He could swear on the same stack of Bibles that he'd never been near the house.

I suppose it was a kind of selfish cussedness that made me want to keep Bernard Temple—and Pyramid Porle for that mat-ter—under my eye, if only for a few hours. After all, I'd discov-ered both of them and I alone knew that the two were linked not only with each other but also with the dead Maddon. What I wanted, then, was to find out what Porle had meant by try-ing to set me against Temple, especially as I now had grounds for believing that Porle's description of him as dangerous and a consorter with rogues had more than personal dislike behind it. And yet I knew, the more I thought, that I wasn't doing the right thing in keeping back or delaying information that ought to be at once in the hands of the police, so I made a bargain with my-self. If the police asked, me about Miss Smith, then I'd naturally be ignorant. If, however, they asked me if I'd seen anyone at all, then I'd tell them about Temple. At the time that seemed to me a fair compromise. Now I look back at things I think I was playing a risky and a tricky game.

But if I was to be ignorant of Miss Smith, then I had to ring Porthaven at once, otherwise I couldn't explain my presence in the house and the fact that I was apparently waiting for the police arrival. So I looked up the number and then dialled. What I said you can guess. You can guess too the astonishment at the other end.

"And you say there's no woman there!" asked the station sergeant.

"I've just told you so," I said with a show of indignation.

"Rum business to me," he said, and I heard his grunt. "Give me your name and particulars, sir, will you?"

I gave all I thought was necessary and then he told me that an Inspector Galley had already left for Cleavesham and ought to be there at any minute. I said I'd certainly wait, and that was that.

As I hung up I caught sight of something. I had seen it at very close quarters before and had noticed nothing unusual, but this second look brought a question. That ash-tray with cigarette- and match-ends had very little ash. If all those cigarettes had been smoked, where had the ash gone? Each of the easy chairs by the table was surrounded by carpet, and a caller would surely not have flicked all the ash on that carpet, whatever Maddon himself had done. And when I got down on hands and knees and examined the carpet there was only the least suspicion of what might have been ash.

Then, before I'd had time to think of an explanation, I heard the toot of a horn. A car was nosing its way along the short grass track that led through the wood from the road to near the front gate. Two men got out and the taller, so I guessed, was the In-spector, for he had a good look round while his subordinate waited. Then they came down the path and I met them at the front door.

"Inspector Galley?" I said.

"Yes," he said, and stared pretty hard. "And who are you?"

I told him how I'd found the body and rung Porthaven after he'd left.

"It was a Miss Smith who rang us," he said. "Isn't she here?"

"Come and see for yourself," I said, and stepped back.

He had a look, at least in the one room. "You go right through the house, Bill," he told his colleague. "I'll stay here. And you haven't seen any woman at all?" he asked me.

"Never a woman."

"Then she got the wind up. Didn't like staying with a corpse, perhaps."

He had a good look at the body, and when he got to his feet gave a sudden sniff.

"Scent of some sort. Do you smell it?"

I said it had been much stronger a few minutes before.

"Believed in scenting herself up, that Miss Smith—if her name was Smith," he said. Then he lifted the receiver and dialled. He told somebody it was all right and the doctor could come, and from the quality of his final O.K., I gathered that something had given him a special satisfaction. As he hung up, Bill—whose other name was Hope—came back. He'd been right over both floors, he said, and hadn't seen a thing.

"Now, sir, before we start we'd like your finger-prints," Galley said to me. "Only so that we don't get them mixed up with any others."

"You won't find any of mine," I said. "I've had these gloves on all the time."

He gave me a look that was interested, to say the least of it. Then he gave Hope a look. I suppose I didn't look any too ornate that morning, even if I was well washed behind the ears. I dress for comfort, not effect, and of the three pairs of grey flannel trousers in the room, mine were the baggiest. As for my old tweed coat, Bernice threatened years ago to change it for a flag or balloon.

"You always wear gloves when you're out?" Galley asked me.

I thought I'd get friendly. "Not very often," I said. "They're useful though, when I'm doing a burglary job." He gave Hope another quick look. "So you do a bit of burglary occasionally?"

"One must live," I said, but he still didn't see the joke. "Well, we've only your word that you didn't take the gloves off," he said. "You'd better let us take your prints." Hope took them and then Galley questioned me again. "You said you lived at a house called Ringlands.'"

"Not 'lived'," I pointed out. "I'm staying there with my sister. I arrived last night."

"From where?"

"London."

"You knew you were coming to an area? What about a permit?"

"I'm afraid I haven't got one," I said.

His eyebrows lifted. "But you know the regulations?"

"If I didn't," I said, "it was my business to make myself acquainted with them."

"There we are then," he said. "I'm afraid I shall have to report it to the Chief. It'll be for him to decide. Have a look round this room now, Bill, and see what you can see." I sat in the unscented armchair and watched the routine I'd watched a hundred times—chalk marks round the body, copious notes in notebooks, this and that gingerly touched with gloved fingers and an occasional puff of powder at a possible print. And Galley was a good enough man at the job, even if he was spreading himself for my benefit. He found two hairs on the chair and left them where they were, and he noticed the two kinds of cigarettes and the lipstick marks, and he had Hope try the ash-tray for prints, and from the way it was afterwards put aside I gathered they'd found something on it.

Steps on the front path announced the arrival of the doctor. He was a dug-out, for the regular police surgeon was in the Army, but he certainly knew his job. It was his opinion that the gun was small calibred and the shot fired from fairly close. Time of death he gave as roughly between 5.30 and 6.30 that morning, and Galley didn't ask him how he knew.

Galley and Hope went through the dead man's pockets, and while they made an inventory the doctor got into conversation with me. He had practised in Porthaven for forty years before his retirement, but had never attended Maddon. Ringlands he knew well enough and had met Helen, but as we were talking quietly, Galley didn't gather a more favourable impression of myself. Then the telephone suddenly went and Galley took the call. I heard little except, "Very good," and "Right-ho," and the final, "Good-bye."

"A bit of luck, doc.," he announced. "The Chief was at Bycliffe and he thought if there was nothing doing he'd push on to Hastings to see somebody, so he rang the office on spec., and they told him about this."

"Did he take his car or his bike?" asked Hope.

"His car, I think," Galley told him. "What should he take his bike for?"

"Well, he won't be here for a bit," Hope said, and then looked over at the doctor. "Someone must have kept this place clean, the way it looks everywhere. Suppose you don't know, sir, if he had anybody in?"

"I believe he had young Mrs. Beaney, just along the road," the doctor said. "It won't do any harm to ask."

"Slip along and fetch her, Bill," Galley said, as if the idea had been his own. "You needn't tell her too much so long as she comes."

Out went Hope, and Galley took off the receiver. I'd expected an ironic twist or two as I've told you, but I didn't anticipate what was going to happen.

"About that woman calling herself Smith who rang you up," Galley was saying. "What sort of a voice had she? . . . You know what I mean. Was she a lady, or what?"

"I see," he went on. "Tell me this then. Did she strike you as anyone who'd make themselves up? . . . Yes, paint and powder and all that, and lipstick and a cigarette smoker. . . . You can't say!"

He heaved an exasperated sigh, then his voice had a sudden urgency.

"I say; there may have been some truth in that yarn about her sick aunt. Have the bus from Cleavesham met and question the conductor. . . . I know it may be too late, but we've got to take a chance."

He hung up and then gave me a look, and I didn't know why. But I met it unblushingly. And then one of those queer silences fell on the room. The doctor sheered off and stood looking out of the window, and Galley was idly moving the papers on the desk. I sat contemplating the mess into which my cussedness had landed me and wondering if with any gracefulness I could call off the wild-goose chase of Miss Smith. But most of all I was thinking of Bernard Temple—people's warden, church worker, and a vital cog in the war effort of Cleavesham—and trying to reconcile all that with a stolen wad of notes and the look of sheer malignancy on his face when he had swung his leg and kicked a dead man in the ribs.

CHAPTER IV
WITCH-DOCTORING

MRS. BEANEY WAS doubtless called "young" to distinguish her from an ancient mother-in-law, for she was best part of fifty. She was tallish and gaunt with legs like a robin's and the general look of an adventurous crow, and I very much doubted if the relationships between her and her late employer had been other than strictly business ones. I didn't see her at close quarters, however, only through the window as she approached with Hope, and as the idea was not to scare her with a look at the body, she was interviewed in the dining-room. The doctor went in too and I was left alone with the corpse. I don't think that had quite struck Galley at the time, and he was probably too interested in questioning the woman to worry if I should bolt. I was interested, too, in what Mrs. Beaney might be saying and I actually moved towards the door to try to overhear. Then I thought better of it and returned to my chair.

Then I noticed something. That ash-tray had two lips. It was fashioned, in fact, like a sweet tray, and on one of the lips—quite large they were too—Hope had shown up a very clear print.

Bush, Christopher

The Case of the Platinum Blonde

Dean Street Press
(1944) 2018

RM

July 2018

15.95

What was more he had left his apparatus on the desk flap, and at once I had my ears pricked for the sounds from the other room. But though Hope had dark powder as well as white I was too scared to make a dusting and press it on paper, for I mightn't have had time to blow the powder off and make a fresh dusting. But I did make a copy of that print and with infinite care, counting the ridges and noting them down, and all the time my ears were strained for the sounds from that other room. I reckoned I'd make a good job of it and it was lucky that I'd finished, for Hope came in and then went out with his apparatus to take Mrs. Beaney's prints. A few minutes after that Mrs. Beaney left and the three came back to the room.

"Temple," Galley was saying reflectively. "Do you know him, doctor?"

"I've heard the name often enough," the doctor said, "but I've never attended him."

That was a good time for me to chip in with the little I allowed myself to know. It was quite gratefully received.

"How did his name crop up?" I asked.

"I don't see why I shouldn't tell you," Galley said, after a glance at Hope. "Mrs. Beaney said he was the only friend this Mr. Maddon had. Used to call a fairish bit."

"She never heard them having a quarrel?"

The question startled him, and because I'd hit a nail clean on the head.

"I'm afraid I can't go into any more details," he told me rather curtly. "But you might tell us where this Temple lives."

When he knew he gave Hope another look and said it was interesting. What he meant was the point he'd seized on—that if one followed the field-path, one actually passed his cottage. Then, before he could ask me anything more, there was an interruption.

"Here's the Chief now," Hope suddenly said.

Galley instinctively pulled himself up and straightened his coat back. I squinted round through the window and saw a man placing a bicycle against the front gate. As he came down the path I saw that his soft felt hat was soaked and his waterproof was dripping too.

"A bit wet, sir?" Galley hailed him.

"Just a bit," Chevalle said, and jokingly. It was an attractive voice, but what I was wondering was if it would be quite as pleasant by the time he had finished with me. And it wasn't any too promising when Galley button-holed him and took him into the other room, where I guessed he was being told about myself.

Chevalle looked a soldier. He was about five foot ten and carried himself well, and he had what I might call a parade-ground poise. The clipped moustache took something of the heaviness from the face and the square jaw, and his eyes were the kindly sort. When he came into the room and looked across at me, there was actually a smile in them.

"Your name's Travers?" he said. "Mine's Chevalle. I'm the Chief Constable. And you're staying at Ringlands with your sister, Mrs. Thornley."

"Yes," I said. His voice was pleasant and the accent somehow familiar. The West of Scotland was how I placed him at first, and then, from the smooth, unforced sounding of the final 'r's' I changed to Northern Ireland.

He merely nodded and smiled and then began busying himself with Galley and the doctor. I sat down again.

If Galley knew his job, Chevalle knew it even better. There was no fuss and no display but he covered the ground and he found what Galley had missed.

"Curious?" he said, and sniffed round the chair. "I've smelt that scent somewhere. But doesn't it strike you as funny, Galley, that this Miss Smith should have stayed here long enough to have left her scent in the room and"—his eye went to the cigarette-ends—"and smoked three cigarettes."

"Two, sir," corrected Galley.

"You sure? I thought you said three."

He had a closer look and then took up the thread of thought.

"Even two cigarettes would take a quarter of an hour at the least. All that time she was here with a dead man, and yet she was scared to stay on and wait for the police."

"If you ask me, sir," Galley said, "there's something fishy all round."

"There usually is in murder cases," Chevalle told him dryly, and then caught my eye and smiled. "But what did the woman do with herself all that time?"

"Perhaps she was the one who went through this desk."

"Everything is as you found it?"

"Not a thing touched, sir," Galley assured him.

"Then the desk was gone through in a hurry. That wouldn't have taken a quarter of an hour. And if she was genuine, why should she be such an incredible fool as either to search the desk and leave it like this when she knew she was going to ring us, or to do it after she'd rung us? She didn't even tidy it after she'd rung us."

"I know, sir," Galley said and shrugged his shoulders. "Did they ask at the station what she was doing here at all?"

"I believe she said she happened to be coming by."

"Then she could only have been coming along the field-path from the village or to the village," Chevalle pointed out. "That doesn't explain why she came to the house. You say Mrs. Beaney said nobody ever came here except tradesmen and occasionally Mr. Temple."

"But Mrs. Beaney only comes in of afternoons, sir."

"True enough," Chevalle said. "But what's that in the grate?"

He had spotted the tiny heap of ash and was on his knees at once. The two corners of cardboard were brought out with gloved fingers, and his eyebrows lifted at the sight of them. But he could make nothing of them and Galley put them in the envelope.

"Which way did this Miss Smith go out?" he was asking Galley.

"Don't know, sir. Both doors were open."

"I found the back door opened," I broke in. "The front door was locked and bolted and I opened it myself."

"Then she went out the back way," he said. "Perhaps we'd better have a look."

Galley asked what about the body? Another minute and he and Hope were carrying it out to the ambulance in which the doctor had come. As I stood by the door with Chevalle, watching them, a woman went by on the path towards the village. She had a good look back before she passed out of our sight.

"That was Mrs. Beaney," I said.

"I know Mrs. Beaney," he told me wryly. "She's off to give the village the news. I wouldn't mind wagering that by the time you get back to Ringlands, Mrs. Thornley will be telling you all about it."

"I know her sort," I said. "But you know my sister pretty well, don't you?"

"She's a very good friend," he said. "And a very good sort."

He must have thought it odd that I made no comment, but I happened to be thinking. I liked Chevalle. I had taken to him from my first sight of him, though perhaps I had been biased by Wharton's praise. In any case, and on a sudden impulse, I pulled out Wharton's letter.

"I don't know if you've time to glance through this. It's from an old friend of yours and mine."

"Indeed?" he said, and was smiling as he unfolded the letter. Then his expression changed and there was quite a look of concern on his face when he had finished reading it.

"My dear fellow, I'm so sorry. I had no idea."

"Why should you have had?" I said.

"And your sister never told me of your . . . your activities."

"The last thing she'd do," I said. "I don't think she wholly approves of my peace-time association with the police."

He laughed. "Well, we can do with you down here. Galley's steady and reliable and all that, but he hasn't a lot of imagination. He's only had his rank for the last three months. His predecessor, an excellent fellow, was killed in a raid. But I'll talk to you about all that later."

"Not if you're thinking of dragging me into this case," I said. "I'm an invalid. Go easy's my motto!"

Galley and Hope were coming back and we left it like that. The first thing we all did, for I tagged along uninvited, was to look outside the back door. Chevalle and Galley spotted the first heel-mark at the same moment. Hope was told to make casts, and then Chevalle had a look round.

"What I'm wondering," he said, "is how the woman got in. Maddon must have let her in. Therefore he knew her. And very well too, or he'd have put on a collar and tie."

"What woman?" I ventured.

"The woman who killed him," he said. "Whether she and Miss Smith were the same person remains to be seen. Personally I'm inclined to doubt it."

The cigarette-ends were now in an envelope and the silky hairs in another. Then during a last rummage Chevalle found a hair-pin. It was a light bronze and probably belonging to the woman of the hair. That too went into an envelope and so did the ash-tray. Then I was left alone again while Chevalle and Galley inspected the upstair rooms.

"They've been searched too," Chevalle told me when he came down. "Wonder what was being looked for?"

"Why not the old, old story?" I said. "Blackmail letters."

He stared, then raised his eyebrows. "That's a mighty good suggestion. I often wondered where Maddon got his money from."

There didn't seem to be anything for me to wait for, so I said I'd be going. I added, for Galley's benefit, that if I was wanted I'd be somewhere at hand.

Chevalle strolled with me to the front gate. "It's rather short notice," he said, "but I'd like you to come and have supper with us to-night. Sevenish. I expect I'll be free enough by then."

"I'd love to come," I said, "if you're sure I shan't be in the way."

"Don't you worry about that, my dear fellow," he said. "But about in there," he said, and nodded back at the house. "Got any ideas?"

"One or two," I said, and at the moment I hadn't the faintest intention of telling him the half of them. "Maybe to-night they'll be worth telling you."

"Sure they're not now?"

"Dead sure," I said. "But I'd like you to do a couple of things—only because I think they're going to help. One is, keep an eye on Temple. Put a man on his tail."

"Temple!" he said. "What on earth do you know about Temple?"

"Don't know yet," I said. "I know he didn't kill Maddon, but I do know too that he may have an idea who did."

"That's a mighty strong statement."

"If you care to trust me till this evening I may make it stronger," I said. "As for the other thing, I'll tell you without being too enigmatical that it's also bound up with Temple. And it's this. Forget all about Miss Smith."

I've rarely seen a man so taken aback. His face, tanned as it was, seemed to flush, and I thought it was with annoyance. After all he'd every right to be furious at the calm presumption of an outsider like myself of whom he knew nothing at first hand. But it wasn't annoyance. It was sheer bewilderment.

"But she's . . . she's important. She's vital," he said, or rather stammered. "She's simply got to be questioned."

"So you *can* question her, and in ten minutes' time," I said. "But I don't think you'll be doing any good."

That bewildered him even more.

"Look here, Major," I said. "I know where you can lay your hands on her but I'm not quite sure what might happen if you do. In another half-hour I may be sure. She doesn't know me but I know the way to make her talk and I'd like to try it. What about it?"

"You go ahead then," he said.

I had been deliberately sheering off, and all I had to do then was to call back that I'd be seeing him that evening and be giving him some news. If I'd looked back after that I knew I'd have seen him staring after me and wondering just what I was—cheap bluffer, witch-doctor, or just someone who'd made rather too apposite an appearance at that house.

But I wasn't giving myself a headache over that. I was congratulating myself on having got out of an awkward fix. I might

not be clean out but at least I had gained time, and I was suf-
ficiently sure of my mental dexterity to have no qualms about
justifying myself when the showdown came that evening.

And there was no denying the fact that I had been undeserv-
edly lucky. First, Galley had been too busy to ask me to give an
account of everything that had happened on my arrival at the
house and when he had had the time, then Chevalle had turned
up. He had been busy too, and then, just when I had sensed that
he was about to ask me for a statement, I had taken the wind out
of his sails by that hocus-pocus about Temple and Miss Smith.

Not that Chevalle had a monopoly of bewilderments. There
were the devil of a lot of things I couldn't understand. Take the
time of the murder, for an example. Maddon struck me as one
who'd sit up late and rise very late. Mrs. Beaney, for instance,
came to clean up in the afternoons. Yet he had been up and fully
dressed—not too meticulously I admit—at well before six o'clock
that morning. Admitted that the absence of dirty china showed
that he had had no morning meal. But what of the lady? She
must have been up even earlier, for she had had to come from
somewhere.

Then suddenly I stopped in my tracks. Wouldn't it fit the
case better to assume that the lady had arrived the previous
night? That Maddon might or might not have met Porle at elev-
en o'clock as the notice on the door had insisted, did not much
affect things, for the lady might have been in bed and asleep by
then. But in the morning she might have had to be up and away,
and Maddon had got up too, intending to get breakfast. Maybe
some of those cigarettes had been smoked the previous night.

I liked that theory, even if it did conflict with something
which you may have spotted for yourself. But it wasn't an urgent theory needing immediate testing. Bernard Temple and
Pyramid Porle were far more urgent, and strangely enough it
was Porle who intrigued me most. He had been far too good a
prophet for my liking. It takes a hell of a lot of knowledge, and
inside knowledge at that, to predict the night a man's soul may
be violently required of him.

*　　*　　*　　*　　*

It was well after eleven o'clock, but I knew I'd have ample time to get back for a one-o'clock lunch. I stepped out, nevertheless, along that path to the village, and as I walked I noticed how easy it was to conceal one's movements. The tall, sheltering hedges of hop gardens were often on both sides of me, and the hedges of fields and meadows were interspersed with oaks, and tall enough for concealment if one cared to stoop. The path went uphill and down and twisted round, but the last two hundred yards were straighter and more level, and I kept my eyes about me as I neared Temple's garden. But he wasn't there and I knocked at the front door. The chances, I thought, were well against his being in, but almost at once I heard a movement inside the house.

It was he who opened the door, and he stared at me for a moment, trying evidently to place me. The previous evening I had been reasonably well dressed and had worn a rather chic grey hat, but in a second he had spotted me and was giving that dental smile and bowing slightly from the waist up.

"Major Travers, isn't it?"

"Sorry to trouble you, Mr. Temple," I said, "but I rather wanted to ask you something about war savings generally. My sister didn't know, but I thought you would."

"Come in, sir. Come in." He was ushering me with waving hands into a cosy little room on my right. Through a door on the left I caught sight of an elderly woman peeling potatoes at the kitchen sink.

"Sit down, sir. Sit down. Sorry I can't offer you a drink. Unless it's not too early for whisky?"

"It *is* too early," I said. "Even if it weren't I'd never drink a man's liquor in war-time. By the way, I caught sight of you this morning, but I was too late to catch you up."

"Of me?" he said. "But I haven't been out of the house this morning. Where did you think you saw me?"

"Coming by the garden gate of Ringlands," I said. "Sorry, I must have been mistaken. A pretty fool I'd have looked if I'd gone chasing some stranger."

He forced a chuckle at that and I weighed in with some footling question about interest on Defence Bonds and whether it could be left at compound interest in Treasury Bonds and with no payment of income tax. Very patiently he showed me the various fallacies in that unhappy idea.

"Well, I'm much obliged to you," I said.

"You're not going already," he protested. "It's so rarely I get visitors." Then he added quickly that he meant interesting ones.

"I'm afraid you can't put me into that category," I said. "Oh, by the way, have you heard the news? They tell me there's been a murder in the village!"

"A murder!" His surprise was superb. "You're surely not serious."

"Indeed I am," I said. "You can take it from me that it's true. A man named Maddon, who lives at Five Oaks."

"Maddon!" He stared, then shook his head. "Who should have wanted to kill Maddon?" Then he fairly whipped round on me. "Do they know who did it?"

"Not that I've heard," I said. "But you knew him of course." He darted me a quick look, so I added that I meant in his official capacity of war-savings secretary.

"Not a pleasant man," he said, and shook his head again. "I'm afraid he wasn't popular."

"A good customer of yours, was he?"

"Another collector was concerned with that," he said. "I don't think, though, that he ever subscribed. In fact, I remember he boasted to me not long ago that he'd never bought a certificate."

"Well," I said, getting to my feet and introducing some comic relief, "it's a damn nice reception you've given a stranger. Staging a murder as soon as he gets here."

He gave a beautiful dental smile at that and then I came to the opening for which I'd been ready as soon as I stepped inside that room. Before I'd knocked I'd wondered both what and how much to say, but the patience cards laid out on the folding table by the window had given me an idea. And, without any boasting, I knew Temple would be putty in my hands, for he was the fawning, ingratiating sort; itching to climb from one society stratum to another and always on the look-out to insinuate himself into this and that. There had been something revealing and almost pathetic in the way he had let slip that he rarely had interesting visitors. Helen, for all her lack of snobbery, is very much the *grande dame*, and maybe he thought I might be worth cultivating too.

"You're a patience fiend, are you?" I said as I looked across at the table.

"I find it a great solace at times," he said and gave me an apologetic look.

"I play a lot, too," I told him, and then appeared to remember something. "I don't expect you to believe me, but I could have made a fortune out of cards. Oh, no," I said. "Not the gambling. That's a mug's game. By telling fortunes!"

"Really?" he said.

By now I was fingering the cards and idly manipulating them into a pack.

"If it interests you," I said, "and if you promise to keep it to yourself, I'll try it on you."

I could almost hear the thoughts whirl in his brain. And then he knew it was absurd to have any suspicions of me, and he was smiling deprecatingly.

"I'm afraid I shouldn't be a very interesting subject."

"You never know," I said. "Got a sheet of writing-paper handy?"

He fetched one at once. Then I got him to shuffle the cards while I turned my back. Then I told him to lay them out in three different-sized heaps.

"What's your age, by the way?" I said. "Strictly in confidence."

"Forty-eight," he said.

"Then no heap is to contain more than twenty-four cards," I said, for hocus-pocus like that is always convincing. "And remember the number in each heap because I'm going to jot them down and make a preliminary calculation."

That was all done and I put the paper in my pocket and approached the table. He drew a chair forward for me and I sat down. First, to make the mumbo-jumbo still impressive, I took the third card all the way down from each heap and discarded the rest. Those third cards I laid out on the table in a square of four cards each way.

"This is most extraordinary," I began. "I ought to have explained that I can't tell about the past or the future, only the immediate present, so to speak. What's happened today, for instance."

There I picked up a card and laid it aside. "Have you come into a nice little sum of money to-day? Not a lot, perhaps. A hundred or so?"

I looked up at him and he was scared stiff.

"Mind you," I said, and was looking down again. "I can't always be right. Perhaps I picked out a false third card, but that's what these cards tell me."

"As a matter of fact I did have some money come this morning," he said, and his voice had hardly a tremor. But he was aware of what tremor there was, for he began a noisy clearing of his throat. I was picking up another card.

"Also to-day you've had a tremendous surprise," I went on, and as if to myself. "What the cards actually say is that you've lost a dangerous enemy and are likely to have made a friend. And another interesting thing," I said as I picked out another card. Then I shook my head. "But I think that must be wrong. It says you met a certain lady for the first time. The contact is very close. Very close indeed. In fact," I went on, and laying two other cards on top of it, "I'd even go so far as to say that I've never seen a closer contact. It's as if this lady were almost part of yourself. Your wife, for instance." Then I gave an elaborate shrug of the shoulders and pushed the remaining cards to a heap.

"I'm afraid you'll regard me as a bit of a boaster. If you haven't been out of the house this morning, then I'm all wrong, or the cards are. Perhaps I picked them out wrongly after all."

I had blethered on to give him time to recover himself, and when I got to my feet I was smiling apologetically as I met his look.

"It was really very good, in a way," he said, and his voice was none too steady. "The letter this morning did tell me that an uncle of mine had died, and he and I weren't on the best of terms."

"Good Lord!" I said, glancing at my wrist-watch. "I'm afraid I must fly. Got another call to pay before lunch."

He was uncommonly quiet as he showed me out. He did put out a dampish hand and hope we'd see more of each other.

"Most certainly we will," I said. "Do you know Chevalle, by the way? A very clever fellow, I believe. I only asked because I'm dining with him to-night."

Then before he could get a word in, I smiled, nodded, and moved off. And I'd left him with the devil of a lot to think about, particularly that wholly unnecessary and clumsy reference to Chevalle. And I'd by no means finished with Bernard Temple. After lunch, though he didn't know it, he was due for an even bigger shock.

I looked back as I neared Lane End, for I was rather expecting Temple to be watching me, but there was no window that looked my way, and in any case I decided it might complicate things even more to my advantage if he knew what that second call of mine was. But once in the short lane I was out of sight, for the hedges were tall. Smoke was coming from the house-chimney, and I guessed Pyramid Porle would be in.

But he wasn't. The plump woman who answered my knock, and was wiping wet hands on her apron, said he had gone out and she didn't know when he'd be back. I said I wouldn't leave a message for he'd know who I was.

As I came to the end of the short lane again I thought of something highly important, and as I'd seen a telephone kiosk outside the post office I thought I'd telephone from there. But when I reached it, who should be inside it but Porle. He had his back to me, so I hurried past, and I'm positive he didn't see me. Then I had a beer at the Wheatsheaf and a pipe and a sit dawn. There were only two people there, and the landlord told me that everybody was busy turning hay after the storm. When I reached home, Helen said I looked as if the walk had done me good.

While she and Annie were busy putting on the meal I rang up Five Oaks. Chevalle answered.

"Still there then?" I said. "Any developments?"

"Not worth talking about," he said. "What about you?"

"Not bad," I said. "I think you can count on Temple's coming to see you either this afternoon or evening. All the same, I'd have him watched."

"It's done already," he told me. "You yourself left his place half an hour ago."

"Good," I said, and had to chuckle. "But one thing. Gross interference on my part, but have you sent Maddon's prints to the Yard?"

There was a silence, and I knew he hadn't.

"Thanks for the tip," he said. "I own I hadn't thought of that."

"Good," I said again, and: "Be seeing you round about seven to-night."

That afternoon Helen apologised at having to go to Porthaven to change her library books and do some special shopping. In the apology was an invitation, but I said I'd defer Porthaven till my pins were more used to pavements. That afternoon, with the house virtually my own, I looked up Temple's number and then rang. It was a direct call that couldn't be traced.

Between my teeth was a handkerchief and a stout fastener gripped my nostrils, and altogether my voice was like nothing on earth, unless it revealed an even more startling ancestry than the precious, eunuch tones of Temple himself.

"Mr. Temple?" I said.

"Yes," he said unctuously. "Who's speaking?"

"You wouldn't know me," I said, "but you did me a good turn the other day and I want to do you one. The police know all about your friend Miss Smith."

Then I rang off. But that afternoon I read my book with an eye on the front gate, for if by a miracle Temple associated me with that anonymous call, and plucked up courage to pay me a visit, then I was going to do a disappearing act. But it was an enjoyable afternoon, and I did more than one chuckle when I thought of the letter I'd write that night to George Wharton.

CHAPTER V
BASSETTS

JUST BEFORE I was ready to set off for Bassetts, Helen said there was something she ought to tell me, but for the life of her she couldn't remember what it was. It wasn't anything to do with the murder, for we'd exhausted that subject long ago. And she'd told me, in strict confidence, one very interesting thing. Temple had said Maddon had boasted of never having bought a certificate. I didn't tell Helen that, but when I was fishing for information about Maddon she did let fall that he was an excellent subscriber and bought a complete Savings Certificate from Mrs. Chevalle every week. How to reconcile those two statements I didn't know, but I did intend at some fortuitous moment to question Temple again.

"It will do you all the good in the world," Helen said, referring to the fact that I was dining out. "Fortunately she"—that was Mrs. Chevalle—"won't be there. They're on speaking terms and no more, and that kind of thing is so awkward."

We were walking down the path to the front gate then, and all at once she gave an exclamation.

"I know what I wanted to tell you. That man Porle. He's gone away."

I nearly said, "My God, no!" What I did say was, "How do you know?"

She said he was on the Porthaven bus that she'd taken. At Porthaven she had gone right on to the terminus but Porle had got off at the railway station and had had two bags and a trunk, the latter in the boot of the bus.

"He's probably gone off on a holiday," I said, as if only mildly interested. "When he comes back I'll have to return his book."

But the news was highly disturbing and I quickened my pace as I walked. There was a back path through the woods which I could have taken, and though I didn't know then that it wasn't a short cut, I wished I'd taken it, for it seemed imperative that Chevalle should have had that news at once. I should have said, too, that I pride myself on punctuality, and so by the time I was walking up the short drive to the pleasant-looking modern house, I must have been a good five minutes early. Then a voice hailed me.

"Hallo!"

"Hallo!" I said, and had a look round. Then a little girl emerged from the shrubbery by the drive. She looked a delightful little soul, and remarkably pretty. Her fair hair was trimmed level across her forehead and it gave her an old-fashioned look.

"I've been playing hide-and-seek," she announced.

"Good," I said. "But not by yourself?"

"Oh, yes," she told me. "It's very nice playing by yourself. Then you can't be caught."

I laughed. "There is that in it. Do you know, I hadn't thought of that."

"Have you come to see my daddy?"

"Yes," I said.

"Then you will have to wait," she told me. "There's a man with him. They're in the study."

"Then I'll have to talk to you instead," I said. "What's your name?"

"Clarice Chevalle," she said. The words were pronounced very solemnly and distinctly.

"That's a lovely name," I told her. "I wish I had a name as nice as that."

She laughed at that. When she had looked so solemn I could see her father in her. Then a voice was calling from the house.

"Clarice! Where are you, darling?"

We had been moving towards the house, and almost at once a girl appeared in the front porch. She too had fair hair, and she might have been the mother of the child, so strong was the resemblance. Hers was a placid face and the eyes gentle and friendly.

"Major Travers?" she said and smiled gravely at me when I nodded. "I'm Mary Carter. Major Chevalle told me to tell you how frightfully sorry he was, but he's engaged for a few minutes. Will you come in or would you like to look round the garden?"

"The garden," Clarice said.

"There you are," I said. "Out of the mouths of babes and sucklings."

"But it's bedtime, darling," Mary told her. "It was only special being allowed to stay up so late."

There was a call from the porch and we turned back. Chevalle was there and Clarice was running to him. He smiled as he gathered her up and hoisted her to his shoulders. His free hand clapped me on the back.

"Sorry to be late. Only just got rid of my visitor. He left the back way."

"We're all going round the garden, daddy," Clarice said.

"Oh, no, we're not, young lady," her father told her, but she only laughed. He rubbed his cheek against hers till she wriggled away and then he set her down.

"How long to supper, Mary?"

"Ten minutes."

"Good," he said. "You take this pest of mine and Major Travers and I will talk over a little business."

I had seen Chevalle and Mary Carter together for perhaps two minutes, and yet in that brief time it seemed to me that there was between the two some deep and intimate understanding. I had no more to go on than a look and a smile, but those can be eloquent things.

"That was Temple with me," he was saying as he took my arm and steered me round to the left. "Were you responsible for sending him?"

"Maybe," I said. "But what was his yarn?"

"Extraordinary. He said he called to see Maddon about a War Bond for fifty pounds that he'd induced him to buy. He walked in as Maddon had always told him to do and then saw the body. He also saw Maddon's pocket-book sticking out of his breast pocket and let his War Savings craze get the better of his judgment and helped himself to the fifty pounds. He brought me round the Bond to-night, to hold for the estate. Then he was terrified at what he'd done, he said, and he daren't put the notes back. Then he rang Porthaven in the voice of Miss Smith and beat it."

"A very well-constructed yarn," I said. "It's right enough, except for an addition or two and an omission. He took far more than fifty pounds from the wallet, and the wallet wasn't visible. I know because I'd had a look at it five minutes previously myself. Also he went through all Maddon's pockets, and his desk, though that had been gone through before. And when he couldn't find what he was looking for, he gave Maddon a dirty look and kicked him viciously in the ribs."

"You were there?"

"Watching from the kitchen," I said, and then remembered something. I'd forgotten about Pyramid Porle.

Chevalle had never heard of the man and when I told him all I knew, his eyes fairly popped.

"What about all that God-palaver on the notice," he said.

"Was it blether, just to scare Maddon into something? or deadly serious?"

"I think it was bluff," I said. "If he knew for a certainty that Maddon's soul was required of him that night, then it was himself who was doing the requiring, even if he was a few hours late. I'm pretty sure he'd nothing to do with killing Maddon, but it'll be easy enough to question his landlady about his alibi for this morning. And to find out if he was out late last night."

"I'm afraid I shall have to do some telephoning," he said. "Sorry about it but I oughtn't to be more than a few minutes."

"Picking him up at the railway station ought to be easy," I said. "It's that bolting that I don't like."

There was a sudden screech and we both looked round. But it was only the brakes of the bus from Porthaven stopping at the front gate. I saw a startled look in Chevalle's eyes and then his face suddenly flushed. Then there was a shriek of joy from the porch behind us.

"Mummy! . . . Mummy!" Clarice was running madly towards the front gate. A woman came through and with her the bus conductor setting down a travelling-case and some parcels. I heard Chevalle give a low, "Damn."

The conductor touched his cap and shut the gate. Clarice was pulling at her mother's skirt, and then her mother stopped and lifted her. She kissed her and hugged her close.

"No, darling. You're rumpling my hair," she suddenly said, and set the child down. Then she kneeled and kissed her again. "Mummy's brought you a lovely surprise, darling."

Clarice danced and clapped her hands. "May I have it now, mummy?"

"I'll bring it to you when you're in bed, darling."

We two suddenly came round the shrubbery bend. Thora Chevalle got to her feet and she said never a word.

"How are you, Thora," Chevalle said. "May I take your bag? This is Major Travers. He's having supper with us."

"How do you do," she said. Her hand was elegantly lifted and the wrist gracefully curved, and I was so astounded at having to reach up that I almost said, "Very well, thanks. How are you?" Then Mary was calling from the porch and running down.

"Hallo, Thora. Had a good time?"

"Lovely," she said. "Carry some of these parcels, there's a dear."

Suddenly I sniffed. I don't know what made me do such a ridiculous thing and in the same moment I was looking apologetically at Chevalle. He caught my eye and on his face was a most curious look as if I'd caught him out in something foolish.

"Mummy, you do smell lovely!"

"Do I, darling?" Thora said and laughed.

Chevalle had picked up the case. He didn't look at any of us and his voice sounded formal and strange.

"I have some special telephoning to do. Don't wait for me if supper's ready."

"Of course we'll wait," Mary said, and almost defiantly. We moved on towards the house. Chevalle out-distanced us and Mary was ahead too.

"Take Clarice to bed, will you, Mary," Thora said, and then turned to me. She was carrying nothing but her handbag. "Are you staying in Cleavesham, Major Travers?"

"For a fortnight," I said. "With my sister, Mrs. Thornley."

^

"Lovely," she said. It was her favourite word. "I love Mrs. Thornley. I think she's such a dear."

She passed elegantly on, up the two steps and through the door to the hall. The others had disappeared and we went through a door on the right to a lounge-drawing room. I deposited my hat on a hall chair.

"Do sit down," she said. "Cigarette?"

"I think I will," I said. "Will you try one of mine?"

As she sat in the light of the big bay window, I thought what a good judge Helen had been. I don't think I've ever seen a woman finer looking than Thora Chevalle. Her hair, worn Garbo fashion, was all sheen and lustre, and as near my ideal of a platinum blonde's as I'd ever got. She was tallish; not precisely slim, but with a body that most would have considered alluring, and her make-up was a work of art. And yet that was what spoiled the face; the thin eyebrows giving a touch of the supercilious and the coloured Cupid lips more than a hint of the babyish.

"Ash-tray?" I said, and put one on the cushion by her.

"Thanks," she said, and though I wasn't looking at her I knew she was giving me an appraising look.

"I suppose you haven't heard our local sensation?" I said.

"No," she said, and, "I didn't know there could be a sensation in Cleavesham. What was it? An air raid?"

"Only a murder," I told her. "Someone took a dislike to a man named Maddon and shot him."

"Maddon!" She stared. "The man who lives at Five Oaks?"

I nodded. She was looking away, and breathing a bit hard unless my eyes deceived me.

"Strictly between ourselves it isn't known who did it," I went on. I had come over to the ash-tray to flick my ash in, and there was no mistaking that scent. "But let's talk about yourself. You've been in Cleavesham long?"

"About four years," she said, much more at ease. "We were at Porthaven before that. I rather liked Porthaven but—er—my husband didn't."

"Well, I like Cleavesham," I told her.

"Ringlands is lovely," she said, and was getting to her feet. "But I must fly. My daughter will be getting anxious."

"Did you drop this?" I said, handing her the post card I'd retrieved from the floor.

She looked at it and smiled a bit condescendingly. "It seems to be Mary's. My cousin, you know. She's a great help with Clarice."

She didn't quite know how to make her exit so I helped her out.

"See you in a few minutes," I said, and gallantly held open the door. "And kiss your small daughter good-night for me."

"Lovely," she said, and even now I don't know to what she referred.

I closed the door, listened and then made for the ash-tray. The cigarette-end went into my wallet and so did the post card which she'd held with warm, ungloved fingers, and I'd marked the spot where those fingers had been. Then while I finished my own cigarette I stood looking at the view from the window, for some of the wood across the road had been cleared that winter and through the scanty slender oaks was the distant blue of the Porthaven hills. Then suddenly the door opened and Chevalle came in.

"Sorry about all this," he said. "Galley's got things in hand now and I don't think I shall be disturbed again."

Then he sniffed. I think it was at the smoke, for all at once he was looking at the ash-tray.

"I like that small daughter of yours," I said. "I wish she were mine."

He had been frowning to himself as if in thought. Now he smiled. "She's a great lass," he said. "I wanted a boy but now—"

He shrugged his shoulders and the frown was on his forehead again. Then a petulant voice came from the hall.

"Mary, where's Richard? Surely he's not leaving Major Travers all this time?"

Chevalle's look was grim.

"We seem to be waited for," he said as he took my arm. In the hall was an appetising smell. Through an open door I saw Mary taking over a dish from a young maid. Thora was in the dining-room when we went in. It was to me she spoke, and I hoped the meal would not be one of those trying affairs when two people on bad terms address each other through a third person.

"Hungry, Major Travers?"

"Ravenously," I said.

"Lovely," she said. "Sit here will you, and then you can talk to my husband. Are you frightfully intelligent?"

"Not when I'm hungry," I said, and she said that was lovely.

It was a good meal. Mary was the connecting link between dining-room and kitchen, and once Chevalle got up to carry a heavy dish. For all his wife seemed aware of him, he might not have been there. As for the conversation, we kept off the murder. Chevalle was uncommonly quiet, though we did talk a little about the last war. He had been at Vimy with the Canadians, and as I'd spent a fortnight there too, we tried to find people we'd each known.

Thora cut that short by asking me if I knew Town. She had been staying with an old school friend for a day or two, and had profited by the visit to Hampstead to do shopping in Town. When I said that Porthaven was a bad place for shopping, she asked how I knew. I said that every woman's home town was a bad place for shopping, and she said that was lovely. Mary asked if I was married, and for some reason or other she seemed quite pleased to hear that I was.

We had coffee in the lounge. Thora suddenly developed a traveller's headache and asked to be excused. She even said good-night, as the head was so bad that nothing but bed and aspirins would cure it. Chevalle listened stolidly and I thought Mary looked a bit self-conscious.

"So sorry," I said as my hand went up to find hers. "Perhaps I shall be seeing you again very soon. And you must come to tea with us at Ringlands."

"That would be lovely," she said and after an awkward hesitation and my more awkward holding wide the door, she gave a wan smile and was gone. In the room one felt the inaudible sigh of relief. Mary said she'd leave us to it but Chevalle made her stay. I was feeling a tremendous pity for him, and I knew why he had been so hurried about asking me to supper. That unexpected return of his wife must have been a bit of a shock, and I had a shrewd idea what he was thinking. But when I said I felt a pity, I chose an indifferent word. Perhaps something of the pity was for myself. I liked Chevalle, and during that short evening I had felt something even of admiration, so it was none too easy for me to pretend an ignorance of things and show a complete unconcern for what I knew he was suffering.

But the rest of the evening passed pleasantly enough. Mary asked if I played bridge, and I said I did, though it was my own brand. She said that didn't matter and we could play a new variation that had been invented for three. Great fun it was and I was staggered when I saw it was after eleven o'clock.

"You'll come and have tea with us at Ringlands?" I asked Mary as we said good-night.

"I don't know," she said. "What with Clarice and things, I'm a busy person."

"Busy be damned!" Chevalle told her bluntly. "Of course she'll come, Travers."

She smiled at him for that.

Chevalle said he'd see me half-way home and then he was going to Porthaven.

"Lucky you're with me," I said, for the sky was clouded and after the light of the room I couldn't see a hand before my face. Perhaps that darkness gave him the courage to ask me that question, though hesitatingly, and as a kind of afterthought when we'd said good-night.

"I expect you'll think me a bit of a fool," he said, "but I wish you'd tell me something. My wife and I have had words about cigarettes. You know, she's helping herself to mine and leaving me in the lurch. I've been missing some lately and I'd hate to question the girl who comes in." He hesitated again and I wondered what was coming. "She was having a cigarette with you just before supper, wasn't she?"

"I believe she was," I said, as if trying to remember.

"You don't know what kind it was? I thought there'd be a stub in the ash-tray but there wasn't."

"What do you smoke yourself?" I asked him, and I could just see the outline of his face in the dark.

"Turkish, and very few at that," he said.

"Then she wasn't smoking Turkish," I told him. "They were Virginias or I've never smelt one."

He began a new hesitant apology but I laughed and said I knew what wives were. Then we said another goodnight, and his last words were that he'd probably be seeing me in the morning. I moved off in the dark and then halted on the grass verge and listened till his steps receded in the heavy quietness of the night. As I moved on again I was shaking my head. I even found myself polishing my glasses, a trick of mine when at some mental loss or on the edge of some discovery.

As for my thoughts, they were far from pleasing. There was a new pity, but now centred wholly on the man whom I had just left. There was an annoyance at myself, my interference and my clumsiness, and a shame that I had in a way forced Chevalle into the awkwardness of that question.

The impartiality of the Law might be fine as a shibboleth, but to be a man's guest and use his house for cheap spying was very much beyond the pale. Somehow I should have been glad if he had rounded on me and blasted hell out of me. For he knew perfectly well that I had taken that cigarette-end, and I remembered, too, that look of his when I had made that unpardonable sniff. It was the look of a man caught in some horrible snare, and now I looked back there seemed to be in it some strange appeal.

When I let myself in I found that Helen had put up the black-out, and there was a glass of milk on the table in my room. I had rarely felt less like sleep, and try as I might I could not thrust from my mind the urgency of things that pressed on the brain like a thundery air. So I went to the bureau and took out the cigarette-end and the hair that I'd pocketed at Five Oaks. I laid them beside the stub that Thora Chevalle had put in the ash-tray and a hair I'd found on the divan where she had sat.

Then I scraped some fine graphite from a pencil and dusted that post card which she had held. Under a reading glass I compared it with the copy I had made at Five Oaks of the ash-tray print and to me they looked dead alike. But even then I told myself that the whole thing was lunacy. Others could have bought scent from the same shop from which Thora Chevalle had purchased hers. And she had been in Hampstead when Maddon was murdered, and if not, how in God's name could she have been at Five Oaks at the—for her—unearthly hour of half-past five in the morning? And why? Where was the motive?

A few minutes later I had made a resolve. I was not in the employ of Scotland Yard. As for my duty as a good citizen, that was an affair between me and my conscience. In any case I would never profit from what I might have discovered as a guest in Chevalle's house. What I would do would be to carry on, and with tremendous discretion, my own inquiries, and then, when I was sure, I would review the whole case. But not with anyone else. I would do the reviewing, and with myself.

Much later still, I wrote a letter to George Wharton, and my thoughts were by then as clear as they'd ever been. Perhaps the stillness of the house gave them their clarity, but I do know that when that letter was finished I went straight to my bed, and almost at once I was asleep. This was the letter, put in a stout quarto envelope with various enclosures.

DEAR GEORGE,

I've got plenty of news for you—too much for my liking. I've located your man. Herbert Maddon is his name and he's been living in Cleavesham for about nine years at a superior kind of cottage called Five Oaks. You'll find it on the rough map herewith.

But he doesn't live there now. At about six o'clock this morning he was murdered—shot at close quarters and probably by a woman. I won't add any details because you may read about it in to-morrow's papers. Chevalle has sent Maddon's prints to the Yard and the result may help your memory.

And now I want you to do something for me in the strictest confidence.

1. Herewith a cigarette-end marked A. and another marked B. Find out

   a. if they are the same brand.

   b. If the lipstick is identical. That may be difficult.

2. In envelope marked C is a hair taken from Maddon's house. In envelope D is one taken from another house. Are they from the same head?

3. In envelope E is a paper bearing the prints of a man named Bernard Temple. Has the Yard any records?

As a favour, don't ask me the why and wherefore of all this. But believe me when I say there is no joke about it. I'm only too serious, and if the word conveyed what I really meant I'd even say I was badly scared.

Very many thanks. Helen sends her best wishes. I'm feeling fitter already.

Yours as ever,
LUDOVIC TRAVERS.

P.S. I don't often venture to prophesy but I have an idea the Yard will be called in pretty soon. If so—and still don't ask me why—move heaven and earth to come down here yourself.

CHAPTER VI
DAY OF REST

I WOKE RATHER LATE the following morning but there seemed to be never a sound in the house. Then I remembered it was Sunday, the day of rest. And I told myself that it was very definitely going to be a day of rest for me.

So I lay on for a few minutes and then Annie brought me a cup of tea, and over that and a cigarette I began thinking, and about those two hairs that were in the envelope which I was going to post that morning to Wharton. For when I came to think of it, that hair I had picked off the back of the divan might have been Mary Carter's. Her hair had the same fair, silky length and quality, though she wore it differently. Hers was rolled up in little curls just above the base of the neck, whereas Thora Chevalle's hung heavily, as it were, with a kind of sinuous massiveness, as if it were fine spun metal and not hair at all. Mary's looked like hair, and lovely hair at that. Thora's looked something dramatic, exotic and unusual; something at which to give a covert stare. It was superb and it was beautiful, but it wasn't the kind of hair one would have wished to see on one's own wife. To me there was in it something actually repellent, but then I may be old-fashioned in my tastes.

As for a difference in colouring, I doubted if a layman like myself could see a trace of it in two hairs laid side by side. It was in the mass that one saw the difference: that slightly greenish tinge in Thora's and the hard metallic sheen. And, of course, there was little Clarice's hair. That was rather like Mary's but shorter; cut level to follow the curve of the neck and trimmed across the forehead for a fringe. But its colouring was Mary's, and there you are. It wasn't exactly a question of whose was the hair from the divan. The question was that if the two hairs were different, which was different? Is that getting too involved for you? Then put it like this, and as I thought of it I had a startling theory. Suppose the hair from Five Oaks wasn't Thora Chevalle's at all. You say that doesn't enter into the argument. I say that I could easily get one of her genuine hairs—indeed, if I were to pursue my private inquiries I would have to—and submit it to an expert. If it differed from the Five Oaks one, then whose hair was that?

And so naturally we come to more of the devil's advocate style of argument. But what about that startling theory you just mentioned, you will ask. Well, I'll leave you to find it for yourself, and here are the thoughts that prompted it. The Chevalle household I knew none too well and I had only my observations of the previous night to go on. But the old eternal triangle was there right enough, I was dead sure of that, if in rather an unusual form. Chevalle and his wife had finished with each other, and only the child kept them together at all. That, and the fact that a man in Chevalle's position could not possibly give his wife either genuine or faked grounds for divorce. I guessed that Chevalle was in love with Mary, and she in love with him. But I knew him to be a man of the strictest honour—his self-discipline of the previous night was an instance of that —and he would be prepared to live out his days with the help of that same discipline, and make a brave enough show. But what of Mary? Would she have been prepared to let him go on sacrificing himself and herself for the ease and comfort of a woman who had probably shown herself worthy of neither?

Well, that is what I was thinking. If you don't see the germ at least of a startling theory, then I'll tell you in advance that Wharton spotted it soon enough. And when Wharton has a theory it isn't an airy flashing thing like mine. It's usually the genuine article.

Breakfast was over, the Sunday papers arrived, the morning was gloriously fine, and life wasn't so bad after all. I sat in the little summer-house in a deck-chair and watched a score and more of our planes heading for France, and then the church bells began to ring. That was a pleasant sound, in the open country. In Town they seem to me both clamant and discordant.

The front gate opened and in came a man. I spotted him at once for Helen's friend Commander Santon, and not only because of his game right leg. He didn't spot me, however, and when he had rung the bell and was standing waiting, I had a good view of him. He was certainly a good-looking fellow, and by that I mean a man's idea of what good-looking is. He had clear-cut patrician features—chin a bit weak perhaps—and sleek black hair and dark eyes. A neat slim figure too, and his age would be about thirty-five. His face was tanned almost too brown. He wasn't wearing a hat but his clothes were just a bit too natty for my liking, especially the razor-edge to the grey worsted bags.

Nothing seemed to be happening in the house, so I made myself visible.

"I expect my sister's upstairs, dollying up for church," I said. "My name's Travers."

"I'm Santon," he said, and I liked his smile.

Then Helen suddenly appeared.

"Morning, lady," he said, and gave her an exaggerated bow. "I trust I find you well."

Helen had evidently been used to such humorous displays of old-world courtesy, if that is what it was.

"I thought you were away," she told him calmly.

"How could I stay away," he told her. "I was back yesterday morning. Too busy to see anybody, though."

We cleared up the matter of introductions and then Helen was asking what the conference had been like. I gathered it had been at Southampton.

"The usual blether," he told her. "I expect you read all about it. Lord Kindersley made a damn good speech. The others weren't much."

"You're not going to church?" Helen said as she ran an eye over him.

"Sorry, lady; can't be done," he said. "I really came to call on your brother—after seeing you, of course. Dewball told me he was here."

"Well, don't lead him into any mischief," Helen said, and moved off down the path.

We saw her off at the front gate and then I asked Santon if it was too early for a drink. He said it was never too early or too late, so I fetched a couple of bottles of beer and placed another deck-chair. Then we got yarning about things generally, and there were two things I liked about him. He didn't throw his weight about by telling me naval secrets—if he knew any, and doubtless he did—and he was ultra-modest about himself. He told me a lot about what other people did at Crete, but except that a lump of shrapnel hit him in the knee he mightn't have been there at all. That he would be very popular with the ladies I had no doubt. Helen had evidently fallen heavily for his brand of humour, and the fact that he didn't mention his wife to me was another sign.

"Another bottle?" I said when the first two were dead men.

"Not just now," he said. "Tell you what, though. We'll have a stroll to my place and then see how we feel."

I was taking the glasses and the two dead men to the kitchen door, and he said we might as well go by the back path. The chestnut had grown pretty tall and it would be shady. So we went that way and a delightful walk it was. As we came level with where I had judged Little Foxes would be, and a new path turned right, I happened to mention the murder of Maddon.

"I wish I'd been here," he said. "It must have turned the whole place upside down. A curious old boy. I suppose you never met him."

"As a matter of fact, I did," I said, and told him about that evening encounter on the path.

"I could never quite get to the bottom of him," he said. "He always struck me as the sort of cove who had something up his sleeve. And it was something that made him damned superior. I don't mean he was rude. You just felt he was having a private laugh at you."

"That's just how he struck me," I said.

"Well, he's gone, and be damned to him," he said unconcernedly. "All I worry about is losing a customer. He didn't buy a single certificate till about three months ago and then he started having one every week."

That was interesting news and I made a mental note to question Temple more closely. But we had come through a little gate, and the now private path was leading by a small enclosure that backed into the woods behind us.

"What's this?" I said, waving a hand at the miniature hay-field.

He laughed. "My God, no wonder you ask! That, my dear fellow, is a tennis court. Hasn't been played on since the war started. My wife was awfully good," he said, mentioning her for the first time. He waved a hand round at the ruins of perenni-al borders and the charming reed-thatched summer-house that overlooked the court. "She used to spend the hell of a lot of mon-ey over this sort of thing. Whole-time gardener and a couple of maids and so on. Dewball and I just do what we think we will."

A tall beech hedge, lovely doubtless when clipped but strag-gly now, shut off the tennis court from the back lawn and the house. That lawn was quite tidy and even the beds of young as-ters and zinnias had been weeded.

"A nice garage you've got there?" I said.

It lay well back in a shrubbery at the point of a long V. One arm of the V ran by the front of the house—with lawn between it and the front hedge—and so to the short gravelled drive and the front gates. The other arm went to the back of the house, and that had been useful for tennis guests to park their cars in the shade. As we entered the garage I caught sight of a kitchen garden and an orchard behind it.

"Room enough here for two big cars," I said.

"We used to run two," he said. "This little Morris for when I was home, and the missis's Jaguar. Not a bad place, do you think? Water laid on here. Electric switch here. Even a pit. Dew-ball and I made that."

"As neat a garage as ever I saw," I said. "What about petrol now? Get plenty?"

"Just enough," he said. "That War Savings job does me pret-ty well."

We strolled along to the back of the house and as soon as Santon was inside, he gave a holler.

"Tom! Where the hell are you?"

"Coming, sir," a voice said, and Tom Dewball appeared rubbing his hands on a green baize apron. He was a cheerful soul of about fifty, and he gave me a genial, "Good morning."

"This is Major Travers, Mrs. Thornley's brother," Santon said. "Whether I'm here or not he's to do as he damn pleases. He can even pick the ruddy strawberries."

"Very good, sir."

"What about staying to lunch?" Santon asked me, suddenly thinking of it and obviously pleased at the idea.

"Lord, no!" I said. "My sister'd have six fits."

"Some other time then," he told me reluctantly. "And, Tom, get a couple of chairs out here and some beer—if you haven't drunk it all."

I told him it was a good job he had all that War Savings work on his hands or he'd have been bored stiff.

"It's been a godsend," he said. "Otherwise I'd have been like those whiskered old coves who think life's heaven to sit all day with a glass glued on the Channel."

"Couldn't you have had a shore job?" I asked him.

"As a matter of fact I could," he said. "Somehow I didn't fancy myself with my backside polishing a chair." Tom Dewball brought bottles of beer, a folding table and a couple of chairs.

"An old naval man, is he?" I asked Santon when he'd gone.

"Of sorts," he said, whatever that meant. "His lungs went wonky and he got his ticket. They're all right now."

"He looks a useful man."

"He has to be," he said, and grinned. "He's cook, housemaid, valet, gardener and the whole perishing issue. The only thing he knows nothing about is a car."

"Talking of War Savings," I said, "I met another of your collectors the other evening. A chap called Temple."

"Temple," he said. "My God, what a twerp!" Then he shot me a look. "You're no friend of his, I take it?"

"God forbid," I said hastily.

"He's the oiliest ruddy specimen I ever ran across," he said. "Always trying to nudge his way in somewhere. What little trick do you think he tried when we had our War Weapons Week? I didn't know it till it was too late or I'd have given him a hell of a kick in the pants. He had the idea of setting aside all the big houses for himself to make a personal call. You see the idea?"

"Trying to gate-crash Cleavesham high society," I said. "I didn't like the look of him a bit. In fact I preferred Maddon. And talking of Maddon, I wonder whether Chevalle's got any ideas about who did it."

"Shot, wasn't he? That's what Dewball heard in the Wheat-sheaf."

"I heard that too," I said. "But something ought to be found out soon. Chevalle's a good man, I take it?"

"You know him?"

"Well, he's the friend of a friend of mine," I said guardedly.

"He's a quiet old stick," Santon said, and was frowning slightly. "I expect he's good at his job. His military record is damn good."

"I met his wife last night," I said. "She's a good-looker."

"Much younger than he," he said quickly, and then proceed-ed to qualify it. "I mean she looks not much more than thirty. He's best part of fifty."

"Well, whatever her age she's a damn good-looking woman," I said.

"All right if you like that particular type."

"Don't mistake me," I said. "I've got plenty of vices, thank God, but women aren't included. My appreciation's aesthetic so to speak."

"You've got plenty of time yet," he told me, and asked if I was ready for another bottle. I glanced at my watch and saw it was half-past twelve, and at once was getting to my feet. I also remembered the letter in my pocket and he told me where there was a box in the hedge opposite the back Bycliffe road. In any case there was no hurry, as letters weren't collected before three that afternoon.

We agreed on a meeting in the near future, and I set off for home by the main road. When I got in, Helen wanted to know if I'd had a good time.

"A most enjoyable morning," I said. "I don't know when I've enjoyed one more."

"You liked Commander Santon?"

"Very much," I said. "Mind you, he's a generation younger than myself."

"What do you mean?" she asked me.

All I had meant, in my private mind, was that I could feel closer, and that more quickly, to a man of my age—like Chevalle—than I'd ever get to Santon.

"Young feller-me-lads of his age move too quickly for me," I said.

"He's certainly a terrible flirt," she said, and smiled to herself. And she didn't see my quick look. Helen's a mighty presentable woman and still well under forty.

I had a good lunch, so good in fact that I felt like a sleep after it, so I went back to my old seat in the summer-house. I'd just got nicely off when Helen came to tell me I was wanted on the telephone.

It was Chevalle, and though he was ringing from Porthaven, I knew somehow that he didn't like to face me after that extraordinary question of the previous night.

"Sorry to worry you, Travers," he began, and his manner seemed normal. "One or two things I thought you ought to know."

"That's very good of you," I cut in.

"The inquest," he said. "Eleven to-morrow morning. We shan't need you, you'll be glad to hear. Temple's coming clean about what he saw and so on. A very plausible story, I should tell you."

"But you're still keeping an eye on him?"

"You bet," he said. "If the verdict's the usual—I don't think it can be anything else—the funeral will be the following morning."

"What about the bullet?"

"What our man calls .234. Quite small. Italian, probably. We've sent it up to Town."

"And our Pyramid friend."

"Nothing yet," he said. "He took a ticket for Town and that's all we know. There's always a rush on that particular train. Still, we're hoping something will turn up at the London end."

"His landlady?"

"Oh, yes," he said. "He told her a sister of his had been taken seriously ill, but the post office told us they didn't deliver any telegram. And he was out the previous night, by the way. Nothing unusual, the landlady said. Now and again he went out to study the stars."

"The devil he did," I said, and as there didn't seem anything more to say at either end I thanked him again and hung up.

But I stood there for a minute or two, polishing my glasses and trying to recapture the tone of his voice. There had been no cheery salutation, no quip and no mention of a future meeting. Everything had been perfectly polite, though I had seemed to feel something of the stilted and unnecessarily formal. In fact, as I hooked my glasses on again, I knew somehow I had been right, and that for reasons known only to us two he had preferred to telephone rather than look me straight in the eye.

It was three o'clock, so I went up to the bathroom and had a cold splash to freshen me up. Then I thought I'd take a short stroll, but when I peeped into the sitting-room to ask Helen if she would care to come, I found her with a book on her lap and her eyes closed. So I set off alone and on a course which I thought would be largely new—through the village and along the Bycliffe road to the fork and then back by the lane that ran behind Five Oaks.

I found I'd made a bad choice. The Green and the houses round it made a lovely picture that sunny afternoon, but beyond it came the first bungalows, and thereafter the road was more of an emetic. I thought of "Sussex by the Sea," and the good folk of Sussex who sing their anthem with a fervour akin to tears, and I thought of Camber, and Winchelsea Beach and Shoreham and Peacehaven, of all of which that Cleavesham half-mile was a ghastly miniature.

Then I saw something that took my mind off pink tiles and railway carriages, for coming towards me was Bernard Temple.

In his go-to-meeting garments, and with a gold watch-chain across his waistcoat he looked a highly respectable citizen.

As we neared I could imagine him looking frantically for a hedge gap with even a semblance of a path beyond it, but there was no dodging me.

"Afternoon, Temple," I hailed from twenty yards, and my tone was geniality itself.

I guessed what he was feeling. He would have liked to pass me with an utter indifference, or perhaps a slight curl of the lip, but he just couldn't summon the moral courage.

"Good afternoon," he said, and all he had achieved was a manner slightly frigid.

"I think you owe me a vote of thanks," I told him with a kind of roguish heartiness.

"Indeed?" he said, eyebrows rising.

"That little trick I played on you," I went on. "Getting you to go to Chevalle. Getting you out of a remarkably nasty hole, in fact."

He shot me another suspicious look and said nothing.

"I was in the kitchen," I said. "From the moment you entered the house I was watching you. From the time you stuck your head inside the door till the moment when you kicked Maddon in the ribs."

That scared him. Chevalle, if he had seen him since the interview, hadn't told him that.

"You may not believe it," I said, "but I shan't tell Major Chevalle that I've met you this afternoon. It's not my business to tell the police everything, though when I knew you'd seen him I did confirm what you'd told him. Now I'd like to ask you a question or two in return. Just what was it you were looking for in his desk?"

He couldn't meet my eyes. Then he made as if to speak, couldn't get the words out, and finally managed to spin me the yarn that he'd spun Chevalle, about fifty pounds for a War Bond, and his collector's zeal getting the better of him. But for me there was a variation. He'd looked in the desk first and when the money wasn't there, then he'd caught sight of the wallet. It wasn't worth while calling him a liar.

"I'm not going to argue that with you," I told him. "But you know that if I cared to open my mouth I could make you a lot of trouble. But here's an easy question. You told me Maddon boasted to you that he'd never bought a War Savings Certificate. My information is that that was true up to three months or so ago, but—and this is a fact—ever since then he's bought one every week."

"But I didn't know that," he said. "Believe me, Major Travers, I honestly didn't know it."

"When did he do that boasting to you?"

"Not more than a week ago."

"You'd swear that?"

"It's true," he said, and spread his hands in a gesture of vehemence.

"I want the information for my own satisfaction," I said.

"And I'm warning you. If what you've told me isn't true, then I'm going to open my mouth to Chevalle."

"Major Travers, I'll swear on anything you like that it's true," he said passionately.

"Well, I believe you," I said. "Know anything about a man named Porle?"

"Porle," he said, his manner eased as by a miracle. "The curious old fellow who lives with Mrs. Harmer at Lane End?"

"That's the man."

He shrugged his shoulders. "I've never even spoken to him. I've heard about him, of course. The whole village has."

"Well, thanks very much," I said. "You can trust me, and I hope for your sake I can trust you."

A nod and I was moving on. I believed what he told me about Maddon's boast. If you ask why I should be concerned about such a triviality and what amounted only to the proof that Maddon was a boastful liar, then I can honestly say that the thought in my mind was the reconciliation of conflicting statements, and the hope that such reconciliation might throw—if only for Wharton's benefit—some additional light on Maddon himself. Also, mine is the kind of mind that hates loose ends and is irked, as I've told you already, by the most trivial of mysteries. What I didn't know at the time, though you should know it now, is that the information which Temple had given me was the most vital in the whole affair.

I got past the bungalow outbreak and cut back along the lane. In its sudden shady relief, and with Five Oaks nearer with each step, I began thinking of Maddon and War Savings, and then it struck me that there was a perfectly harmless explanation of the presence in Maddon's room of Thora Chevalle's cigarette stubs, hair-pin and hair, and finger-print. Mrs. Beaney was the one who could shed light on that—or couldn't she? Would she say she had emptied the ash-tray, when out of laziness or from lack of time she'd done nothing of the sort? But the scent; that couldn't be explained away by a War Savings' visit. In a day it would practically have gone, for though it had been fresh enough when I had entered the room, it had been only a faint odour to Chevalle an hour or so later.

The walk by that brick lane was not too interesting. I did notice that the telephone was available all its length, for a wire led to a farm just short of Five Oaks. I was to remember that later, but at the moment all I knew was that if I didn't quicken my pace I should be late for tea. As it was, I reached home as tea was on the table, and after it I spent an early evening with one of Helen's library books. Then, soon after supper, I was called to the telephone again.

"Who is it please?" I asked, for the caller would give Annie no name.

"Galley, sir," the voice said, and then I remembered it. "The Chief thought you'd like to know about those prints we sent to town. We've just had a call from the Yard. Nothing doing."

"Bad luck," I said. "And thanks very much."

Most of the bad luck, I was thinking, was Wharton's, for the odds were now that for the rest of his life he'd be teasing his wits to give a name and circumstance to what would remain a vague and irritating memory. Also, I could tell myself, I had lost the possibility of a perfectly good drink.

Part Two
THE LADY FOUND

CHAPTER VII
LITTLE BY LITTLE

BREAKFAST WAS EARLY on the Monday morning and soon after it Helen appeared dressed for going out, and Annie brought the bicycle to the front door.

"Where are you gallivanting off to?" I said.

"War Savings' day," Helen told me briskly.

"I'd have thought Saturday the best day," I said. "Aren't most of the men paid then?"

"Then or Friday," she told me, "and a lot of the women too. But Saturday's the shopping day. They don't know till the Monday what they can really spare."

"Live and learn," I said, and that was that. But Helen was in on time for lunch, even if she did go off again soon after. I thought the opportunity a good one for a visit to the Wheatsheaf, though I loathe drinking after meals.

There were only three men in the bar and they were talking about the inquest. Questioning the landlord would be nearer the mark, for he had been on the coroner's jury. I asked what the verdict was, and was told "Murder at the hands of some person or persons unknown." The landlord evidently expected me to be impressed by the sonorities of all that, and I duly frowned and gravely nodded. Then I gathered that Temple's evidence had been the sensation, but only his fortuitous discovery of the crime and expeditious ringing of the police. Nothing had evidently been said about War Bonds, and wallets, and Miss Smith.

"What sort of a man was this Maddon?" I asked, and within ten minutes I had plenty of information, and much of it conflicting. To the claim that he was a gentleman came the objection that he did his own garden and cooked his own meals. But it was agreed that he spoke educatedly, and it was suspected that he was a Londoner.

"The house was his?" I asked.

It was his, I was told. At first he hired it furnished from old Mrs. So-and-so, and when she died he bought it lock, stock, and barrel. A bargain too, they reckoned, considering the present price of house property.

It appeared, too, that Maddon, though keeping himself very much to himself, used to pay frequent visits to Porthaven, travelling, of course, by bus. But he was tight-fisted. When I asked for instances I was told one in which my sympathies were wholly with Maddon, and my respect for his courage. For Sussex, as you may or may not know, has long milked its resident, dormitory class of population; indeed, one might regard such milking as one of the county's major industries. So, when Maddon arrived, the first to seize on him was the local Horticultural Society, expecting a fat subscription. But the approach was the usual subtle one—a letter to Maddon saying it had given the Society much pleasure at its last meeting to appoint Herbert Maddon, Esquire, a Vice-President, and they would be delighted if he would so act. Maddon, so I gathered, wrote back a scorcher. I could well believe it, and I'd have loved to have read it.

After that, the other village bodies went to work more warily, but with no better luck, for Maddon subscribed to never a one of them. With one exception. It was the pre-war custom of Sussex to indulge on Guy Fawkes' Night in processions, fireworks and bonfires and to mulct the spectators for subscriptions to charities. Maddon sent—and unsolicited—the incredibly large sum of a pound to the secretary of the Cleavesham Bonfire Boys, with the remark that nothing was so gratifying to his advancing years as to find that people could still make jackasses of themselves.

As for the rest of that day, nothing much happened. Galley did ring up after supper, saying that the Chief thought I might like to know what happened at the inquest. Before he could ring off I asked him if they'd discovered any relatives of Maddon. He said they hadn't found a trace of one. From all they'd discovered he might not have a relative in the world.

The fact that it was Galley who had rung me was again significant, though of course Chevalle might have been a far busier man than my special pleading had credited. After all, I remembered he'd have those local burglaries still on his hands as well as this business of Maddon, and doubtless his office was as cumbered with routine, official returns and red tape as any other war-time concern into which bureaucracy can contrive to insinuate itself.

But what I was thinking, as I waited for sleep that night, was that in the morning I'd be hearing from Wharton. But I was to be disappointed, for no letter came. Then I stayed in the house that morning, hoping, rather preposterously, that he might ring me when he'd found the answers to some of my questions. In the afternoon I took a very short walk and only at tea-time, and from some remark of Annie's, did I remember that Maddon had been buried. Annie said there were only a few of the curious ones there, except, of course, the undertaker from Porthaven and his men.

It was only a few minutes after that when the telephone went. It was Chevalle, and as soon as I heard his voice I was wondering what he was going to tell me.

"Afternoon, Travers," he began. "Sorry I've been too busy to see you."

"Don't worry about that," I told him. "I knew you'd be up to the ears."

"I thought I'd let you know I'm throwing my hand in," he said. "I've got in touch with the Yard and they're taking over."

"I think you're doing the right thing, if I may say so," I said. "It looked a pretty tricky case to me, and you people are overworked as it is."

"Glad you agree," he said, and he sounded relieved. Then he seemed to heave a sigh. "Well, that's that. Hope to be seeing you soon."

It's not a bad feeling at times to have a long-shot of a prophecy come true, but I wasn't feeling any too happy. To me there was only one explanation for Chevalle's retirement from the case, and it was the one that prompted the prophecy. I knew that whoever came down from the Yard would have a harder job on hand, now that Chevalle was out of things. Even as a layman he couldn't be forced to give evidence against his wife, and whatever it was that he had discovered—and it had to be pretty damning—would be locked up tight in that cold brain of his. And I doubted if even Galley would have been given the faintest glimpse of the truth.

It was about half-past nine that night, and I was thinking about bed, and how the morning must bring a reply from Wharton, when I heard a ring at the front door. Then I heard Helen's voice and a second voice which seemed curiously familiar. Another moment and I knew it for Wharton's.

"Delighted to see you," Helen was saying, and Wharton was insisting that the pleasure was all his. I've often wondered why women fall so heavily for George. Maybe he has IT or the modern variety known as OOMPH, or maybe again it is the air of forlornness with which he can speciously clothe himself, so that they feel an immediate urge to mother him. But of all the little tricks and adaptations in George's vast repertoire—and within an hour he can be hearty, oily, majestic, virtuous, pathetic, Rabelaisian and a pious old humbug—his handling of women is an achievement which one might reasonably call supreme.

"Ludo's in here," Helen said as she opened the door. "Annie's not in bed yet so we can soon put up the blackout. Mr. Wharton to see you," she announced triumphantly.

"He's looking very much better," George told her, still up to his old tricks and looking at me with a sideways peer, like a blackbird on a lawn. "Good cooking and fresh air; that's what he wanted."

"Mr. Wharton's staying at the Wheatsheaf," Helen told me. "Now I'll leave you to talk."

"Now I can get in a word," I said to George. "Do you mind if I ask you how you are? I believe that's the correct thing."

"I might be worse," he told me unctuously, and began taking off—of all things for a warm June evening—that navy blue overcoat of his with the velvet collar. "Only got down a couple of hours ago. Saw Chevalle at Porthaven and then got myself fixed up at the Wheatsheaf."

Annie came in with two bottles and glasses on a tray, and she was smiling at him as if she were thirty years younger. Wharton got to his feet with a flourish, and a "Well, well. And how are you?"

"Good work, George," I said when she had gone. "And so you managed to get sent down here then."

With a vast assumption of humility he told me an old fool like himself was all that could be spared. In any case things shouldn't take very long.

"Any special reasons for predicting that?" I asked.

He said there weren't, except that the smaller the locality the easier the case. Then, when he'd taken a pull at his glass, and wiped his walrus moustache with a handkerchief like an embryo table-cloth, he asked me to tell him all I knew about things.

Well, I played strictly fair. I told him exactly what happened at Five Oaks, and the clues that were found and who found them. I went on to my visit to Temple and the queer case of Pyramid Porle, but I said nothing about the evening I'd spent at Bassetts.

"That's much what Chevalle told me," he said. "But you were being a bit of a Smart Alec, weren't you? Why didn't you tell Chevalle about Temple and Porle straightaway?"

"You know how it is, George," I said guilefully. "We all fancy ourselves at times. And it worked out well in the long run."

"Not with this man Porle it didn't," he told me. "Did you get his prints?"

"They may be on this book," I said, showing him the copy of *The Great Pyramid Explained.*

He snorted. "Probably been pawed over by half the village. But what was his game?"

"Don't know," I said frankly.

"A bit touched, was he?"

"A bit of a crank, yes, but remarkably sane. I'd even call him astute."

"Looks to me as if he'd been watching that man Maddon for some time," Wharton said to that. "He knew Maddon and Temple were pals. I take it he meant Maddon when he told you that Temple was mixed up with rascals?"

"That's how I took it," I said. "But going back to prints. Those I sent you for identification were Temple's."

"Temple's were they?" He said it so off-handedly that I knew he had something up his sleeve. I'd be a fool if, after fifteen years of George, I couldn't read him like a banner headline.

"What was his Yard record?" I asked.

"Who said he had a record?" The glare went and he allowed himself to smile. "Rather funny about Temple. Did I ever tell you that story about the tombstone inscription? *'Here lies William Longbottom, Poet and Painter; born in 1853, died 1879, aged 26 years.'* And underneath the Latin quotation—'*Ars longa, vita brevis.*'"

I warned you that George could be Rabelaisian. I laughed, though I'd heard it before. If you see the point of the joke, then you have a flippant mind too, and if you don't, there's no harm done.

"But what's that got to do with Temple?" I wanted to know.

"Tell you in the morning," he said. "You and I are going to pay him a little visit. But I'll give you a clue. When I heard his real name, then I remembered him. And you ought to too." He snorted. "Always boasting about your memory."

"I'm damned if I am," I said. "That's your speciality, not mine. But about Maddon. You still don't remember who he is?"

"Funny thing, isn't it?" he said aggrievedly. "On the tip of my tongue, so to speak. Still, I'll win that bet before the week's out, or my name's Robinson."

I must have looked startled at that flagrant transference of the term of that bet for he was asking if I'd thought of something. I said I was wondering if he'd any news of those other samples I'd sent him. He countered by asking if I thought him a magician, and again I knew he was hiding something in that crafty old brain of his.

"Going already?" I said. It is true the beer was finished but it wasn't much after eleven o'clock and he was a night bird if ever there was one.

"Got to get a night's rest," he said as I helped him into that ancient overcoat. "Can you be at that Five Oaks place at nine o'clock sharp? Chevalle and that man of his are handing over."

I said I'd be there on the dot, and I was.

Chevalle went out of his way to be genial with me that morning, but I think he was putting on an act for Wharton's benefit. George himself was in great form and plumb in the centre of the stage. First he made me go through again everything I'd seen, and when the time came for Temple to enter, then I had to be Temple. Not a good performance, I fear, with George obviously hinting that he could have done it twenty times better himself. After that, we came to the various clues and each was handed over, including the ash-tray and the casts of the heel marks. Of the scent there was only the faintest possible trace, but George ran his nose, or rubbed it, all over the chair and professed to have a pretty good idea of what that scent had been.

"What about that fellow Porle?" he said. "Any more news?"

"Devil a bit," Chevalle said. "As far as we're concerned he's gone up in smoke. And the smoke's gone too."

"We'll get him," Wharton said grimly. "And without much fuss. Anything else you'd like to show me now?" There was a paying-in book of Barclays Bank, Porthaven, and the significant thing was that the manager had revealed that for the last two years Maddon had never drawn out a penny.

"Any cheque books available?" Wharton asked.

"Never a sign of one," Galley cut in.

Wharton had a look at the paying-in book. "Looks as if he paid something in once a fortnight. Where'd he get that from? No property in the village?"

"None at all," Galley said. Chevalle, significantly to me, was keeping his mouth shut. "And the post people say he never got registered letters."

"People don't always register letters with notes in them," Wharton told him. "What's your idea, Major?"

"What do you think I called you in for?" Chevalle told him with an attempt at humour. "I might perhaps repeat a suggestion of Travers's, if he doesn't mind—that he was blackmailing someone." He shrugged his shoulders. "On the other hand, I don't see who the devil he could have been blackmailing."

"What's wrong with the scented lady?" Wharton asked him blandly.

Chevalle shrugged his shoulders again.

"Dammit all, she's real enough," Wharton told him with humorous expostulation. "Mind you," he went on, the smile giving place to a frown. "I see your difficulty. It isn't just a question of combing this village for all the women with the right coloured hair. You might call this village part of Porthaven, and you can't search that. And she might have come from any part of England, and be back there by now."

Chevalle had been frowning away, and now it looked to me as if he too were making a decision to lay at least some of his cards on the table and leave things to Wharton with a better conscience.

"All the same," he said, "she had to get here somehow. If she walked from Porthaven she'd have been seen. The buses haven't anything to report about a strange, fair-haired woman either the previous night or the next morning. Men were working in the woods practically all round here and no one saw a sign of a strange woman."

"Ah, well," said Wharton resignedly. "We'll have to try again. You're lending me Inspector Galley here, and he can get busy along the same lines."

I wondered if he'd noticed the queer sort of challenge there had been, to me at least, in that use of Chevalle's of the repeated word "strange" when he referred to the woman. But he'd seen nothing unusual: nothing, that is, to incline him to the belief that the woman had been a local one.

"No other papers, letters or documents?" he asked.

There was nothing. The bank, however, held certain investments that had been made from time to time. Maddon had been a shrewd speculator, for he had held off the markets till he had judged the slump at its lowest and then had invested practically every penny he had had at the bank. The year's rises in values must have added fifty per cent, to the worth of his holdings. The bank, Chevalle said, automatically collected his dividends, so the moneys he took in from time to time could not have been from warrants cashed with local tradesmen.

"What about the bed or beds?" Wharton asked.

"Only one bed in use, sir," Galley said, "and that was a double one. No trace of a woman in the room."

"The bed was made?"

"Yes, sir, and by himself. Mrs. Beaney said anybody could tell a man had made it."

"Well, one thing stands out clear," Wharton said. "This Maddon took every care to hide his identity, and his business, and he made a good job of it. People don't do that unless they want to be hermits or else are up to something remarkably fishy. No photographs, by the way? Of him or anyone else?"

Chevalle shook his head. "Only the post-mortem ones I showed you last night."

Wharton grunted, which was apparently his opinion of their value.

"Well, I think that's about all," he said. "You're a busy man, Major, and I look like being one too. You'll furnish me with a relief for the man you've lent me, so that there can always be somebody here at the phone? Only for a day or two?"

Chevalle said that whatever Wharton wanted, he'd only to speak.

"Good-bye for the present then, and good luck," he added, as he held out his hand. A smile and a nod to me and he was off. Galley went with him to the front gate and pumped up the rear wheel of his bicycle for him. George had a thorough good look through the house, and then the plain-clothes man was left in charge and George and I moved off to the village. Galley was to go on with those inquiries about a fair-haired stranger.

As he walked along the field-path towards the village, George talked about everything but Temple, and it was plain that he didn't want to reveal an inkling of the surprise he had in store for me. But George was always a secretive soul and I put it like that because his antics in that respect were more amusing than irritating. He loved hugging little pieces of information to himself and making a mysterious mountain out of a matter-of-fact molehill. He liked to throw scorn on a suggestion, and then to explore it to see if there was anything in it after all, whereupon he would appropriate the good in it and affect a mighty indignation if reminded of its origin.

But as we neared Temple's cottage I had to remind him of something.

"One thing I don't want you to mention to Temple, George, and that's the little matter of his kicking Maddon in the ribs."

His stare became a glare. "And why not, pray?"

"Because I promised him I wouldn't let it go any further," I said. "If he finds he can't trust my word, then I shan't be able to wheedle anything else out of him."

"And what *have* you wheedled out of him, as you call it?"

"If it hadn't been for me he'd never have gone to Chevalle," I said, and then was telling him to pipe down, for we were right on Temple's garden.

There was no sign of him there so we went to the front door, and I drew George in close, so that we could not be seen through the windows. I had expected the woman to come, but it was Temple himself.

"Morning, Temple," I said cheerfully. "I've brought a friend of mine to see you."

He shot a look at Wharton and it was plain that he didn't know him.

"A nice place you've got here," Wharton burst in, and was already through the door. "Wouldn't mind a little place like this myself."

"This way, gentlemen," Temple said, but he didn't give that dental smile of his. "The room's a bit untidy, I fear. I've been busy over War Savings' accounts, as you see."

"No need to apologise," Wharton told him, and Temple was beginning at once to look relieved. Nobody who didn't know him could suspect Wharton of either malice or guile. At the worst he might have been peddling insurance, or vacuum cleaners.

"Will you sit down," Temple said to me, for Wharton was already making himself comfortable. Then Wharton gave a kind of sigh.

"A real nice cosy little place, as I was saying, Mr. Broadbeam."

Broadbeam flashed back to Longbottom, and I half-smiled, thinking of Wharton's anecdote. But the smile faded at the sight of Temple's face. It was rather pallid and unhealthy-looking, but at Wharton's apparently innocent remark it flushed to the colour of a dead ripe tomato.

"Let me see," Wharton went on reminiscently. "Four years was what you got, and you came out in '34. Did you come straight down here?"

I was afraid Wharton was going to indulge in one of those baitings in which I have known him fairly revel, but I loathe that kind of sadism, whatever the excellence of the reasons, and I loathe Wharton when he indulges in it. Perhaps he saw the look on my face for his tone took on more sorrow than irony.

"Very nice to hear you've been going straight," he said. "I'm not the one to rake up the past. My name's Wharton, by the way. Superintendent Wharton of New Scotland Yard. I remember your case very well."

Temple managed to speak. He had been moistening his lips and shaking his head, and now he was spreading his hands as he made his protest.

"But you've got nothing against me now." The words gave him a new courage. "Why should you come down here and set people against me?"

Wharton gave a look of the most innocent bewilderment.

"Set people against you? Why, my dear sir, Major Travers here will tell you that he didn't even know your real name till I just addressed you by it! God forbid that I should throw a man's past in his face." Then he snorted indignantly. "It's evident, my dear sir, that you don't know the man you're dealing with."

It was hard not to tell George that he'd said a mouthful. What I did do was to try and set Temple's mind more suavely at rest.

"Superintendent Wharton's quite right," I said. "Nobody in this village is going to know anything about your history. Provided, of course, that you play fair with us."

His lip drooped at that, but I didn't know whether it was in a sneer or from pity for himself.

"You see, you've been keeping bad company," Wharton chimed in. "Our information is that you were a close friend of Maddon. What have you got to say about that?"

"But I wasn't a friend of his," he said, and then as if he had given something away, "And if I was, he was perfectly respectable, wasn't he?"

"Now you're asking us for information," Wharton said. "But just between ourselves, what was your opinion of him? Taking him all round, so to speak."

"Well, he was no friend of mine," he said, and shrugged his shoulders. "I was seeing him fairly often because I was always at him to subscribe to War Savings. I regarded him as a man with plenty of money. Major Travers will tell you that my zeal for War Savings sometimes made me . . . well, over keen."

"Quite understandable," Wharton told him graciously. "But you didn't like him, I take it."

"I didn't," Temple said, and he sounded as if he meant it. "He had a nasty, sneering, superior manner. Very irritating at times."

"Tell me," Wharton said, and leaned forward confidentially. "Do you think *he* had a past?"

Temple's face flushed again but his answer was prompt, even if he avoided Wharton's eyes.

"I don't think so. I gathered the impression that he'd lived abroad, in the Colonies or places like that, where he'd had to be alone a good deal, and he'd got to like it." Wharton tried to get more information about that but with little success. Temple couldn't remember any specific reference to Colonies. Everything was very vague, in fact, though Temple insisted that his own intuitions had been consistently strong.

"Well, we won't keep you from your work," Wharton said at last and got to his feet. "My word's my bond and what's been said here is highly confidential. And I can guarantee Major Travers's discretion too. I take it we can call on you, very discreetly, from time to time to hear if you've any news? You may remember something—about Maddon for instance—that would help us."

Temple said with simulated enthusiasm that he'd be delighted. Then, somewhat nervously, he was saying that Cleavesham would never be the same to him again, and as soon as a convenient change suggested itself he would be leaving the village.

"I don't know that I blame you," Wharton said. "The only thing is that until this business of Maddon is over, you'll have to stay put. And one more thing. I hate to say it, but it'll pay you hand over fist to co-operate with me. I'm putting no pressure on you—that's the last thing I'd do—but if I remember rightly the police never recovered all the cash that was missing on a certain occasion. You wouldn't like inquiries made as to what you're living on now." His hand went pontifically up as Temple began a protest. "Not another word, my dear sir. Forget all about everything, just as I'm going to do as soon as I'm out of this door."

"One of your best efforts, George," I said as we strolled along towards the Wheatsheaf.

"The Old Gent's a long way off dead yet," he told me with a sideways nod of self-appreciation. He was fond of little deprecatory allusions like that.

"What about Porle's rations?" I suddenly asked as I caught sight of Lane End Cottage. "What's he going to do for food, now he's bolted?"

"Go to a hotel, of course," he told me. "Go from hotel to hotel I should have said. But you don't seem very interested in our friend Broadbeam?"

"Should I be?" I said. "I thought you'd told me all you thought good for me to hear."

"You will have your little joke," he said. "A bank cashier, that's what he was. Highly respectable. Sidesman at church and secretary of this and that. Tremendous outcry when he was arrested. Must have been some dreadful plot. How could anybody think any wrong of that dear Mr. Broadbeam! But it was only about ten thousand he'd done the bank in for. Been keeping two homes going for one thing, though that didn't account for all the money. Four years he got, and that was in 1930 if I remember right."

"Married, was he?"

"Didn't I tell you so? Only once though. The other place he had was a flat in Town where he kept a pretty lady. His wife died during the trial, by the way. No children, if I remember rightly."

We had gone past the Wheatsheaf and were nearing Ringlands. George said he had some telephoning to do and perhaps Helen would let him use her 'phone. As we came within fifty yards of the house Helen came to the front gate and a woman was with her. As she turned, the sun glinted on her hair.

"Who's that?" Wharton asked quickly.

"Mrs. Chevalle," I said, and he gave a curious grunt.

CHAPTER VIII
NEARER AND NEARER

"DO YOU KNOW Superintendent Wharton?" Helen said, and: "This is Mrs. Chevalle?"

"Happy to meet you, ma'am," Wharton said, and the approach that would have seemed ridiculous in me seemed perfectly natural to him. "I know your husband pretty well, but now I know why he never gave me the pleasure of meeting his wife."

Helen laughed. Thora Chevalle, to my surprise, didn't say it was lovely. She was looking the least bit nervous, but enough, I thought, for Wharton to notice.

"You're down here on business?" she said.

"That's it," Wharton said, and all four of us were inside the gate by then. "Trying to lend your husband a hand. Can't have murders happen in a place like this and do nothing about it."

I was watching her. George's smile was so paternal and his tone so remote from murder that she was beginning to relax.

"It's a horrible word, 'murder'," she said.

"It is," agreed Wharton, "and we'll say no more about it. You're an old inhabitant here, Mrs. Chevalle?"

"Oh, yes. We've been here some years now," she said.

But Wharton was staring at something. "Keep still," he said, "but there's a wasp or a bee crawling on your hair."

She gave a little shriek but George waded in to the rescue. I couldn't see just what happened for he had whipped out his huge handkerchief and was telling her to keep still, and then announcing that he had it. She gave another little shriek as he drew the handkerchief away, and tugged at her hair. Then she giggled. But Wharton was stepping through the crazy-paving path to the lawn, removing the wasp and treading it into the ground, and he came back with a valedictory wiping of his hands.

"Bravo!" I said. "I've heard of nothing so gallant since Francis jumped into the lions' den and rescued the lady's glove."

"I think it was *very* gallant of Mr. Wharton," Helen said.

"Oh, my poor hair!" Thora was saying. "Is it an awful fright?"

"It'll do till you get home," Helen said, and none too kindly, I thought, but the mirror was produced from the bag all the same and Thora took a coquettish peep at herself.

"Have you a cigarette on you?" Wharton was asking me.

"Do have one of mine," Thora said promptly. Wharton's protest was feeble. I ironically held the lighter. Thora said she wouldn't have one herself and I said it was too near lunch. Then she said she would have to fly, and inside two minutes she had flown.

"Nice little garden you've got here," Wharton said to Helen. "Most attractive."

"It *is* rather nice," Helen said. "Annie and I did most of it ourselves."

"I knew it!" Wharton said. "I said to myself, this is Mrs. Thornley's work!"

"It's nothing like the gardens of Pulvery, of course," Helen added deprecatingly. "But these veronicas make a lovely splash of blue, don't you think? And I must show you our special peonies."

I sheered off to the house and left them to it, not that I was missed, but there are times when George is spreading the soft soap a bit too thickly. And I didn't like the way he'd fastened on to Thora Chevalle. I had thought it exaggeration for Chevalle's benefit when he had claimed to catch a scent of the Five Oaks perfume, but I might have been wrong. The fact that my sense of smell is none too keen is no proof that his isn't abnormal. And Thora Chevalle had been heavily enough scented that morning, for I had the perfume still in my nostrils when I was in my room. Then there had been that clumsy subterfuge to get a hair of hers; clumsy because it was obvious and risky, even if it had apparently succeeded. And that asking for a cigarette when he didn't smoke one a month, and a minute before had his cold pipe in his hand.

It was not till a good twenty minutes later that he left, and without doing that telephoning on which he'd been so keen. Helen came back all smiles and humming to herself.

"Wharton like your garden?" I asked politely.

"I really think he did," she said.

"What were you gossiping about all that time?" I let my smile become a bit arch. "I'll bet it was about Mrs. Chevalle."

"Of course it was," she said. "She *is* rather an overpowering person to meet for the first time. You can't help being interested in her."

"Wharton's the world's prize Parker," I said. "And I'll bet you didn't leave much untold."

"Why, Ludo, what a thing to say!" she told me with a pretence of indignation. Then she smiled, and I thought with a definite satisfaction. Even Helen can be catty at times. "But we did have a really good gossip."

Lunch would be on in five minutes, she warned me, and I said it couldn't be too soon for me. But what I did was to stroll round the back way to that spot on the lawn where Wharton had trodden with his elephantine foot on a highly convenient wasp. As I anticipated, there was never a sign of a wasp there, even allowing for the devastating completeness of the annihilation.

I found myself at a loose end after lunch, so I took the morning paper to the summer-house. But I couldn't settle to it, and soon I was thinking about the case again. What first came into my head was something I had gathered at the Wheatsheaf that morning after the inquest. Someone had remarked that Temple was an older inhabitant than Maddon. There had been a bit of an argument about it, and finally it had been established that he had been in the village for two years before Maddon arrived. But now I was remembering that the main ground for proof had been that a certain somebody, who was people's warden, had died in a certain year and that Temple had taken over the office.

That led me to a train of thought. I was far from believing the various yarns that Temple had spun to account for this and that. I had facts to go on, I could tell myself, and two facts stood out remarkably clear. One was that Temple had helped himself to Maddon's money, and that though he had been forced to hand back fifty pounds, he was still in possession of a tidy balance. Then there was the fact that he had hunted with a feverish haste through that already ran-sacked desk. As an addition, and to clinch those two facts, was the kick in the ribs he had given the dead man, and the look of utter malignancy that had accompanied it.

Now to me those facts added up to this. Maddon had known Temple as Broadbeam. He had discovered that Temple was living at Cleavesham and had dug himself in as a highly respectable and worthy inhabitant, so he had come to Cleavesham himself and had then proceeded to blackmail Temple. But he had not skinned him alive. He had been satisfied to do the milking regularly as against killing the cow for the sake of beef and hide. That was Maddon, the financier and shrewd investor. What Temple had expected to find in that desk was the blackmail instrument—accounts of the Broadbeam trial, photographs, and so on—and hence that vicious kick when the frantic search produced nothing.

That naturally brought me to Pyramid Porle. What was his game? He, as Helen had confirmed, was expecting to come into money, and he had spoken to me of certain financial enterprises in hand. So it seemed to me that Maddon alone must be the source of that coming windfall, and there again it looked as if Porle was a blackmailer and applying the screw by his own peculiar methods. If so, there was a highly intriguing triangle, with Maddon milking Temple and Porle after the milk. As to why Porle had bolted, I thought I could explain that. He would expect the police to find that notice he had tacked to the door. Maybe when he had heard the news of the murder, his informant had added that the police had their eyes on someone, and then Porle had panicked.

Yet I was sure that neither Porle nor Temple had had anything to do with the murder. Porle just wasn't the sort to commit a murder, and from my special hidey-hole as unseen witness I had seen on Temple's face and in his every action the certainty that a dead Maddon had been both surprise and shock. The interest of the two men therefore lay in what they revealed about Maddon himself. I was largely interested in that for Wharton's sake and because I too was keen on discovering the whole history of Maddon. And a knowledge of Maddon might reveal the identity of his murderer. And there I suddenly thought of something startling. Temple had definitely expected to find something in the desk. But it hadn't been there, and, what was more, the police had discovered nothing. Therefore the murderer had taken it. And why should the murderer take it? What was the point? To use it against Temple and so keep Temple's mouth shut? But shut against what? For once I was stumped for a theory. And yet I know now that if I had eaten less for lunch and had been feeling more mentally alert, I could have found an answer, and so for the second time in that case there was a vital clue right under my nose, and myself not able to see it.

Perhaps I should have arrived at it in a few minutes if Annie had not called to me that I was wanted on the 'phone. It was Santon.

"Hallo, Major," he said cheerfully. "Got anything on this afternoon?"

"Devil a thing," I said.   ^

"Well, I've got to see a man at Bycliffe and then another in Porthaven. Like to ride round with me?"

"I'd love it," I said.

"Right-ho, then," he told me. "I'll pick you up at three."

I went up to get myself into more ornate garments and then thought I'd stroll along to the house and so save his petrol. There was ample time, and as it was an afternoon of merciless heat I thought I'd take the back path through the woods, so I left word with Annie that I'd be out to tea and then set leisurely off.

Just as I'd passed the cross paths I met Mary Carter. We both smiled like very old friends.

"Off shopping?" I said, eyeing the basket.

"Isn't it a nuisance?"

"You mean points and things," I said. "What's Clarice doing?"

"She has to sleep in the afternoon," she told me.

"A bit of an effort, isn't it?"

She laughed; a lovely, infectious sort of laugh. "Oh, yes; there's always rather an argument."

"And Mrs. Chevalle?"

"She was busy with a caller," she said. "Someone to see Major Chevalle, but he buttonholed Thora instead. I didn't catch the name. A Mr. Warden I think it was."

I didn't enlighten her, though I might have done so tactfully enough, but I think I was just the least bit startled at Wharton's pertinacity in following up what could have been to him only the ghost of a clue. At that moment there came a fortunate diversion for a grey squirrel ran across the path almost at our feet.

"Isn't it a shame that the farmers shoot all the squirrels," she said.

I told her the difference between the grey and the red. In fact, I said, if I had a nice little rifle and some ammunition, I'd try to eliminate some grey squirrels myself.

"I hate the thought of shooting anything," she said, and there was nothing affected about the remark. "And I hate guns. Thora had a little gun—revolver I suppose you'd call it—in a drawer of hers I had to go to one day and it was just like seeing a snake."

"Perhaps you were a squirrel in a former existence," I told her laughingly.

"Not much of a squirrel about me," she said. "I don't know what I was. A camel probably."

There seemed a quiet irony in that allusion to beasts of burden. I changed the subject to that of our next meeting and suggested tea on Sunday, and the invitation to be passed on to Mrs. Chevalle and Clarice. Then we smiled a good-bye to each other and went our ways. I was still smiling as one does when something pleasant lingers in the mind. Mary Carter lingered in mine so that not even the thought of Wharton at Bassetts, or a gun in a drawer, could move her from it. A real man's woman, I was telling myself, and that was the highest mark my appraisement could ever give. And a fine wife she'd have made for Chevalle if their world had gone less tragically awry.

I still had time to spare when I reached Little Foxes. Dewball was mowing the tennis court with a scythe and making heavy going of it. He paused while we agreed that it was a blazing hot day, then Santon heard me and came through the hedge arch.

"Hallo!" he said. "Glad to see somebody in this ruddy village who's on time. But you shouldn't have walked all this way."

He hadn't been waiting, he said, but he was ready when I was. So we moved off to the garage. The Morris saloon had had a good wash down and a polish and very nice she looked. He was finicky about cars, he told me. Liked to see them natty. Had an idea they went better. Just like golf clubs. Clean ones always seemed to improve his game.

Off we went and I must say it was very pleasant, with the windows down and he driving fairly slowly so that I could have a good view of the countryside.

"A pity you weren't here for our Wings for Victory week," he told me amusedly. "We might have stung you for a nice little sum."

"You'd have had your work cut out," I said. "Oh, and something I meant to ask you. That War Savings' rally you were at, at Southbridge. I know the town pretty well. What's it like since the Blitz?"

"The hell of a mess," he said. "You'd never recognise it."

"Lucky they missed the Civic Centre," I said. "Or wasn't it?"

He didn't follow that.

"It wasn't everybody's idea of perfection," I explained. "Rather like an elaborate cornflour shape. Can't touch the Norwich one."

"Don't know Norwich," he said, "but the Southbridge one's still there—or most of it."

"I hope that big concert room is intact," I said. "I'll certainly hand it to them over that. I expect that's where your rally was."

He laughed. "I'm no ruddy architect. A damn big room with a platform that's all I know. That's Bycliffe, by the way. Perched on top of that hill."

"A fine view out to sea," I said.

"Not so good as you'd think," he told me. "The Hun has given it a pasting or two."

The hill was steep and winding and he had to drop into bottom gear. But the view from the top was really superb, even if the sea was hidden by the far cliffs. A pleasant, straggly village it was with a fine old church and green, and it was quite near the church, and under a huge chestnut tree, that he drew in the car.

"I shouldn't be more than twenty minutes," he told me. "What are you going to do? Have a look round? Or there's a wireless in the back if you'd like to switch it on."

I said I'd be perfectly happy either sitting in the car or strolling round. But I thought wirelesses in cars had gone out of fashion.

"I like to listen to the news when I'm on the run round," he said. "As a matter of fact, this particular set was one my missis had in hers and I snaffled it when I sold the car."

I sat on for a minute or two and I couldn't help smiling at nothing in particular; just the thought of the sailor's fondness for gadgets, and how full of beans Santon always was. Then I thought I'd stretch my legs. So I got out and took a stroll past the church in search of the best view from the hill. It seemed to be from the churchyard wall so I went through the swing gate. A man was tidying up the churchyard by swopping the grass from paths and graves. He was making heavy going of it, but from a quite different reason from that which had made Tom Dewball sweat. Tom had been coping with a heavy crop. This was only a nuisance crop and dry at that, so that the swop had nothing at which to bite.

"Afternoon, sir," he said, and straightened himself and wiped the sweat from his forehead with the back of his hand.

"A warm afternoon," I said. "A pity you couldn't have cut that grass last Saturday morning when the rain was on it."

"Rain, sir?" he said. "Not on Saturday there weren't."

"But surely," I said. "That was when we had the thunder-storm."

He had caught the "we" and was asking if I was staying in Bycliffe. I told him I was from Cleavesham and he grinned.

"Now I'll show you, sir," he said, and made a sweep with his arm in the direction of the Channel. "Them storms always come from over there, right as far as you can see. Then they split up. One lot go out to sea and just catch Cleavesham, and the other go more round like, then they sometimes join up. But not once in a hundred times do we catch anything of it. Regular galling, it is. You can sort of see the rain dropping on Cleavesham and here there ain't so much as a drop what'd lay the dust. And something else I'll tell you, sir."

We stood there yarning about vagaries of weather and when I happened to glance at my watch I saw that I was late. So I slipped him a tip to drink my health and hurried back to the car. It was another five minutes when Santon turned up. He was full of apologies and blasting hell out of those who got muddled in their War Savings accounts.

I suggested tea, if there was anywhere handy. There was—a quite nice guest-house place. I bought a basket of early tomatoes there for Helen and another for the Chevalles, and it was nearly five o'clock when we got on the move again. Towards Porthaven the road was far less interesting, and the town itself I never did like, with its stucco-fronted boarding-houses along its garish main parade. Now, with its beach all barbed wire and concrete, bombed gaps in the stucco, and plaster peeling from its walls, there was a bravery about its tawdriness.

I sat in the car till Santon had finished his last job of work, but it wasn't a long one, and it was still short of six o'clock when we reached Bassetts. The front door was open and no one in sight, so I deposited my basket of tomatoes and sprinted back to the car. As I was closing the front gate Clarice hailed me.

"Hallo!" I said. "Playing hide-and-seek again?"

"Was it for me, that basket?" she said.

"Young lady, you see too much," I told her. "Do you know you're coming to tea with me on Sunday?"

I left her to think that over.

"An old-fashioned one that," Santon said. "Takes after the old man."

"I like them like that," I said. "Mary's a charming girl too."

He didn't make any comment on that, perhaps because I was telling him that I'd walk the short distance to Ringlands. But he wouldn't hear of it, and deposited me and the tomatoes at the front gate.

"Very good of you," I said. "And thank you for a damn good afternoon."

"We'll have one or two more," he told me, and then grinned as he moved the gear to reverse. "A bit more lively next time."

"No you don't," I told him, but he only laughed as he backed the car round. I smiled to myself too, as I went down the path, and then the smile became slightly cynical. So Santon thought of Chevalle as "the old man." That put me in the same category too.

"Had a good time?" Helen said.

"Very nice indeed," I told her. "Bycliffe's a very charming spot."

She smiled at the sight of the tomatoes, and then told me I'd missed Wharton. He'd come to beg to use the telephone and then had stayed to tea.

"He would," I said, and then guilefully: "I hope you collected the cash for his calls."

"My dear, he was frightfully extravagant," she said. "He rang supervisor to ask the charges and how much do you think they were?"

"Ten bob?" I said airily.

"Twelve and sixpence!"

"No wonder Income Tax is ten bob in the pound," I said. "And did he say anything about seeing me?"

"Yes, he said he'd be seeing you in the morning."

"Very good of him," I said, and she looked at me as if I'd uttered some blood-curdling blasphemy.

I was just in time for some of the news, and as we listened to it I was paying a very formal attention. Those calls of Wharton's, I thought, must have been to the Yard. Maybe he had been telling them he was sending them another platinum hair. And another cigarette, perhaps, and with lipstick on it. Maybe he had even wormed out of somebody—and he wouldn't have stopped short of questioning Clarice—just where Thora Chevalle was supposed to have spent that short holiday in town, and he was arranging to have the friend closely questioned.

"What makes you so restless?" Helen asked me, for I had got to my feet and was polishing my glasses. "Has the afternoon made you too tired?"

I sat down again and said it was probably an uneasy conscience. She didn't take it at all flippantly, even if she did smile faintly as she told me with a hint of reproof that that was what came of spending an afternoon with Commander Santon.

CHAPTER IX
THE SHOWDOWN

I DIDN'T SEE Wharton the following day. When I came down to breakfast I found a note for me, sent from the Wheatsheaf. He had been recalled urgently to Town, he said, but would be back late that night and hoped to see me the morning after that. I wondered when he had actually left for Town, and after breakfast I went to the Wheatsheaf and had a word with the landlord, who was doing some hoeing in his garden. He said Wharton had left Cleavesham last night by the eight o'clock bus to catch the eight-thirty from Porthaven, a train which would get him to Town about ten-fifteen.

It seemed to me that getting to Town at that time of night wouldn't mean any sort of conference, but more probably a full day ahead and the need to be on the job in the early morning. What that job was I could very well guess, but I didn't let it worry me too much. As far as Thora Chevalle was concerned, the case was acquiring an inevitability and nothing I could do would deflect or deter. If she were guilty, then she was guilty, and tragic though the results might be for people in whom I was already more than interested, justice had to take its course. If she were innocent, so much the better. Wharton was tremendously discreet, I'll say that for him, and no possible suspicion of scandal would be attached to her name.

Well, the morning of Wharton's arrival came and as soon as breakfast was over I was sitting waiting, and with an eye on the front gate. It was not till about half-past nine that a dark coupe drew up and Wharton got out. I was at the gate before he had opened it.

"I won't come in," he said. "If you're ready we'll go straight off."

"A nice little car," I said, running an eye over it. "How did you induce anyone to trust you with this?"

"I'm not tramping about and waiting for buses at my time of life," he told me. "Five Oaks is where we're going first. Thought I'd like a word with that Mrs. Beaney."

He moved the car off. George drives as if he'd bet someone a thousand pounds he'd never have an accident, and if so he's running a risk for some day a tricycle will run into him from the rear. But the twenty miles an hour gave me time to talk.

"Have a busy day in Town?" I asked.

"All over the place," he said. "Didn't get back here till nearly midnight."

"Find anything out?"

"One or two oddments," he told me after a bit of thought. "You'll hear all about it later."

It was no use questioning him when he was in that sort of mood. Somewhere up his sleeve was a surprise for me, and George wasn't one to reveal an inkling till the spectacular moment of revelation came. So I turned the conversation to the weather, and by the time he'd told me how hot it had been in Town he was drawing the car in by Mrs. Beaney's cottage.

We sat in her little living-room while Wharton did the questioning. As sharp as a ferret, that woman was, and I guessed that by noon at latest the village would know each word that Wharton had spoken, and probably a bit more for luck.

She had never seen a sign of a woman in the house, she said. She didn't think Mr. Maddon had been one for women. The only one who ever came was Mrs. Chevalle, and she knew that because Mrs. Chevalle called on her first. Sixpence a week she subscribed and she knew that wasn't much, but it all helped. Afterwards Mrs. Chevalle went straight on to Five Oaks.

"Mrs. Chevalle called as usual last week?" Wharton asked.

"Oh, yes, she called," Mrs. Beaney said, and, "Was there any reason why she shouldn't have called?"

Wharton laughed roguishly. "You leave me to ask the questions, Mrs. Beaney." His face straightened. "All I'm trying to get at is whether everything was normal last week, right up to the time he was murdered. Apparently it was. You noticed nothing unusual about him?"

It was plain that she'd have liked nothing better than to mention a something, but she had to shake her head.

"Now that ash-tray that was on the little table," Wharton went on.

"Ash-tray?" she broke in. "I don't remember no ashtray."

"Come, come," Wharton said. "Surely Inspector Galley or someone asked you about the ash-tray?"

"No one mentioned no ash-tray to me," she said.

Wharton described the ash-tray and told her that ciga- rette-ends and match-ends had been in it. Had she ever seen any sort of ash-tray when she'd come to the house? She said she hadn't. Mr. Maddon didn't smoke much and he threw his ends anywhere; usually in the fire-place, which she always cleaned up. But she admitted that there might be things like ash-trays which she'd never seen in the house. What with the work she had to do there and the little time to do it in, she hadn't a minute to herself, not that she was one to poke in other people's drawers and cupboards.

Wharton switched the attack. Did Maddon ever have any gossiping moments, and if so, what had he ever let fall about himself? The question aroused Mrs. Beaney's indignation, but only because Maddon had made things clear when she first arrived to do the cleaning. Obviously she had tried to get him to talk with the hope of finding matters for gossip, but he had laid down the position with a rather caustic asperity.

"Not that I was one to talk, as I told him. I come here to work,' I said. 'And I'm not interested in other people's business,' I said."

"And a very good rap on the knuckles for him too," Wharton said. Then he was giving one of his wheedling looks. "But just between ourselves, what did you make of him? Did you think he'd been married, for instance?"

"He was very neat and tidy," she said after a bit. "And he did some of his own cooking and made his own bed. I used to get his tea for him. High tea, they call it, a bit of fish or something, or a pudding."

Before Wharton could speak she was remembering something.

"There's the photo! I haven't never shown it to nobody, but I'll let you see it. Found it, I did, as if he'd thrown it away, and I kept it myself because it reminded me of my poor sister Ada when she was a girl."

She was rummaging in a drawer and Wharton's eyebrows lifted as his eyes met mine. It was what was known as a cabinet photo; a print mounted on stiff cardboard, and it showed a girl of about fifteen fitting on a chair, with a boy of about ten or twelve standing behind her, his hand on her shoulder. Behind was a backcloth representing distant mountains.

"Rather Victorian," I said when he'd passed it to me. "Probably taken best part of forty years ago." Then I noticed something else. "Someone's cut the photographer's name and address off. If I remember rightly, they used to be in silver letters on the mount."

"I know where it was took," Mrs. Beaney told us. "I happened to see it once before, on his desk, and it was took at Windsor. That's what made me take to it so. My poor sister lived at Windsor."

"There you are!" Wharton told me. "That's what comes of having a good memory. I told you we'd hear something from Mrs. Beaney. And I suppose you didn't remember the photographer's name?"

But that was beyond her. Wharton got to his feet and began the usual well-soaped thanks. The photograph he'd return in a day or two, he said, and in the meanwhile Mrs. Beaney had better keep quiet about it. The police might consider she'd been withholding information, and if they turned nasty, that might mean trouble.

We drove on to Five Oaks. The plain-clothes man who was sunning himself in a chair at the front door, ear cocked for the telephone, scrambled to his feet at the sight of us. Wharton told him genially to sit tight, and what he did himself was to write a letter and put it and the photograph in a stout envelope from his attaché-case.

"I'll get this rushed up to Town from Porthaven," he told me. "A pretty forlorn hope hunting for a photographer who was in business forty years ago, but you never know."

"Going to Porthaven, are we?" I asked, when we were back in the car again.

"One or two things I want to talk over with Chevalle," he told me, and much too casually. "I rather wanted you to be there. Two heads are better than one."

"I know," I said. "Even if they're sheeps' heads. But who do you think those children on the photograph were? Maddon's own children?"

He shrugged his shoulders. "How should I know? What I'm hoping is that there'll be a photographer who's kept records. If so, he might be able to tell us who paid for the photograph. That might give us a start on Maddon's trail."

"You're a bigger optimist than I am," I told him. "Still, you never know. But what are you seeing Chevalle about, George?"

"You'll hear in good time," he told me impatiently. Then he trod hard on the brakes, released one hand from the wheel and looked at his watch. "Plenty of time. Chevalle's had some civic function or other on and he told me he wouldn't be free till best part of twelve o'clock."

I smiled cynically to myself but asked no more questions. Whatever it was that Wharton was going to talk over, it had been of sufficient importance to fix a time for the interview. Why he should want to have me there was an unanswered question that was just a bit disturbing.

We had best part of an hour in Porthaven. George was arranging for the dispatch of his letter, and I found a place to get coffee. At just before noon I rejoined him at police headquarters. A minute or two later we were in Chevalle's room.

Chevalle was in uniform and a fine figure he looked. The two rows of ribbons looked impressive, and they weren't coronation ones, either.

"Hope I haven't kept you two waiting," he said, as he shook hands with us. "Make yourselves comfortable, and then we'll get down to it."

Wharton went to the outer door, opened it and glanced along the passage.

"No chance of anything being overheard?" he asked as he closed the door again.

"Heavens, no!" Chevalle said, and looked a bit bewildered.

"All the same we'll not talk too loudly," Wharton told him, and was drawing his chair in closer to Chevalle's desk. Then he began putting on his antiquated spectacles, and I knew something unusual was in the wind. Chevalle caught my eye and his eyebrows lifted. I gave a quick shake of the head.

"The time has come for some remarkably plain speaking," Wharton began. "I thought it best to have Major Travers here as a trustworthy witness. We can both rely on his discretion, and that what's said here goes no further."

"Aren't you being rather mysterious?" asked Chevalle, and his smile was a dry one.

"Just taking precautions," Wharton told him evenly. "I always do that when I'm on mixed business. Part private, part not."

Chevalle nodded.

"And a talk of that sort is agreeable to you?" Wharton asked him.

"Good God, sir, get on with it!" Chevalle told him with a grim impatience.

Wharton opened the attaché-case, made as if to take something out, then changed his mind and closed it again.

"You'll have to take my word for everything," he said. "Though it's all here if you should want to see it." Then he was peering over his spectacle tops. "The fact is, Chevalle, I want to question your wife."

"My wife!" He shot an inquiring glance at me. "I'm afraid I don't follow."

"Well, I warned you that it was to be all cards on the table," Wharton told him evenly. "I'm putting mine down right-away. My opinion is that you know perfectly well why I want to question your wife."

"Oh?" Chevalle said, and his eyes narrowed.

"Look at it like this," Wharton said placidly. "The first real murder case you've had since your appointment here. A first-class chance for you to show your metal and make a name for yourself. But what do you do? You scarcely touch the outside edges of the case and you throw your hand in." His tone changed to the challenging. "If you're anything, Chevalle, you're a fighter. You're a sticker. Yet you threw your hand in!" He shrugged his shoulders, and the tone changed again. "If it's your wish not to talk, very well, we'll not talk. In that case I shall have to proceed as I think fit."

"Proceed with what?"

Wharton raised hands to heaven, then let them fall. I thought he was going to get to his feet.

"Proceed with questioning your wife. Asking her to make a statement."

Chevalle leaned forward. "You surely can't mean—"

"Oh, yes, I do," Wharton said. "I mean make a statement as a suspect."

Chevalle's eyes narrowed again. "I take it this isn't some kind of joke?"

"What joke there is is of your own making," Wharton told him, and his lips pursed in an ironical smile. "But if you want me to tell you a few facts, here they are. The hairs on that chair at Five Oaks were definitely Mrs. Chevalle's. The cigarette-ends and the lipstick on them were hers, and so was the ash-tray print. I think the scent was hers, but I'm keeping that out."

Chevalle smiled, and it seemed relievedly. "But, my dear fellow, there's a simple explanation of all that. My wife went there every week, as you know—"

Wharton had raised a hand. He said rather grimly that he didn't know a lot of things, and then proceeded to detail them. Why Monday's ash-tray should never have been seen by Mrs. Beaney and should have remained unemptied, and why scent should linger for days.

"It's no use, Chevalle," he said. "Your wife was at that house either late the previous night or early the following morning."

Chevalle's lip drooped. "I see. And how did she get there from Town? By aeroplane?"

"If it's her alibi you're relying on," Wharton told him, "then I've a disappointment for you. I know with whom Mrs. Chevalle was supposed to be staying, and where. I saw the person myself and broke her evidence down, and it wasn't a hard job either. Your wife, Chevalle, had rigged the whole thing with her. She did call at Hampstead and see the friend, but she didn't spend the night there, and the friend doesn't know what she did with herself after that." He heaved a sigh. "That's why I propose to ask your wife where she did spend her time, and why she gave me deliberately false information."

Chevalle sank back in his chair and he was moistening his lips. His fingers were at his chin and he couldn't meet our eyes. He was a badly shaken than, and Wharton knew it.

"Now you know why I wanted this little talk," he said. "We're all friends here, Chevalle. Lion doesn't eat lion. But I've got to do my duty all the same."

"I know." Chevalle's voice had the dullness of defeat. "And I'm grateful. All the same, Wharton, there may be a perfectly natural explanation."

"I hope there is." He shook his head. "I hope for everyone's sake there is."

"Let me tell you something," Chevalle said. "And I never thought I'd tell this to a living soul. My wife and I haven't seen eye to eye for the best part of three years. She goes her own way and I ask no questions. She doesn't even run the house. Her cousin does that." His tone took on a defiance. "So long as she doesn't smirch my name or make things difficult for me here, then I'm satisfied. All the same, she has my name, and I'll fight for that name. That's why I tell you she couldn't have killed Maddon. What was the motive? Tell me that."

"Do you mind if I say something?" I suddenly asked. "Why not?" Wharton said, and I felt Chevalle's eyes seeking mine. But it was at Wharton I looked.

"I'm not butting in on this," I said, "but I'd like to have Mrs. Chevalle's name cleared. The best way to do that, it seems to me, is to lay all our cards on the table, as you said. The worst service I can do is to hold anything back, and I think I know of a motive. If I'm wrong, then Mrs. Chevalle can prove it wrong, and she'll be a step nearer into the clear."

"That's fair enough," Chevalle said. "What is the motive?"

"I think she was being blackmailed."

"Blackmailed! My wife blackmailed!"

I told him about the conflicting information as to Maddon's War Savings Certificates and I instanced the ironic twist in Maddon's make-up.

"So I see it like this," I said. "Temple's information was right. Maddon *did* recently boast that he'd never bought a Savings Certificate and he was speaking the truth, even if he did buy one every week. For he didn't buy it at all. *It was your wife who paid for it.*"

"A bit far-fetched, surely," Wharton said.

"Take it or leave it, there it is," I said.

Chevalle's head suddenly went to his cupped hand and he was rubbing his eyes as if they were tired. When he looked at us again he was a beaten man.

"All right, gentlemen, I give in. Maddon may have been black-mailing her. I don't know. But for God's sake leave me alone."

His voice was rising. Wharton got quickly to his feet and went to him behind the desk. His hand fell on Chevalle's shoulder.

"There," he said, as one would to a child. "You leave it to me. You can trust me, Chevalle. I give you my word."

"I'm sorry." Chevalle got to his feet, shaking his head. "Ever since I had an idea of all this I've been through hell. Some-times"—the voice was rising again—"I've wished to hell I could get this coat off and get back in the Army again and do a man's job." He shook his head again. "And I may do yet."

"Your job is to stay here and take what's coming," Wharton told him. "Personally I don't think Mrs. Chevalle has a lot to fear, but it's up to her. You couldn't use any influence?"

"With her? No. It's your case, Wharton, and I'm out of it." The lip drooped. "If I weren't I wouldn't bring myself to ask a woman of mine to be so good as to tell the truth."

Wharton gave me a backward nod so I began moving off. I saw his hand go out to Chevalle.

"Forget everything. That's my advice. Trust me and I'll never let you down."

"Drive a bit slowly, George," I said when we were just clear of the town. "There's something I'd like to put up to you."

I think that interview with Chevalle had shaken him a bit. There was what I hadn't heard, for it had been a good five min-utes after I had left the room before he came out to rejoin me, with Chevalle still there.

"What was the expert opinion on that bullet?" I began.

"Italian probably," he told me mildly.

"We'll never find out whether or not Maddon had a gun," I said. "But what about Mrs. Chevalle? Doesn't any case against her hang on whether or not she had one?"

"She had one all right," he said. "She let that slip to me herself. Says she used to keep it in a drawer and then it disappeared."

"That's bad," I said. "If she couldn't think of anything better than that, then she's in a nasty jam. She didn't say what kind it was?"

"It was the right calibre, so I judged," he said. "She said a friend gave it to her as a kind of curio some time ago, and she'd forgotten who the friend was." He gave a grunt. "But what was that theory you were talking about?"

"It isn't a theory," I said. "It's a suggestion I'd like to put up to you. Have you met Mary Carter, Mrs. Chevalle's cousin?"

"A pretty, fair-haired girl? If so I just saw her and no more."

"She's the one who holds that house together, George. As Helen may have told you"—I just couldn't help that malicious touch—"she's the maid-of-all-work. Looks after the child and runs the house. Has to be sweet with Chevalle and his wife at the same time. I think she loves the whole three of them, but the wife the least. All the same, she's not the kind who'd do anything to get a friend out of a jam. Hence the suggestion. Thora Chevalle strikes me as just the kind who'd bully Mary Carter and run her off her legs, and then go whining to her for help. What I'm getting at is, why shouldn't Thora have got herself in badly with Maddon and then gone to Mary? What would Mary suggest? That Thora should go to Maddon and try and finally buy him off. Hence the fake holiday. Thora went to see him then, and late at night, but when she came back she could only tell Mary she was in a worse jam than ever. So Mary settled things in her own way. She fixed an appointment with Maddon for early the next morning; slipped along there and did him in and then disposed of the gun." He slowly shook his head. "That slip of a woman? She never'd have the pluck to do that. I had something of the same idea myself but it wouldn't work."

"Don't you believe it," I said. "She's no slip of a woman. She may look that kind, but I'll bet she's got all the pluck in the world."

"Well, I'll have another good look over her," he said. "It's not a bad theory, for you, even if I did have it first. So was that one you floored Chevalle with. That one about the Savings Certificates."

"By the way," I said. "I don't know if you saw to the water in the radiator but the car's steaming pretty badly."

"So it is!" he said, and trod on the brakes.

"She'll last you to the Wheatsheaf," I told him, for we were just passing Bassetts.

But George was the careful kind. Right against us was a pond with a fallen willow in the middle of it and he made me bring water in an empty pint bottle he found in the back.

"Nice handy spot for that gun to have been dropped in," he said as we moved off again.

"You're right," I told him. "Why not have it dragged?"

"Plenty of time," he said. "A whole lot of things will have to happen before we get as far as that."

The trouble was that just how many things and what were to happen, we neither of us had the foggiest idea. And if we had had, then I'd have stripped to the raw and grubbed about in the mud of that roadside pond till I'd found that gun, or knew at least that it wasn't there.

CHAPTER X
CLOSING THE NET

WHARTON SAW Thora Chevalle that same afternoon, and by appointment. Even when talking on the telephone she was already in a flutter, Wharton told me, and it was she who suggested three-thirty as the time for his call. That was because Clarice would be awake by then and could be sent with Mary Carter on some errand to Porthaven, for there was a bus that passed the gate of Bassetts at three-fifteen.

This is what happened at the interview. As I was not there you may think the statement over-confident, but what you are about to read is what George himself told me as quite a dramatic story, and George could certainly dramatise himself, if nothing else. As for any extras, fifteen years of George have taught me all his tricks, as doubtless they have taught him mine. If you should think that you know already what Wharton was going to talk to Thora Chevalle about, I can only say that that interview told me quite a lot of things, and but for it there would have been no last chapter. And so then to what happened.

Thora Chevalle seemed reasonably at ease when she appeared at the already-open front door. Her 'How-d'you do?' was on the gushing side, and she was made up to kill. There was the escorting to the lounge, the patting of a cushion on the chair on which Wharton was to sit, and then the proffered cigarette-case. That gave Wharton a first-class opening.

"You'd never guess where I first saw a cigarette like this," he said, with a pursing of the lips. "Well, not a cigarette exactly. A stub. Two stubs, in fact."

Her interest seemed only polite.

"Yes," Wharton said reminiscently. "It was in an ashtray at Five Oaks."

Her eyes opened wide at that, but she didn't seem anything approaching scared.

"Five Oaks! Why, I've never smoked a cigarette there in my life!"

"I know," said Wharton taking out his wallet. "Here's one of them. And it's got your lip-stick on it."

She gaped again, then had a look. "It does look like it," she told him with a bit of a titter.

"And these two hairs," Wharton said. "They're yours. They were found on the back of an easy chair."

"That would be when I called for War Savings," she said. Then her eyes opened wide again. "But I never sat in a chair. Never in my life."

Wharton was watching her. Her head shook quickly and she gave a little scowl as she said that, as if the thought of calls at Five Oaks was none too pleasant.

"And a still more funny thing," Wharton was going on, "was that your finger-prints were found on an ash-tray there."

"But I've never touched an ash-tray!" She was looking genuinely bewildered. "I've never even seen one!"

"Ah, well," said Wharton with a sigh. "Maybe you fingered it absent-mindedly one day when you were there. You had a lot to think about, you know."

"Whatever do you mean?" she said, and Wharton knew he had been lucky to make that remark so vague. But he was having a pretty poor opinion of her intelligence. "All dressed up to the nines," was how he put it to me, "and the brains of a nit-wit. Hadn't got the sense to see what I'd been driving at from the start. That's why I thought I'd show her my teeth."

"Well, perhaps you'd got used to it," he told her. "But I shouldn't have been very pleased myself if I had to call on a man like Maddon and give him a Savings Certificate out of my own pocket."

Her face went a vivid red, so red that it was as if those scarlet lips of hers had paled. For a moment she panicked badly, and he was surprised when she managed to get some sort of control over herself.

"It's not true," she said, still staring at him wildly. "It's not true."

Wharton got to his feet and looked down at her.

"Stay where you are, Mrs. Chevalle, and listen to me. I'm not here to gossip or tell you fairy-tales. I'm here on business—the business of discovering who murdered Maddon. Look at me, Mrs. Chevalle, and answer my question. Maddon was black-mailing you—wasn't he."

"No," she said. "No. It isn't true."

Wharton shrugged his shoulders. "And what if I can prove it to be true? What if I propose to bring you into a Court of Law and prove there that it's true."

"You'd never do a thing like that," she said.

"So it *is* true."

She sprang to her feet and then tried some dramatics of her own.

"I thought you were a gentleman, Mr. Wharton. I don't think there's any reason for going on like this. I think you'd better go." And then, infuriated perhaps by his unbudging attitude and dry smile: "Major Chevalle will be simply furious when I tell him about this."

"Sit down," Wharton told her, and maybe the grimness of his voice or the look in his eyes scared her, for she did sit down. "I went into all this with Major Chevalle this morning, and he's given me a free hand. He's a man of honour and he has his duty to do, the same as I have. In any case, he's nothing to do with this matter now. I'm in charge, and that's why I'm here this afternoon. I've asked you in so many words to explain certain things in connection with the shooting of Maddon, and so far I'm not satisfied with the explanations you have given me."

"Do you dare to suggest that I'm telling you lies?"

"I dare anything," he told her placidly. "If it were my own mother who'd shot Maddon I'd make her tell the truth. And sooner or later I'll make *you* tell the truth—either to me, more or less in confidence as we are now, or publicly in a Court of Law. The choice is up to you."

"But I *have* told you the truth." Her lip began to quiver then, so he showed his teeth once more.

"The truth? You've told me nothing but lies!" He turned his back on her for a moment and then whipped round. "Look here, Mrs. Chevalle, let me put all this in a nutshell. If you had nothing to do with killing Maddon, it's the simplest thing in the world for you to prove it. Maddon was shot at about six o'clock that morning. All you have to do is prove to me where you were at that time."

"But I've already told you where I was!"

"I saw your friend Miss Taylor myself," he told her. "She blew the gaff. More politely, she gave you away so as to save herself. You wrote her a letter that she was to say you were staying with her. You'd done that sort of thing before, and she was agreeable.

To make it doubly sure you went to see her and you took her a nice little present. A handbag that cost a fiver if it cost a penny."

That was when Thora Chevalle began to cry. Blubber was how George described it. "Her brains might be an excellent case of arrested development," he told me, "but she had low cunning enough to use that handkerchief of hers to collect her wits. If she'd thought of softening me up, she was never more mistaken in her life. She shot me a look to see how I was reacting, and then at last she produced a beautiful yarn."

The yarn came after a final sob and a dab at her eyes with the wisp of a handkerchief. The room was reeking of scent. "Mr. Wharton, may I tell you something in confidence?"

"Isn't that what I'm here for?" he answered.

"Then it's about my husband," she said after a moment's hesitation. "We are not on very good terms, but I think he spies on me, though I never spy on him. That's why I won't ever tell him where I go. I just go on a holiday and it's not his business where I go. That's why I made up that story with Aggie—Miss Taylor." She gave a wan smile. "I do it to annoy him, really. I oughtn't to say that, but you said you wanted me to tell the truth."

"You do it to annoy him," Wharton repeated non-committally. "Well, so far so good. Now perhaps you'll tell me where exactly you *were* at six o'clock that morning."

"You'll believe me if I tell you?"

"I'll believe you when I've been to the place myself and got the additional evidence of at least two witnesses I can trust" Wharton told her.

"But I couldn't do that."

"Do what?"

"Let anybody else know."

"Ah, well," said Wharton heavily, and reached for his hat. "I suppose I shall have to act in my own way."

He was already at the lounge door when she called him back.

"But you can't go like that!"

"Listen," Wharton said, and turned on her fiercely. "If you think I can stay here and listen to all the lies you're prepared to concoct, you're very much mistaken. Where were you that morning at six o'clock?"

"But I can't tell you," she said, and her hand wobbled frightenedly in front of her mouth.

"Right," said Wharton grimly. "Listen to me again, Mrs. Chevalle, for as sure as my name's Wharton, this is what's going to happen. If within two days—by this time the day after to-morrow—you haven't told me, and told me the gospel truth, about where you were, I'm coming here again. And I'm going to take an official statement from you as a suspect in the matter of the murder of Herbert Maddon. Forty-eight hours and the truth, mind you."

"You couldn't arrest me," she told him defiantly.

"Not only can I but I will," he told her. And something in that new attitude of hers must have angered him, for he let out more than he intended. "And within another twenty-four hours of that I'll know the name of the man with whom you spent the night!"

A look of tremendous fright came over her face at that. Her fingers were frightenedly at her mouth again. He waited a moment in case she should choose to speak, but she turned away. Without another word he went out of the house and straight to me at Ringlands. Helen was out, but Annie brought us tea to the summer-house and it was over that that he told me the story of the interview. He was still definitely not himself. I think he was brooding over the question of whether or not he had gone too far, and, of course, there was always in the background the figure of Chevalle, and the avoidance of scandal, and if there had to be a scandal, how far it would affect the public opinion concerning Chevalle himself.

"What do you make of things?" he asked me, and extra-ordinarily earnestly.

"I don't know," I told him slowly. "What I have got is the impression that everything's more blurred."

"How do you mean?"

"Frankly I don't see her so clearly as mixed up in that murder. What she ought to have been most scared of was getting hanged by the neck, but what really did scare her was being forced into admitting where she had spent that night."

"Yes," he said, and pursed his lips reflectively. "All the same, you can't get away from solid evidence. But one thing I must say. I don't think so much as I did about that theory of yours about complicity with that Mary Carter."

"Why not?" I said, ignoring the fact that he had once claimed it as his own.

"Because she'd have given Mary Carter away to save her own skin," he told me. "She'd sell anybody."

"If there was anything in the theory, she may do it yet," I said.

"She'll give no one away to incriminate herself," he told me.

"In any case I could have bitten my tongue off after I'd mentioned Mary Carter at all," I said. "She's a dam-good sort, and if she does have to be brought into things I don't think I'll ever forgive myself."

"No use talking like that," he said. "I'll see her myself this evening. Make a private appointment somewhere over the telephone." Then he shook his head. "It's Chevalle that's worrying me. Not that I think there need be any scandal."

"Of course there needn't," I said. "Even if the worse comes to the worst there'd be no reflection on him. A man of his pluck could live things down. By the way, did you say anything to Mrs. Chevalle about that gun?"

"What was the use?" he said. "She'd only have told me more lies. Besides, you've got to leave liars with a few lies to clothe themselves with. If you strip them naked, they get desperate, and you don't always want that."

"Why did you give her as long as forty-eight hours?" I asked. "Wouldn't twenty-four have brought her up to scratch?"

"It's only one clear day," he said, and, more grimly, "two whole nights. That's when she'll do her thinking."

"What are you going to do yourself?"

"Plenty for me to do," he said. "I might as well get rid of Galley, for all the use he is now. And those other men of his. Then to-morrow I'm going over that Five Oaks place with a micro-scope. And I might start putting the screw on Temple."

"Still worrying yourself about where you met Maddon?" I asked him.

"Wouldn't you?" he said. "Wondering who he was used to be bad enough before: it's been ten thousand times worse since I've been down here. What time is there a bus from Porthaven, by the way?"

We went to the house and looked at the time-table. One was due at Cleavesham at half-past five.

"Then I'll be pushing on," he said. "That's the bus that Mary Carter ought to be back on and I'd rather ring her up from the pub."

I felt a bit restless when he'd gone, so I took a walk through some field-paths I found on Helen's map, and the finding of my way certainly kept my mind off the case. It was well on the way to meal-time when I got back, and almost eight o'clock by the time it was over. Then I had a look at the local Home Guard do-ing an exercise on a meadow opposite Ringlands, but the midges were a bit troublesome, so I adjourned to the house for the nine o'clock news. It was during that that the telephone went for me.

"Major Travers?" a feminine voice said.

"Yes," I said. "Speak up, will you? I can't hear you very well."

"This is Mary Carter. I daren't speak too loudly. Are you there?"

"Yes, I'm here."

"Can I see you to-night? I know it sounds unusual—"

"Of course you can," I cut in. "Where shall it be? Here?"

"No. Not there," she said quickly. "On the path at the back of your house?"

"Good," I said. "When?"

"In about a quarter of an hour?"

"I'll be there," I said, and then she rang off.

I told Annie I was going for a short stroll and she needn't put the black-out up. Then I made my way to the back path, and as I didn't know how much it was frequented, I walked towards Little

Foxes, looking for a side path. Then I found a little ride that had been used for timber hauling, and when I at last caught sight of Mary I was glad I had thought of it, for she was wearing no coat and her light summer frock could have been seen for yards.

"Did you wonder what it was all about?" she asked me as we made our way along the ride. She was smiling bravely enough, but I could see she was perturbed, and that was revealing.

"I think I knew," I told her, and stepped off the track to behind a thick beech clump. "You'd like me to help you; isn't that it?"

"Well, yes," she said. "But it's not me, exactly. It's Thora."

"You trust me?"

"I shouldn't be here if I didn't," she told me quietly.

"I trust you too," I said. "That's necessary, you see. We've got to tell each other a whole lot of things and keep nothing back. Is that a bargain?"

"Yes. It's a bargain."

"Then you begin by telling me what's worrying Thora," I said.

She was full of it, and of indignation too. Wharton had threatened to arrest her for the murder of Maddon.

"It's ridiculous!" she blazed at me. "He must be mad! How could she have done such a thing? And why?"

"Steady, young lady!" I said. "You listen to the other side— Wharton's side."

That calmed her down. By the time I'd finished massing that accumulation of evidence I could see she was badly shaken.

"Where is Mrs. Chevalle?" I asked her.

"Lying down," she said. "She didn't come down at all to-night. She's simply crazy with worry."

"And Major Chevalle?"

"In the house," she said. "I said I had a headache and made that an excuse for a walk."

"Whose suggestion was it that you should see me?"

"Mine," she said. "Thora jumped at it too."

"What was I expected to do?"

"Well," she said hesitatingly, "I thought you knew Mr. Wharton pretty well. Dick told me that, and I thought you'd be able to point out how impossible it was. I mean that Thora should have done such a thing."

"It's all very simple then," I said. "You see, you can't commit a murder if you're somewhere else when it was done—unless you use mechanical means, like a time bomb, and that wasn't the case with Maddon's murder. He was shot, and at a definite time. All Mrs. Chevalle has to do is to prove an alibi."

"That's what I told her," she said. "But she won't. She's just obstinate about it."

"Isn't obstinate a mild word? Would you call a person obstinate who refused to save her own neck? In fact, oughtn't we to ask ourselves if Mrs. Chevalle can or dare say where she was at the time of that murder?"

She gave me a frightened look. Then she frowned as if she were thinking of something.

"Do you mind if I'm uncommonly frank?" I said.

"I want you to be," she told me earnestly.

"Then I'll tell you one of my impressions of Mrs. Chevalle. I think she's the least bit over-sexed. I happen to know the relationship between her and her husband, and my view definitely is that she has to have a man in the offing somewhere." If I'd been arguing with Wharton I'd have left out those last four words. "To be blunt, I think she was not spending a holiday with a girl friend. In fact, Wharton proved to her that she'd told him lies about that. You see what I'm getting at?"

"Yes," she said, and bit her lip.

"And you don't disagree?"

She shook her head.

"If what I think is right," I went on, "then everything's explained. She didn't do the murder, but she daren't prove an alibi. If she spent that holiday with some man, then she gives Chevalle grounds for an immediate divorce. And she'd lose the custody of the child. Unless, of course . . ."

"Unless what?"

"Unless she really did shoot Maddon."

"Yes, but *why* should she shoot Maddon?"

"It's our belief, and Mrs. Chevalle hasn't denied it, that Maddon was blackmailing her."

Her eyes opened wide at that.

"If a woman philanders extensively," I pointed out, "then she lays herself open to being found out. The world's a small place. Or Maddon may have known of some earlier indiscretion."

"How horrible people are!"

"Human nature," I said, and then there was a long half-minute of silence. There was a smell of honeysuckle from a thorn clump near us, and the whole dusk was still and scented. Never would there be so intimate and so lonely a moment.

"Will you tell me something, Mary?" I said gently.

"What is it," she asked, and as if she felt that intimacy too.

"You needn't tell it to me," I said. "Just say it."

"Say what?"

"You love Chevalle, don't you?"

She was holding herself very still and the smile was for herself.

"And if I do?"

"And he loves you?"

"And if he does?" she said, and then at last looked at me.

"Nothing," I said. "I just wanted to be sure."

"Life's queer," she said. "Hasn't it treated you queerly sometimes?"

"Not as much as I deserved," I said. "But you didn't say it as some people do—as if you had a grievance?"

"I'm not bitter about things," she said. "In a way I suppose, I'm happy."

"Tell me about yourself," I said. "When you were a girl and everything."

She told me, and there wasn't a lot to tell. Thora's father and hers were brothers, and each made his own way in the world. Thora's father began as a bricklayer and rose to be a master builder. Mary's father made his way by scholarships and became a music teacher. He was gassed in the last war and then I gathered the small family of three had a bad time. Thora's father helped surreptitiously, but he had against him his wife and Thora herself. They were ashamed of the poor relations and

Thora was jealous of Mary's success in winning a scholarship to a good school.

Though Mary spoke with no bitterness, I gathered that Thora thought that as a poor relation Mary should have had the usual schooling to fourteen or so, and then have gone to work to support her parents.

"My mother died first," Mary said, "and I left school to look after father. He died only a month later. I was eighteen then and I got a post as nursery-governess. Then Thora married and Clarice came, and Thora persuaded me to come here."

"Where she could at last definitely have you in a position of subservience."

"Not altogether that," she said. "Besides, I was glad to come."

"How does she really treat you?"

"It's how she treats Richard that's so . . . so galling," she said. "She's maddening. And he never says a word."

"But you," I said. "How does she treat you?"

"Sometimes I hate her!" She said that with a passionate vehemence. "She's selfish, and mean and paltry . . . and horrible. Then she'll be decent for a bit. Not to Richard—to me. Then it begins all over again."

The shadows of the wood and the gathering dusk made her almost invisible now, but I caught a glint of her hair as she suddenly turned.

"What's the time? Richard will wonder whatever's happened."

"I'll see you home," I said. "There oughtn't to be anybody on the path now."

"No, no," she said. "There's another path to the road. I'll go that way."

"Then I'll see you as far as that," I insisted.

We went quietly and it was only as we neared the road that I remembered something.

"You still haven't asked me what I can do to help," I said.

"What *can* you do?"

"For her, nothing," I said. "She can save herself if she wishes. For you—well, I don't know. Stick your chin out and keep it out."

I felt her smile at that. "And what can I tell Thora?" she asked as we stopped at the last stile.

"Tell her to tell the truth. Wharton's a hard one where duty's concerned. Whatever he's said he'll do, then he'll do it."

"I'm sure she'll never tell."

"Well, do your best," I said. "If it will help in any way you can use my name."

"Perhaps I will," she said, and hesitated, foot on the stile. "I don't know how I can repay you."

"There's nothing to repay," I said. "But you can answer me one last question if you like. It's this. Was to-night the first time you had an idea that she was suspected of having anything to do with Maddon?"

"But, of course!" she said. "That's why it was such a shock."

She went then and I followed her after a minute or two. It was close on black-out time, so I made my way up to bed at once, but sleep came far too slowly. Yet somehow, with the interests of Mary Carter and Chevalle so much nearer and more personal, I should have been glad that my theory of Mary's complicity had been proved so utterly wrong. Perhaps the knowledge did please me, but it brought other trains of thought, and it even brought a wholly new theory. So startling was that theory that I actually sat up in bed and found myself reaching out to the bedside table for my glasses.

Then a happier thought came and drove it from my mind, for I suddenly remembered a character who seemed to have dropped out. Pyramid Porle—and I couldn't help smiling to myself at the thought of him. The bland satisfaction on that pudgy face of his when he came by me that night after affixing his gaudy notice. The magnificence of his gestures, his florid courtesies and his superb unbendings.

"Yes," I was telling myself just before I slipped into sleep. "I must certainly ask Wharton what's being done about Pyramid Porle."

CHAPTER XI
EVE OF ACTION

THERE WAS TO FOLLOW a day of comparative inaction; of lull, if you like, before the last shattering event. For me it was a day of odds and ends, and though I didn't know it at the time, its apparently trivial events were pregnant with information. Take the new theory of mine, for instance, which had made me sit up in bed. The morning exhibited it in a pretty poor light and I knew it had been the ephemeral off-spring of dark woods, the scent of honeysuckle and the trustfulness of a pretty woman. Yet before that day was out I had reinstated that theory and thereafter, whatever I said openly or did, it remained in the background of my mind.

In the morning I took a stroll round to the east of the village and as it was still half an hour to lunch-time when I came to the Wheatsheaf, I thought I'd look in. Five men were there, not counting the landlord. One was watching a game of darts, and one of the four contestants was Wharton. He gave me only a nod as if I were a casual acquaintance.

All the pots had just been filled so I had only myself to pay for. Wharton's side had got their double and were well away, and George was crowing. I uttered a silent prayer for the others to get going, and doubtless in answer, they did. And to some purpose. A double top, a treble twenty and a double nineteen—a hundred and eighteen. Wharton grunted, then threw his darts. Three ones that all skimmed the twenty. Then the enemy popped up with a treble eighteen and two twelves, and George's lead had vanished. His partner chipped in with a fifty-four and George cheered up again. Two more throws from the others and it was all over. Fifty-two the last man wanted. His first dart was a twenty, his second a sixteen and his third caught the wire of the double eight and stuck the right side. The onlooker hastily emptied his mug and hoped for a refill by the losers.

George paid up with a good grace, but he didn't ask me to have one. When he'd finished his tot he asked, for the benefit of the room, if I had come about that little matter. I said I had, if he wasn't too busy. With a "Better luck next time, sir," in his ears he led the way to his room.

"Never saw such a lucky thrower as that little fat fellow," he told me. "What brought you round? Found out something?"

I said I'd come to ask him the same question, and his reply was an immediate snort. He'd got rid of Galley and the man, and had gone through Five Oaks with a sieve and a microscope and hadn't found a thing.

"No news about that man Porle yet?" I asked.

"I rang up only this morning," he said. "Nothing about him at all. They're checking taxis now. He probably had to have one, with all that luggage."

"What about intermediate stations?" I asked.

"All been tried," he said. "He didn't get off there."

"And Temple?"

"He was out," he said. "I might have a look at him this afternoon."

"Have you got that photograph handy?" I asked him. "That one of Mrs. Beaney's."

"Do you think Maddon really threw it away?" he said as he unlocked his case.

"I don't," I said. "I think she helped herself to it. And if you ask me, I think it's the last thing Maddon would have thrown away."

His eyebrows raised at that. "You think it was part of his blackmail equipment?"

"Don't you?" I said, and waited while he had a good look at the photograph himself.

"That girl," he said, and frowned. "Nothing of Mrs. Chevalle in her."

"For a very good reason," I said. "She wasn't born when it was taken."

He gave me a glare at that. "That boy too. Doesn't remind me of anybody. Unless it's Temple."

"Temple!" I said, and reached for the photograph. "Don't know, George. I don't see much resemblance. Not that there would be. All boys look alike. At least when they're being told to watch for the dicky-bird." Then I frowned. "And yet—"

"And yet what?"

"Well, let's see where logic gets us," I said. "We think Maddon was blackmailing two people. Mrs. Chevalle and Temple. The photograph couldn't have been used against Mrs. Chevalle, and therefore it was used against Temple. Temple was in jail for four years and Maddon saw him there. Maybe Maddon was a member of some visiting commission, or Maddon might even have been in there himself."

"Oh, no," he said. "If so we'd have had his prints."

"I'd forgotten that," I said. "But that doesn't bust the theory. You know the claim that if you stand at the entrance to Piccadilly Tube Station long enough you'll see everyone you ever knew. That holds just as good for the front at Porthaven in peacetime. Maddon saw Temple there and recognised him."

"Very pretty. Very pretty indeed," he told me. "Now if you'll only tell me what that's got to do with the photograph of a boy and girl, then I'll see what can be done." He snorted. "You and your theories!"

"You want everything handed out on a gold salver," I said. "I admit it isn't a photograph of Temple in prison costume, but you'll admit it ought to tell us something, if only we could find out what it is. It was important to Maddon. It was the only photograph we know he had. And it was dangerous, or he wouldn't have cut off the photographer's name and address."

"Well, that's a dead end too," he said as he locked the photograph up again. "There isn't a photographer in Windsor who was established there all that time ago. We've got the names of one or two who were, but that's a forlorn hope."

"You never know your luck," I told him. "But come and have another drink and cheer yourself up."

But he wouldn't do that. His lunch was almost due, he said, and so I left him to it. He also told me he had a hunch that Mrs. Chevalle might crack up that afternoon, so he was staying at the pub, just in case.

I thought he was being rather optimistic, though I took good care not to hint as much. My own idea was that Mrs. Chevalle wouldn't weaken till the moment of formal arrest, and then she'd spin a yarn with a bit more truth in it, in the hope of gaining more time. She'd have few scruples in making accusations against others and making herself out some sort of a victim.

But I wasn't worrying too much about Mrs. Chevalle. What I was thinking about was that new theory of mine, for something had already happened that morning to give me new faith in it. What I was looking for, then, was another fact or two to make that theory a really workable one, and it seemed to me that that photograph was a vital link in a chain of evidence if only I could fit it into its right place. But by the time I was back at Ringlands I had given up the attempt as hopeless. For the life of me I couldn't fit that photograph in, and yet the annoying thing was that something more than intuition kept telling me that it *could* be fitted in. Later in the day, I told myself, I'd have another crack at it. For the moment, fitting that photograph into the theory was rather like trying to explain the murderous proclivities of Jack the Ripper by gazing at a print of The Maiden's First Prayer.

As soon as I got in, Helen told me that Commander Santon had rung me up. He wouldn't leave a message and said I could ring him at any time before two o'clock. I rang him at once.

"Morning, Major," he said, still bright and breezy. "How are you this morning?"

"Not too bad," I said.

"Like a little jaunt to-morrow?"

"What time?" I said, thinking of Wharton's zero hour.

"The morning. Elevenish. Back for lunch."

"Good," I said. "I'll be at your place round about eleven."

"Don't do that," he said. "I've got to go to the village, so I'll call for you on my way back."

Mary called that afternoon at about half-past three. Helen was doing some weeding in the borders so I stayed put in the summer-house and watched them going round the gardens. It was only when they came down the front path that I put in an appearance.

We chatted for a bit and I thought it was rather artistic the way I contrived to maintain an argument with Mary that made it necessary for me to go with her a little way along the road.

"Was I flattering myself too much," I said when we were out of earshot of Helen. "Or didn't you come to see me after all?"

"I did and I didn't," she said.

"Well, tell me how things are going."

"I don't think Thora slept much last night," she said. "I thought she looked ghastly when I took her a cup of tea early this morning. Then she went out and when she came back she was much more cheerful. I wondered if Mr. Wharton had changed his mind and let her know."

"Not he," I said. "If she's banking on that, she's due for a shock. But you don't think she's made up her mind to own up?"

"I don't know," she said, and frowned.

"Did you have to use my name?"

"Not actually," she said. "I said I'd been thinking things over. Then when I asked her to tell me if she'd been spending that time in Town with . . . with somebody else, she was simply livid. She used the most dreadful language, I simply had to go out of the room. But she dared me to say a word to Richard. She said she'd kill me if I did."

"I wouldn't worry about that," I told her. "But where did she go this morning?"

"I don't know," she said. "I looked into her room to see if she wanted anything—she hasn't been downstairs at all since yesterday afternoon—and she was gone. Then just before lunch she came into the kitchen when I was there. She seemed so changed I shouldn't have known her."

"And now?"

"When I came away she was playing with Clarice as if she hadn't a care in the world."

"Well, keep smiling," I said. "This time to-morrow we'll know far more about things. And the Major; he isn't at home?"

"He always has lunch out," she said. "Nowadays he rarely gets home till just before seven. This morning he went out on his bicycle somewhere."

"If I had Government petrol you wouldn't see me on a bicycle," I said.

"Oh, but he's frightfully conscientious."

I thought it best to turn back then, but just as we were saving good-bye, I thought of something.

"Strictly between ourselves, and going back to that holiday of Mrs. Chevalle's, did she ever give you any explanation of why she came back a day early?"

"A day early!"

"Yes," I said. "She should have come back the next day. I was with Major Chevalle and he seemed very surprised and annoyed."

"Then he must have misunderstood me," she said, "or else I must have told him wrongly." She smiled. "I can prove that I expected her back."

"How?"

"Did I look surprised?"

"Come to think of it, you didn't," I said.

"Was there enough food ready for all of us?"

"Yes," I said, "and a noble meal it was. And there we are. Major Chevalle must have misunderstood. I'm dead sure he was not only surprised but highly annoyed into the bargain. He didn't say anything to you afterwards?"

"He wouldn't do that," she said. "We never talk about Thora. I can't think when we last mentioned her. Once he used to step in if she was particularly beastly—to me, I mean—but that always led to dreadful scenes."

I clicked my tongue.

"It's nothing really," she told me, and smiled. Then she was holding out her hand again.

"See you on Sunday," I said, and at once she was frowning.

"Don't you think that rather depends?"

"Yes," I said. "I'd forgotten about certain things. Still, keep that chin of yours up and we'll be having tea on Sunday after all."

But as I turned back I didn't believe that for a moment. It certainly did all depend, and on far too many things. But the most important thing of all was one that never occurred to me.

I was rather restless after tea, for every minute brought zero hour a bit nearer, and there was the likelihood, also, that at any minute anything might happen. So I thought I'd take a short walk, and as I was getting ready for it, a framed photograph in my bedroom set me thinking of Mrs. Beaney's photograph again.

I wondered, for instance, why she had taken the photograph at all. Maybe it did remind her of her sister, but it was just as likely that she saw a possible resemblance to herself, and wanted to exhibit it to some of her cronies as taken in some far-off days when her family was really something. I wondered if Maddon had cut off the bottom inch on which was the photographer's name and address, and it seemed to me that that was the last thing he would have done. If he were using it as a hold over the person he was blackmailing, then those details were the important thing, for without them the photograph was unauthenticated, and merely a photograph of two people who might at that age have been anybody.

When I set out, then, it was towards Mrs. Beaney's cottage, and I was lucky enough to find her in. She recognised me at once, and was telling me that she was alone and her husband who was haying, wouldn't be in till heaven knew when. I took that for friendly gossip and not as an invitation to frivolity.

"Well, I won't come in," I said, but she was already backing to the living-room, and I had to follow. Then she asked if I'd like a nice cup of tea. No trouble at all. She was just making one for herself.

"It's very kind of you, Mrs. Beaney," I said, "but I'm in a great hurry. What I've really come about is—"

"I know," she said. "To do with poor Mr. Maddon."

"In a way, yes," I said. "But really to give you the chance of earning some money."

That made her eyes pop.

"That photograph of the two children," I said. "If you can find me the strip that was cut off from the bottom, I'll give you a pound note."

On her face was the whole story—the fool she'd been to cut it off and burn it. But whoever'd have thought!

"We'll never find that, sir," she told me, and the sorrow was guilefully for me. "Why, that must have been cut off years ago!"

I didn't tell her otherwise.

"Of course," I said. "But I thought there might just be a chance that you'd seen it lying about somewhere."

"If I do run across it," she told me, "I'll let you know at once. You're staying with Mrs. Thornley, aren't you, sir?"

I gave an unnecessary yes. That woman probably knew what I had for lunch, if not tea. And she wasn't going to get anything out of me by specious promises.

"Try thinking again, Mrs. Beaney," I said. "Imagine you're looking at the bottom of the photograph and you see the word Windsor. What else do you see?"

What she did see was some sort of catch in my question. That woman was wilier than a weasel.

"All I did was to cut the bottom off to make it regular," she said. "It was all torn when I found it. That's why I knew he didn't want it."

"Wasn't there anything at all besides the word Windsor?" I asked, and jingled my loose change.

She licked her lips. Then she did remember something.

"Come to think of it, sir, there was. I remembered at the time how funny it was."

"Why was it funny?"

"Well, because it ended in an O."

"A name ending in an O?"

"Yes," she said, "and now I come to remember it, it began with an O."

"Now we're getting on," I said. "A man's name beginning with O and ending with O."

Through that cross-word puzzle brain of mine flashed every such word, and a pretty poor flash it was. Othello was the only name, though I did add Otranto and Oswego, Ohio and Oviedo, which are place-names. Then I did think of a name.

"Orlando? How about that?"

"That's it, sir! Orlando. I thought what a nice name it was."

"It's just the kind of fancy trade-name a photographer would take," I said. "I congratulate you on your memory, Mrs. Beaney."

"Well," she said complacently. "I never was much at school, but I did have a good memory. I'll say that for myself."

I slipped her two half-crowns. While her voice was saying that she didn't expect anything of the sort, her hooked fingers were closing over them.

"And if you should think of anything else—of which you can be certain, mind you—you must let me know," I said as we parted at the door.

Quite a good quarter of an hour's work, I thought to myself and I hadn't a notion just then how good it would prove to be. Orlando I still thought a capital name. Neat but not gaudy. A bit of appeal in it, a bit of romance and a certain artistic reticence. So pleased was I with the discovery, in fact, that as soon as I got home I rang George.

"Orlando?" he said grumpily. "Who the devil would have a name like that?"

"Orlando Gibbons," I said flippantly, "but he was rather before your time. And I've known photographers with even more highfalutin names than that. Look up the Telephone Directory and see."

The upshot was that he said he'd try it, and he said that none too graciously. When I asked if there was any other news he almost bit my head off. George too was feeling the approach of zero hour.

The following morning I woke soon after six o'clock, which was two hours too soon, and when I'd tried for an hour to get to sleep again, I got up instead and took a stroll round the garden. At breakfast I had to force myself to eat, for I had no more appetite than a small boy who's due in a few minutes to set off to the Zoo.

The Times came, and when Helen had had her usual quick look at it, I took it to the summer-house and tried to settle down to the cross-word. But I just couldn't do it. My eyes kept going to the front gate, so I went back to my den and there my ears were always cocked for the telephone. But it was well on the way to ten o'clock, and I consoled myself with the thought that in just about an hour I could safely set out for Little Foxes. Then I remembered that Santon was calling for me and I wondered if I might take a short stroll instead.

I decided I hadn't better. Santon might have changed his mind about the trip or Wharton might ring up. When I looked out of the window I saw Helen at her weeding, so I joined her. She soon found me a trowel.

From time to time I glanced at my wrist-watch, and when at last it was a quarter to eleven I straightened my back and said I'd better be getting ready for Santon. The soil was dry as a bone and my hands weren't too dirty, I thought, and just then I heard the sound of car brakes. It was Wharton's car at the gate, and he was getting out in the devil of a hurry.

"Morning, Mrs. Thornley," he called. "Can't come in."

Then he was beckoning to me and urgently.

"Hop in," he said and opened the near door. "Some-thing's happened up at a place called Little Foxes."

"That's just a few yards on," I said, too taken aback to ask the right questions. "Commander Santon's place."

He had already shot the car on with a jerk.

"What is it George? What's happened?"

"You show me where the house is," he told me snappishly. "Then we'll both know what's happened."

We were practically already there. There wasn't any need for him to ask if the house was Little Foxes for Santon was coming out to the road and holding up his hand.

"Commander Santon?" Wharton said as he scrambled out.

"Yes. You're Superintendent Wharton?"

"Yes," Wharton snapped at him, but I was looking at Santon. His fingers were twitching and he looked as if he'd had the devil of a shock.

"Well, what is it?" Wharton was asking him. "What did you send for me for?"

"It's Mrs. Chevalle," he said. He was trying to go on, but the words wouldn't come out.

"Yes, yes," Wharton said impatiently. "Mrs. Chevalle. What's happened to her?"

"She's shot herself," he said. "Shot herself in my garden."

Part Three
NO MORE LADY

CHAPTER XII
A CASE OF SUICIDE

SANTON WENT LIMPING on ahead and at a quicker pace than most could have made with that game leg. Wharton had to stride to keep alongside him, and I brought up the rear.

"Why did you send for me?" Wharton was asking him. "I know you said something but I didn't catch it. The 'phone was bad."

"Chevalle asked me to send for you," Santon said. "I'm afraid I was a bit flustered."

"He's here?"

"Why, yes," Santon said, and seemed surprised at the question. His voice was much steadier, by the way.

"Was he here after it happened?"

"He was here when it did happen," Santon said.

"Must have been the devil of a shock," I said.

"Why, hallo, Travers," Santon said with a quick look back, as if only then did he know I was there. "This way Superintendent."

Wharton had been making for the front door, but Santon went past it and towards the garage and then sharp right. We went across the lawn, through the hedge arch and on to the yellow, newly mown tennis court. I don't know why we went all that way round. It seemed to me afterwards that we might just as well have gone straight down the path from the main gate. And if you want to follow what I mean, and just what took place that morning, below is a rough map of Little Foxes as I drew it later.

Chevalle was standing in front of the summer-house as if waiting for us, and his face, usually the colour of old polished leather, now looked almost yellow. Wharton gave him a quiet good-morning and went right on.

Thora Chevalle was lying on the summer-house floor, and it somehow seemed incongruous to me that she should be wearing a hat and a short coat. The hat had been knocked aslant when she fell, and was almost hiding her face. By her right hand was a little automatic.

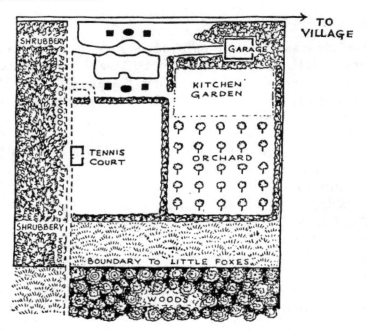

Wharton got down on a knee and moved the hat with a finger, and by the still sleek platinum of her hair I could see the browny-red mark where the bullet had entered. A small wound, and rather like that in Maddon's skull, but upwards slightly and not so cleanly through the temple.

"The doctor ought to be here at any time now."

That was Chevalle. I had not heard him come up and neither apparently had Wharton, for he gave him a quick look and then got to his feet.

"He'll do no good when he does come," he said, and the very gruffness of his voice was a sympathy. "A bad business, Chevalle. I wish to God I weren't here."

Chevalle said nothing. Some of the colour had come back to his cheeks, but his face was set and impassive. Wharton let out a breath and then ran an eye slowly round.

That summer-house was well made. Its floor was of stout boards and each side had a metal-framed window that ran from front to back. In the back was a door, and all the front—but for knee-high boarding and opening—was open to the tennis-court. There was a table in one corner and stacked against it were four wicker chairs. Another chair had fallen and it looked as if it was the one on which Thora Chevalle had been sitting.

Wharton took a look through the side window. The path to the woods curved behind the summer-house, but there was a perfect view of the front gate. As he turned, Santon anticipated the obvious question.

"We might have come here that way," he said, "but I wasn't thinking. I'd got the house on my mind and . . . Well, perhaps you understand."

"I know," Wharton said, and nodded understandingly. "But someone had better tell me something about it. What have you got to say, Commander? After all, this is your house."

Santon moistened his lips. Then he was shaking his head as if he didn't like the job.

"Well, tell me what happened," Wharton said with a touch of impatience. "How'd she come to be here at all?"

"It's all so extraordinary," Santon said, still shaking his head. "I don't see how you can believe it."

"A curious statement?" Wharton said. "You're a man of honour. Why shouldn't we believe you?"

"Well, perhaps so," Santon answered lamely. "And there's Major Chevalle. I wouldn't like to hurt his feelings." Chevalle said nothing. He mightn't even have heard. "Feelings or not," Wharton said, "I want a statement." Santon shrugged his shoulders.

"Very well then, here it is, and I give you my word it's what happened. Yesterday morning it started, really. Mrs. Chevalle came to see me. I thought it was about War Savings' business, but it wasn't, and when she started talking I honestly thought she was out of her head." He'd been looking away up till then, but now he gave Wharton a look clean in the eye. "She said you were threatening to arrest her for killing old Maddon!"

"Yes?" said Wharton calmly.

Santon looked surprised. He'd evidently expected some explanation from Wharton. He looked pretty blank for a moment.

"Well, what was I to think?" he said. "I told her she must be crazy and she said she was—nearly. I tried to laugh her out of it. The upshot was that I thought there must be something behind it, so I said she had only to prove an alibi and that she could do standing on her head, so to speak. She said she couldn't. I asked her why and she wouldn't tell me. Then I humoured her for a bit and got her to go home." He shrugged his shoulders as if it were all still a mystery. "I didn't know what to do. It sounded so damn silly to me—I mean her killing Maddon. I mean, why should she? Sounded absolutely crackers to me."

"Yes," said Wharton. "I expect it did. But just why should she have come to you at all?"

"About that? Well, frankly, I don't know. We're good friends, of course. Always have been. And we're associated on this War Savings' business, which means she's in and out of here a goodish bit."

He shot a look at Chevalle, but Chevalle's face still showed nothing.

"Chevalle mustn't mind my saying so," he said, "and I'm open to correction if I'm wrong, but I gathered from her that he was the last person she wanted to confide in. That's really why I didn't ring him up yesterday."

"And this morning?" Wharton asked.

"This morning she rang me up about nine o'clock and said she had to see me. I tried to choke her off. I told her I was going out to Upford, which I was. I was picking Major Travers up at eleven, at Ringlands. She said, if I didn't see her she was going to shoot herself!"

Wharton raised his eyebrows.

"Well, what could I do? I said if she was coming she'd better hurry, and even then it was best part of an hour before she actually came. I'd got rid of Dewball—he's my man—by sending him off to Hiver's Wood to cut stakes for the tomatoes and I told him to cut a couple of hundred for the zinnias while he was there. Then she turned up. I thought there was going to be a scene, but there wasn't. She said she was going away and would I take her to the station in my car. She'd practically finished packing, and she'd sent Mary and Clarice to Porthaven. Not Porthaven station, though. Cambridge, that's where she wanted me to take her. When I tried arguing with her, she pulled that gun out of her hand-bag and said if I didn't do it then she'd shoot herself!"

"And what then?"

Santon shot Wharton a look. I thought myself that the calmly official voice wasn't too helpful.

"Then I had to think, and think quick. I said I'd do it, but the battery of the car was out of order, and it'd take me a few minutes to put it right. Also I'd have to ring Major Travers about the trip being off. Instead of that I rang Chevalle and told him to come here at the double. I couldn't tell him any more, in case she should overhear, except that his wife was at Little Foxes and threatening to shoot herself. Then I went back to her—she was in the lounge—and said if she'd go home I'd call for her there in about ten minutes. She wouldn't budge. I think she knew I was trying to double-cross her."

He gave Chevalle another look.

"That really suited my book better, because Chevalle would find her here when he got here himself. So I got on with the car battery, and then she came out to watch. I pretended to be furious. I said what would anybody think who happened to call. She said she couldn't stand being in the house alone. So I said, 'Why don't you sit in the summer-house?' Then she said perhaps she would. And that was the last I saw of her. I heard Chevalle's car, and as soon as he came through the gate I called to him. I had to take a risk about that, but I hoped she was in here."

"Give me the exact words, if you don't mind," Wharton said.

"Well, I was on my back, making a show in case she suddenly turned up again. I didn't actually know at first that it *was* Chevalle. I said, 'That you, Chevalle?' and he said, 'Yes, it's me,' or something like that. I said, 'Hang on just a second and I'll be there.' Then practically at the same moment I heard the shot. 'My God!' I said, 'what's that!' By the time I was out from under the car he was gone. He thought the shot came from just behind the house, so he went through the front door. I sprinted after him, and then I remembered the summer-house."

"You got here first?"

"I think we both got here together," he said, and gave Chevalle another look.

"Here's the doctor," Chevalle said quietly.

The doctor—the same elderly man who'd been at Five Oaks— was looking inquiringly through the hedge arch.

"Who told you to come here, Doctor?" Wharton asked him, and it was a question I should have thought of myself.

"Commander Santon rang me," he said, and looked surprised.

"I had to go to the house to warn those people who were waiting for me at Upford, so Chevalle asked me to ring the doctor and then you," Santon explained.

"And what is it this time?" the doctor asked breezily.

But there was nothing of the flippant on his face when he saw what lay on the floor.

"No need to worry about time of death," Chevalle told him quietly. "She died just as I got here."

"My God, Chevalle, I'm sorry."

Chevalle shook his head and turned away.

"Got the ambulance?" Wharton said. "Then you'd better get her away. I'll lend you a hand. Through this door here."

He slipped on a glove and picked up the gun by the barrel and laid it on the table by the hand-bag. A quick chalk mark round the body and he was ready. I caught a look which told me to stay.

I watched from the window. In the drive I could just see the rear of the ambulance where the doctor had parked it by the house. Then Santon was clearing his throat close by me, and I turned.

"Mind if I put that car of mine in and shut the garage?" he asked. "Too many gipsies about here for my liking."

"Do," I said, and then looked round for Chevalle. He was standing with his back to me at the far end of the court, but as Santon moved off, he turned and came slowly back.

"Saying it's inadequate enough, God knows," I said, "but I'm sorry about all this, Chevalle. If only I could have done something—"

"Neither you nor I nor anyone could have done anything," he told me quietly. "But it was kind of you to say so, Travers. I know you meant it."

We heard the ambulance move off and in a couple of minutes Wharton was back.

"Where's the Commander?" he was asking at once. "That's all right," he said, when I explained. "All the better without him for a minute or two. Now what about you, Chevalle? Like to tell me your side of things?"

"There's nothing to tell," Chevalle began, and his voice was quiet but perfectly calm. "Everything Santon said was correct. He rang me and said my wife was at his place and threatening to shoot herself, and would I come at once, and I did. When I got inside the gate he told me to wait a minute—"

"You saw him?"

"Saw him? Of course I saw him. He was just getting out from under his car. Then I heard the shot, and him calling again. I didn't know if it was in the house, or where, so I ran to the front door. There was nothing in either of the rooms so I went out at the back. Then I sort of half remembered where the sound had come from." Wharton nodded. "That's clear enough. But may I ask a question or two?"

"Why not?"

"Well, it may be like rubbing salt in an open wound," Wharton told him with a shake of the head. "But did I gather that you actually saw her die?"

Chevalle stood rigid for a moment or two. "Yes," he said. "I might say I heard her very last breath."

"Well, the doctor thought she might have lived a minute or two after the shot," Wharton said. "But one more question. Why should she have shot herself after all? I took all that threatening to Santon as very much of a bluff."

"You'd driven her pretty hard, Wharton," Chevalle told him curtly. "I'm not blaming you, mind you. I'm stating a fact. As to why she did actually shoot herself, I think it was because she saw me coming in that front gate. She knew Santon had double-crossed her, as he put it."

"She knew this summer-house well?"

Chevalle gave a little grunt. "We've played tennis here often enough. She probably knew this garden as well as her own."

"Well, so far I'm satisfied," Wharton said. "But there's the Commander looking for us."

He hollered to Santon that we'd be at the garage in a couple of shakes, and then he was picking up that little gun by the barrel. It was the kind that could be hidden in a good-sized hand, and as he pointed a finger below the barrel I could only just read the incision marks of name and maker. It was Italian and looked beautifully made.

He broke the barrel and we could see that the six chambers had been full, and one shot fired. He squinted along the barrel and then had a look at the tiny empty case that had been lying beneath the table. Then from his wallet he produced something wrapped in tissue paper. It was a bullet and he showed it to Chevalle.

"The one that killed Maddon?" Chevalle said.

"Yes," Wharton told him and slipped it into the empty chamber. He took it out and slipped it in again and each time it went in smooth and fitted snug.

"What you're trying to tell me is that my wife killed Maddon."

His eyes had narrowed, and it was the first time that morning he had shown any sign of feeling, at least in Wharton's presence. Wharton shrugged his shoulders and began wrapping up that bullet again.

"You're wrong, Wharton," Chevalle told him, and his voice had a cold anger. "It may be the bullet and the gun, but she didn't use it. How could she? Tell me that."

"Now, now, now," Wharton told him, as if to a child. "Surely you can trust me to do what's right? There's going to be no scandal. I give you my word on that." Then he was shaking his head. "But one thing you can't shut your eyes to. Her hand was the last to hold this gun."

"There's still the paraffin test," Chevalle told him dourly.

"I know it," Wharton said evenly. "That's the first thing the doctor's going to do. Inside half an hour we ought to know."

We adjourned to the front of the house for a reconstruction of the brief happenings after Chevalle's first arrival. Chevalle was looking grim and taciturn and I knew that in his heart of hearts he was blaming Wharton for that suicide. The taciturnity seemed to upset Santon. When we joined him he remarked with something of his old cheeriness that perhaps we'd like to look at the garage, and when there was no reply, he gave a quick look at us.

"All in good time," Wharton told him.

It was Chevalle he was placing first, and at the front gate. When Wharton called from the garage he was to enter. Then Santon would call and Chevalle was to halt just where Santon's voice had halted him.

Then the three of us went to the garage. Santon pushed the car out to where it was before and got his legs under the running board.

"I know it doesn't look to you as if I'm doing anything to a battery," he said, "but she wasn't to know that. What I wanted was a position where I could watch for Chevalle and be pretending to do something if she happened to come here again."

"I've got you," Wharton said, and called to Chevalle to come through the gate. Santon was calling then.

"That you, Chevalle?"

"It's me," Chevalle called back, and then halted.

"I didn't think he'd have heard it," Wharton told me. "Did you hear it clear enough, Chevalle?"

"Quite clear enough."

"Right, then," Wharton said. "Carry on, Commander."

"Hang on and I'll be with you in a second," Santon called.

Chevalle strolled on towards the front door, and then Wharton slapped a piece of wood against the garage door to make a bang.

"My God! what's that!" Santon called.

Chevalle was already at the front door and out of sight. Wharton and I moved round to the back of the house to watch him emerge.

"Carry on!" Wharton called to him. "Do just what you did then!"

Chevalle made as if to go towards the orchard, then changed his mind and made for the hedge arch.

"Right!" called Wharton. "That's all I want."

Next came Santon again. He wriggled out from under the car and made for the front door. A moment's halt and he was making for the back of the house.

"Stand fast!" called Wharton. "I think that's about all." We went to the lounge for a brief final talk. Wharton gave a quick sniff as he entered and I knew what he'd caught —that perfume of Thora Chevalle's. But it was very faint, and so was that quick sniff of his, for Chevalle gave no sign that he had heard it.

"About the inquest," Wharton began. "I'll take it off your hands, Chevalle, if you'll tell me the ropes. Tomorrow morning suit you?"

"The sooner the better," Chevalle said, and looked away.

"Well, we're all men of good will," Wharton announced. "We don't want scandal and we're not going to ask for it. What do you say, Commander?"

"I don't know anything about Maddon, and I don't want to," Santon said. "I don't think his name need be mentioned."

"That's just my idea," Wharton told him. "We'll cook no evidence, but all the same there's no need to bring in what's unnecessary. What do you say, Chevalle?"

"What can I say?—I'm grateful. And I'm sorry for some of the things I said this morning."

Wharton's hand went to his shoulder. "You've nothing to reproach yourself with. Still, there we are. You can see me at the Wheatsheaf this afternoon, Commander? Say, three o'clock."

Santon said he'd be there.

"You're going to Porthaven?" Wharton asked Chevalle. "No," Chevalle said. "If Santon doesn't mind my using his telephone, I'll ring the office up. Then I shall go home. I think I ought to be there when Mary gets back."

"Try and get a message through to the doctor," Wharton told him. "If he's made that test, ask him to send the result to Bassetts."

Santon asked rather diffidently if we'd have a drink, but none of us felt like it. Then we caught a glimpse of Tom Dewball coming past the window with a huge bundle of stakes across his shoulder. Wharton was asking questions about him when Chevalle came back.

"If you're going straight home, I'll go with you," Wharton said. "There's just a thing or two I'd like to check up on. See you at three o'clock this afternoon, Commander."

He shook hands with Santon and then we moved off in our respective cars. Mary was still out, but Chevalle's key let us in. Thora Chevalle's bedroom door was locked, but Chevalle said he'd find a key. When he'd gone, Wharton looked in the handbag and there a key was. It fitted, but he didn't use it after all.

Inside the room were a very large trunk, locked and ready to be moved, and a large case that needed only to be fastened. Each was labelled Charing Cross.

"Well, that seems to settle everything," Wharton said, and his sigh was definitely one of relief. "And I can only say I'm sorry. All the same, I don't think I could have acted differently from what I did."

"I was wrong," Chevalle said, and held out his hand. "Don't think me callous, Wharton, but these last few days I've had about as much as I could stand."

"Forget it. Forget everything, as I shall. See you this afternoon, at the Wheatsheaf."

"I'll be there," Chevalle told him gravely.

Then the telephone bell went. It was the doctor ringing from Porthaven to say the test had been positive. Merely a quick try-out, of course, but definitely positive.

"That's that then," said Wharton, and gave another sigh. Then he held out his hand again and with a quick nod was making for the door. As we got into his car and he began to reverse, the bus from Porthaven slowed down behind us and as we headed for the village I saw Mary and Clarice go through the gate.

"A hell of a morning," George said to me. "Whoever'd have thought it!"

I formally agreed with both remarks.

"Looks as if my time down here is pretty nearly over," he went on.

"Unless anything else comes out at the inquest," I said.

He didn't glare, which was what I expected. His tone was positively mild.

"What *should* come out? I don't reckon there was much we didn't run our rule over this morning."

"You certainly made a good job of it," I told him. "But I would like to know one thing, if only for my own peace of mind. I'd like to prove that Mrs. Chevalle *did* kill Maddon."

"I'll rush that gun to Town," he said, "as soon as I get the bullet out of her head. Then we'll know."

I shrugged my shoulders. It was a gesture that would often infuriate him, but now he merely changed the subject.

"You going to be in all day?"

"I may go for a stroll," I said.

He was drawing up the car before Ringlands. "If I don't see you before, I'll see you at the inquest," he said. "I'll try and fix it for eleven."

I waved a good-bye from the gate and made my way down the path. Helen came out to meet me.

"Had a nice ride?" she said.

I motioned her across to the summer-house and told her in confidence what had happened. She was shocked but there was nothing remotely resembling tears. In fact, by the time we were in the house she was showing a mild excitement, and I knew she was visualising the wedding of Chevalle and Mary Carter. What Wharton was thinking at that moment I could probably guess too—how to make a first-class show of doing his duty and at the same time keep Chevalle's name clear.

I was feeling something of the same sort too. But I was not like George, I could tell myself. I was a free-lance, and the owner of a damnably suspicious mind. Things that morning had fallen out too pat for all concerned. Thora Chevalle had committed suicide, and, very conveniently on someone else's property. Chevalle had got rid of a woman who had been an incubus for years, and whose final exploit had been complicity at least in the murder of Maddon. Now everything would be nicely hushed up, and everything in the garden lovely.

And why not? Since I had liked Chevalle from the start and Mary Carter even more, and had detested Thora Chevalle as heartily, the morning's happenings ought to have pleased me enormously. But somehow they didn't. If you wonder why, I can only refer you to that strain of cussedness in my make-up. Things, I told myself, just didn't happen like that in real life, and my personal likes and dislikes were nothing whatever to do with the facts.

Not that I intended to try and put a spoke in anybody's wheel. If Wharton was going to be satisfied, then I should be so too—at least on the surface of things. After all, I was a free-lance and without a vestige of authority. Even if to satisfy my insatiable curiosity I did discover something—and I suspected a good deal already—then I could keep it to myself. There were certainly things I did want to discover, for they were bound up with that fine new theory of mine, and what had happened that morning had gone far towards making it not theory, but incontrovertible fact. Of all the jigsaw, two or three pieces only refused to fit in place, and of them the one that nagged at me most was Orlando's photograph.

CHAPTER XIII
THEORY AND PROOF

THE TIME HAS COME, it seems to me, to lay some of my cards on the table. I want to play fair with you, and at the same time be fair to myself. You will have noticed that I said "some of the cards." That is where the fairness to myself comes in, for you can't expect me to tell the contents of a hand till the last card has been dealt.

As for playing fair with you, that's much easier. I have been mentioning a mysterious theory. Maybe you have guessed what it is, but if you haven't, then here is an inkling. Who was the one to gain most by the death of Thora Chevalle?

That's easy, you may say. Chevalle himself stood to gain most. He was rid of a wife he had come to loathe and despise, and if the killing of Maddon could be glossed over, he had no fear of a scandal that might possibly force him to resign. Moreover, he was now free to marry Mary Carter. Now that motive might seem to any person of intelligence to be so overwhelmingly strong that Chevalle simply *must* have had a hand in the death of his wife. But if it were so, then how could I prove it? Not to Wharton, I repeat, but for my own satisfaction. How would that fit into the general theory of which the death of Thora Chevalle was only a part?

Again the answer seems simple. Prove that Thora Chevalle did not commit suicide, but was murdered. And how could it be proved? There I'm afraid I still have to mystify you. For if the one to profit most by her murder was Chevalle, then the way to prove that he was responsible for it, was to prove that he didn't commit it! To prove, in fact, *that the one who committed the murder was Santon.*

Immediately after lunch that day I got to work on the job of proving to my own satisfaction the theory of which I have just given admittedly only a vague idea. Before I began I made a new bargain with myself. If I discovered anything that implicated Santon, then I would pass it on to Wharton, but if the discovery implicated Chevalle, then I would reserve the right of keeping it to myself.

What started me off so hot-foot was a chance peep into a cupboard in my bedroom, and seeing on the floor a pair of tennis shoes that had belonged to my brother-in-law, Tom Thornley. He takes large nines and I tens, and I found I could wear them, even if they were the least bit tight. Then the idea came, and when Helen and Annie were in the kitchen after lunch I had a look in the hot-press and there found a towel that was long past its best. I took it, and the shoes, and then made my way unseen to the back path.

I was making for Bassetts, and as I came near Little Foxes I kept a wary eye for Santon and Dewball, for after what had happened that morning I wanted to avoid them both. But I got past the house without a sign of either of them, and then suddenly I smelt smoke. In a moment it was drifting across the path, for the wind was in the southwest, and I was wondering if the house itself or a shed was on fire. Then there was something in the smell of the smoke and the fact that it hugged the ground that told me it was only a rubbish-heap burning.

So I went on my way, and then, when the chimneys of Bassetts were visible through the chestnut, I turned sharp right, and set a course by guess and by God. My memory proved reliable and though I didn't strike that little pond by the roadside, I came within sight of it. When I did get to it, I did some reconnoitring. A dense hedge of thorn and holly concealed it and me from the road, provided I kept to the side nearest Bassetts, and that was the side where I wanted to explore. As for the path by which I had come, that was a hundred yards away in the chestnut underwood.

I felt the black water and found it on the cold side, for though it was a swelteringly hot day, that pond was well in the shade. Still, it wasn't too cold, and well in the underwood I stripped to the raw, wrapped the towel round my middle and put on the shoes. With a length of oak fallen from a tree I probed the pool bottom and found it about three foot at its deepest. Then I stepped carefully in. Except from a casual tin or bottle I didn't look for danger from a cut, for a notice was posted by the roadside with a threat of penalties for depositing rubbish, and that pond moreover was too far from the village to have been a general dump.

The first two feet were clayey and slippery and then I sank to the ankles in mud and leaf-mould. My long arms went down and while I cocked an ear for a sound on the road, my fingers were groping methodically, and my feet went forward inches by inches. Then I found something, and it was just as sudden as that. Somehow it seemed ridiculous that I should be holding that gun in my hand, and I smiled at it with all the inanity of surprise. For I'd never really expected to find it. True the pond wasn't large. What was so unsubstantial was the theory that it should be there at all!

It was the sound of a bus or lorry that straightened my face and I nipped out of the pond and squatted well behind the hedge. When the lorry had gone I had a quick look at the gun, and wiped it on the towel. It was a beautiful job of work, and the very spit of the one with which Thora Chevalle had shot herself. Then, with another inane grin, I looked at the incised marks below the barrel. It was the twin of the other. It was, in fact, one of a pair.

I rubbed my legs down with the towel and dressed. The towel was muddied beyond redemption and the shoes a rather soggy sight, so I scraped a hole under a chestnut stub and buried them. That the gun had no prints didn't matter in the least, for the mere evidence of its finding was proof that it was Thora Chevalle's gun. To me it was incontrovertible proof. If she had shot Maddon, then she dared not keep the gun. If she had not killed Maddon, then she had been terrified lest Wharton should find the gun in her possession. In either case she had thrown it into the pond. Or had she induced Mary to throw it in there? Again in either case, I told myself, it came to the same thing.

I slipped that gun into a trouser pocket and made my way back towards Little Foxes. A glance at my watch showed that I had now well over half an hour to wait before Santon should be safe at the Wheatsheaf with Wharton, so I drew off the path, stoked my pipe and sat with my back against an oak. So far I was remarkably pleased with myself. That gun should be given to Wharton and he could send it to the Yard with the two bullets. What would be discovered was that the gun from the pond had fired the bullet that had killed Maddon. And since it was in the pond while Thora Chevalle was killing herself, there could have been no jiggery-pokery about substitution. She had, in fact, not killed herself with her own gun, *and therefore she had not killed herself at all.* Unless, of course, she had owned both guns, and that was highly improbable. Mary had seen only the one. And the two guns looked to me the kind that are kept together in a neat little case.

But the finding of the gun didn't make the next moves any easier, and it was not till well after three o'clock that I began to see daylight again. Off I moved then to Little Foxes, and along the path by the summer-house. To the right I heard a voice adjuring someone not to take his Sunshine away, and when I came round to the little orchard, there was Tom Dewball stoking a bonfire with a pitchfork.

He stopped his singing and rather gaped at the sight of me.

"Hallo, sir? Come to see the Commander?"

"Not actually," I said. "In fact I know he's out."

"That's right, sir. He went out about half an hour ago."

"You seem on good terms with yourself?" I said, and I knew he hadn't been told about Thora Chevalle.

He looked a bit sheepish. "You mean the singing, sir."

"Well, we'll agree to call it that," I said, and grinned. He grinned too.

"I like bonfires," I said. "Always did. And I like the smell."

"The Commander had this one started this morning," he said. "He likes a bonfire too. Then he reckoned we'd better clear up all the rubbish while we had the chance."

He shook another forkful or two while I watched.

"Be all burnt out before black-out," he said. "If not, then I'll damp it down with some of that wet stuff. Don't want to, though, if I can avoid it. It makes the wood-ash so hard to sieve."

He finished the stoking and was leaning on his fork as if disposed for a gossip.

"Didn't I see you with a bundle of stakes this morning," I said.

"Oh, them," he said darkly. "You weren't supposed to see them, sir."

As he knew me for an old soldier he made no bones about telling me about the scrounging. He could have cut plenty of wood from their own strip behind the tennis court, but what was the sense of using your own when other people had plenty they wouldn't miss.

"What did the Commander say to that?" I asked jocularly.

"Lord bless you, sir, he's a bigger scrounger than I am," he told me with a grin. "It was him who sort of threw out a hint for me to go to Hiver's."

"You'll both be hung yet," I said, and then began to move away. Then I artistically remembered that I'd come for something.

"Nearly forgetting what I came here for," I said. "Do you happen to have a copy of the *Porthaven Gazette*?"

"The Gazette, sir?" He shook his head. "No, sir, we don't take it. We used to, but there don't seem to be anything in it except Porthaven news, so the Commander gave it up. The *Telegraph's* all we take now. And the *Mirror*."

"We take the *Telegraph* at Ringlands," I said. "And *The Times*. A bit extravagant these days, but there we are." Then I gave a sigh. "Not that the *Gazette* matters very much. There was something I thought might be in it—that's all."

He told me I could see one at the Wheatsheaf and I said it wasn't all that important. I'd happened to be passing Little Foxes when I'd thought about the *Gazette* or I shouldn't have bothered him. After that he walked with me to the front gate where I saw he'd already begun to stick the zinnias. A quite cheery farewell, and I set out for home along the main road. That Tom would be bound to tell Santon I had called didn't worry me in the least. Even if it did look fishy that I should have called when I knew for a certainty that he would be out, yet he could see nothing suspicious in my inquiry for a *Gazette*. As for the bonfire, that was incidental.

As soon as I got to Ringlands I rang up Wharton. He was obviously busy with Santon and Chevalle, and annoyed at being disturbed.

"Yes," he said snappishly. "Who is it?"

"Travers, George. You can't be overheard?"

"No," he said, and I could imagine him giving a quick look round. "Why?"

"I won't even risk telling you over the telephone," I said. "But as soon as you've finished at the Wheatsheaf, call here and there'll be a little parcel for you, and an explanatory letter. I've got to go to Porthaven or I'd have been here myself."

"Being a bit mysterious, aren't you?"

"Maybe," I said. "But the letter will tell you why."

I said a quick cheerio and hung up. Then I made a neat parcel of the gun with a cardboard box I found in the bedroom cupboard, and after that set about writing the explanatory letter.

When that was done I asked Annie where she kept the old copies of the newspapers. Luckily they hadn't yet gone for salvage. I found the copy of the *Telegraph* that I wanted, cut out a long paragraph and put it carefully in my wallet.

Helen was calling me to tea. When I said I thought of going to Porthaven by the four-thirty bus she said that would save her a journey if I changed the library books. When I asked where the library was, she told me the best way to the main Boots was to get off at the station and then take a passage-way that led behind some cottages. That would bring me out plumb in the middle of the shopping centre, and save the much longer walk now due to a one-way traffic system.

Before a quarter to five I was in Porthaven. The short cut was an excellent one, and when I'd changed the books I asked the way to the office of the *Porthaven Gazette*. Friday was publishing day and the place looked pretty busy. An office boy took me down to a basement where a girl was in charge of the files.

Within five minutes I had found what I wanted. The copy was on sale, and when I got outside I made for a handy park, cut out the best part of a column and placed it with the *Telegraph* cutting in my wallet. The rest of the paper I read till it was time for the return bus. Then I bought Helen a small present with my sweets' points and soon after seven o'clock was home again.

The meal was ready to put on the table, but Helen gave me Wharton's letter first. He had collected his parcel and had then asked if he might leave a note for me. It was brief and very much to the point.

> Good work. I think I've got you. The whole collection's leaving at once, and not through Porthaven. After the inquest to-morrow I shall go up myself. I've got to be dead sure.
>
> If I don't get the chance to see you in the morning, don't worry. I'll let you know in good time when I'm coming back. If you're making inquiries on your own, be careful. One wrong step and everything's kyboshed. But you're wrong about Ch., or did I misread you? The

latter, I think. He's above suspicion and his alibi's perfect. Burn this.

G.W.

I smiled to myself at George's wonder if he'd misread my letter. I'd intended him to be puzzled by making a hint so vague that it was doubtful if it was a hint at all. As for Chevalle, I knew his alibi was perfect. He was at Porthaven when Thora arrived at Little Foxes, and he couldn't have known of the visit. When he reached Little Foxes, Santon could vouch for his alibi, just as Chevalle could guarantee Santon's. As for Chevalle's being above suspicion—well, I knew that too. Chief Constables don't commit murders. Then I found myself idly polishing my glasses, for into my mind had come a line or two of Shakespeare, learned long ago in my prep-school days—

> *But Brutus is an honourable man.*
> *So are they all, all honourable men.*

A classic example of irony, as I'd then been told, and not unapt for this present occasion, and with or without the irony. Season with irony according to taste, I said to myself. Chevalle is an honourable man. So is Santon for that matter. So is Wharton, and so—ostensibly—is Ludovic Travers. We're all of us honourable men.

It was not till a quarter-past eleven that I entered the inquest room at the Wheatsheaf. Except for the jury and witnesses there weren't more than a half-dozen people there, so I sidled in at the back and took an unobtrusive seat. Identification was over and the doctor was concluding his evidence.

I find inquests boring in the extreme, and I'm not going to bore you by a long account of this one. What you ought to know you shall be told, and no more. The doctor's evidence, for instance. There was the gun and there was the bullet, and there was the doctor explaining with meticulous care for the benefit of a very mixed jury the course that bullet had taken and, in answer to an obviously rehearsed question, stating confidently that its course had been dictated by the state of nervous tension in which the deceased had been when the trigger was pulled.

Then George dominated the proceedings for a minute or two, and when George is on his dignity and has made it clear what he is and what he stands for, then what he says is not so much evidence as final and unquestionable fact. But he hadn't a lot to say that morning—only that the prints on the gun were those of the deceased, and consistent with the way the gun had been held and the course the bullet had taken. I thought the evidence deliberately woolly, but the Coroner was very impressed with George. He couldn't help telling the Court how lucky we all were that so distinguished a witness had been available.

The next witness was Mary Carter. She was a good witness too, speaking quietly but to the point. She had seen the gun in a drawer in the bedroom of the deceased. She could not swear that it was the same gun though she was practically certain that it was. In answer to questions, she said the deceased had been very agitated during the last few days. The reasons were that she had come to hate Bassetts and her life there.

"You would regard her unhappiness there as of her own making?" interposed the Coroner.

Mary nervously moistened her lips, then said almost inaudibly that that was so.

The Coroner leaned forward and remarked, also practically inaudibly and for the benefit of the reporter of the *Porthaven Gazette*, that there would be more evidence on that point later. Then came Commander Santon.

It was his evidence that had had the most careful preparation. There was not a single false statement, but the omissions were significant and one deft piece of manipulation was as near perjury as makes no difference. That was when he gave as the reason for Thora Chevalle's mad desire to get away from Bassetts the one that she had worked herself up into almost a nervous breakdown over imaginary grievances. There was never a mention of Wharton or Maddon, and then the Coroner, obviously a friend of Chevalle's, put in a beautifully timed leading question.

"Tell me, frankly, will you, Commander. Did the deceased give you the impression that she had grounds for jealousy?"

"Good heavens, no!" Santon said. "There was nothing like that at all."

"Well, there's always likely to be gossip," the Coroner said, and once more as if to the reporter, "and that's why it should be scotched at the outset. But go on with your evidence."

By the time he'd finished Santon had related everything, even the visit Thora Chevalle had made the previous morning. But there was no long-drawn description of the position of himself under the car and timings. What was emphasised was that no sooner was Chevalle inside the gate than the shot was heard. Santon concluded, his voice almost inaudible from obvious distress, that when Major Chevalle had entered the summer-house it had been in time to see his wife die. Then he stepped down, and it was plain enough that he had the sympathy of the Court in the trying predicament in which he found himself.

There was a little flutter as Chevalle took the stand. In a clear dispassionate voice he confirmed Santon's evidence. The Coroner began putting questions.

"This is going to be very painful for you, but I must ask you to make every possible piece of information available to this Court. The question of your wife's unhappiness, for instance. Can you tell us to what it was really due?"

Chevalle's eyes narrowed for a moment, and he hesitated. Maybe the Coroner had made a variation in the wording of the question.

"I don't think I can," he said. "It was just that we'd come to differ on everything. We were temperamentally different. I was much older, for one thing, and occupied with my work. She liked excitement, perhaps, and things that I didn't care for. Or had no time for."

"I understand. And on what precise terms were you?"

"Oh, no terms at all," Chevalle told him. "Speaking terms perhaps, and no more. Of recent weeks not that."

"You quarrelled?"

"Never. The situation had got beyond quarrels."

"Exactly! And the house? Your wife still looked after that?"

"No. Her cousin, Miss Carter, had looked after it for some months—with a helper who came in most afternoons. My wife didn't like housework."

"That was a grievance with her, that someone else should be running the house?"

"Why, no!" Chevalle said, and looked surprised. "She was only too pleased. If you'd like evidence—"

"No, no," the Coroner cut in hastily, and then gave a look at the jury. "The jury can ask questions if it so pleases. But one last question myself. Would you regard your wife as highly strung?"

"Yes," Chevalle said, and very quietly. "Temperamental and highly strung."

And so to the brief summing-up. A philosophical and kindly discourse I thought it; apt as a summary and comprehensive. I liked the bit about the queer unaccountable turns that married life will take and the dictum that though marriage is a legal institution, no human law can force compatibility on the constitutionally incompatible.

And so to the verdict, and the only one possible—suicide in a moment of temporary insanity. There was the not-unexpected sympathy with Major Chevalle and the relatives of the deceased. I'd forgotten them and was guessing that the elderly man in the second row was probably the dead woman's father. When later I saw him shake hands with Chevalle I knew it. It was a very happy touch, I thought. It showed that Carter knew perfectly well the faults and limitations of his dead daughter, and that his sympathies were with Chevalle. It didn't show it as crudely as all that, but still it was a happy touch.

But I didn't linger on the scene. The very moment the proceedings were over I slipped out at the back and through the side door of the pub to the road. Then, as I was walking home, it struck me that I'd let my taste for irony get the better of my sense of judgment. It was true that there were certain things that I alone knew, and even more that I suspected, but had I been quite fair to Chevalle, or for that matter, to Wharton? Why wash the dirty linen in public for the delectation of the dirty-minded? Why shouldn't Chevalle's good name be guarded? And Mary Carter's? Why drag in Maddon when the dead woman was little more than a suspect in embryo? And by being loyal to Chevalle, Wharton stood to lose more than he had gained, for he might have made a fine public show by telling even the little he suspected, and a sensation by the announcement that in the opinion of the police the dead woman had owned the gun that killed Maddon.

What I was feeling, in fact, was a revulsion. I had eaten too much of the case, and my mental stomach was announcing the fact, with that cheap irony of mine the principal symptom. So I was pleased at the thought that for a day and more I should be without Wharton, and if I once more let the case become an obsession, then the responsibility would be entirely my own. And I actually lived up to the good intentions, perhaps because there was nothing at the moment which I had a hope of finding out. Then, to show the queer way things work out, something presented itself on a gold platter.

It was after tea on the Sunday, and Helen had tragically reminded me that Thora Chevalle, Mary and Clarice should have been with us.

"Extraordinary how quiet Cleavesham has been ever since I've been here," she said, "and then, as soon as you get here, Ludo, we have two people getting killed."

"The imputation being what?" I asked flippantly.

"It isn't funny," she said. "It's just queer."

"It is," I said. "But surely you aren't as stagnant in Cleavesham as you're trying to make out?"

"It's quiet," she said. "That's why I like it. A few bombs and not half what anybody expected."

In a minute I was asking her what she was smiling at. "Just thinking of something," she said. "We did have one excitement. Our Wings for Victory Week."

"I gathered that was a bit of a riot," I said. "What were the high spots?"

"There were several," she said, still smiling to herself. "The best was a monster treasure hunt, on Mr. Groom's meadow. The one on the left as you come to the corner."

"Well, tell me about it," I said. "Whose idea was it?"

"Mine, really," she said. "Commander Santon was most enthusiastic. He improved on the idea enormously."

I can't remember her description, but it was quite funny. Maybe if I'd known all the locals I'd have found it as funny as she did. The prizes—the treasure, if you like—were hidden at various places all over the meadow, and Santon had rigged up concealed speakers which he controlled from a central tent on a vantage spot. It was rather like the game we played when young, saying hot and cold when the seeker got near to or far from the missing object. The really funny thing was when a certain old lady—a busybody and notorious gossip—had a concealed speaker suddenly bark at her that she was hot.

"My dear, she simply leapt!" Helen said. "I never saw anything so funny. I honestly believe she thought it was the devil himself in the ditch. I laughed till I cried."

She had a good laugh even then. I thought it rather funny too.

"What was the old lady's name?" I said.

"Mrs. Beaney," she said. "The one who used to work for Mr. Maddon."

"But she's not old."

"My dear, she's over sixty if she's a day," Helen told me.

"Well, the story's funnier now," I said. "I hope she didn't get a prize?"

Helen said, regretfully, that she got third prize. I said that wasn't so funny.

The Sunday wore quietly on and nothing looked like happening. Then, just after the nine o'clock news, Wharton rang from Town.

"Thought I'd let you know I'll be down first thing in the morning," he said. "The nine-thirty at Porthaven."

"What's happened to the car?" I asked.

"Don't think I'll need it any more," he said. "The idea here is that everything can stand as it is."

"And the armoury?"

"Everything dead right," he said. "The Pond one, the Five Oaks bullet, and the other O.K. Tell you more tomorrow."

"I'll meet you at the station," I said. "I'll have news for you too."

"What news?"

"Too dangerous to tell now," I said.

"You can lower your voice, can't you?"

"It'd still be too dangerous," I told him.

"But, dammit, can't you give me an idea?"

"Very well then," I said. "It's about a princess with a beautiful head of golden hair. A bed-time story, but only for grownups. A wicked fairy killed her and I know how and why."

CHAPTER XIV
HAPPY MEETING

As soon as I was downstairs that Monday morning I rang Chevalle at Bassetts. If he was going to Porthaven, I asked, would he give me a lift. He said he usually left at nine, but if that was too early for me he could wait.

"No, no," I said. "Wharton's coming down by the nine-thirty and I'm meeting him, that's all. Nine o'clock will suit me fine."

I also told him he wasn't to pick me up at Ringlands, as a post-breakfast walk would do me good. As things turned out, I was just coming up to Bassetts when he brought the car out at the front gate.

He was looking a different man from when I had last seen him. More his old self, and confident, and noticeably cheerful, and he was quite amusing about the fight he was still having with the bus company to get them to run a handier morning service. But we were getting to Porthaven too quickly for my liking.

"Would you mind pulling up for a minute or two?" I said. "There's a rather important matter I'd like to talk over with you."

At once his manner had a subtle change. The real man was no longer there but was covered, as it were, by a film of wariness.

"I told you Wharton was coming back," I began. "He's been making certain inquiries and he's got the answers."

"Answers to what?"

"I may be hurting your feelings," I said, "but he's got the answer to the question of your wife's suicide."

"Question?" He gave me a look. "Surely there wasn't any question."

"The verdict of a coroner's court is one thing and hard fact is another," I said. "Especially when the fact emerges well after the verdict. To be frank," I said, "your wife didn't commit suicide."

His eyes narrowed, which was a trick of his when in thought.

"It may be painful for you to have things reopened," I went on.

"It's Wharton's business, not mine," he said. "Even if it weren't, duty's duty."

"Well, what I wanted to ask was, could you be at Santon's place at two-thirty this afternoon. Wharton wants to go into things on the spot."

"If I'm definitely wanted—yes."

"Then you can do Wharton another favour," I said. "You fix the meeting with Santon. Make any excuse you like, but don t mention Wharton. We'll turn up on foot by the back path."

"I'll arrange it at once," he said, and then shifted slightly in his seat. "Any advance information available?"

"There is," I said, "but Wharton thinks it will rather spoil things if you know it beforehand. I don't quite know what's going to happen myself."

"Right," he said, and it seemed to me with relief. "And that's all?"

"That's the lot," I said. "Unless you ring the Wheatsheaf to the contrary we'll see you on Santon's tennis court at half-past two."

He dropped me at the foot of High Street, which I said was near enough. Wharton's train was due in five minutes, and I thought I'd try Helen's short cut the reverse way. It was the most amazing coincidence that I did. It was like finding the gun in the pond. What happened, happened so quickly that it was plumb ridiculous that it should have happened at all.

It was like this. I was making my way along that narrow walk between the gardens of little semi-detached villas. After each pair was a side path, as a kind of tradesmen's entrance, and I squinted through each one on the right towards the railway in case I should catch sight of Wharton's train. When the gardens began to close in towards the walk, there was only a narrow strip between me and the backs of the villas. Then by chance my eye ran idly up to the bedroom windows, and at one of them I saw a face. It was turned sideways to me as if its owner was reading a book. I took a second quick look, for something in that profile had seemed familiar. Another second and I was making for the passage-way by the side of that house, for the owner of that face was no other than my old friend Pyramid Porle.

A dozen schemes flashed through my mind before I knew they were all unnecessary. Porle was the last man to run away. Then I had to smile to myself: not only at the thought of Pyramid Porle, but the astuteness that had thrown the police clean off the scent. All he had done when he had left Cleavesham was to deposit his luggage at the entrance to the short cut, carry his bags to the pre-arranged snuggery, and then return for the trunk. Unless it had been remarkably heavy he could have carried it that forty yards and up the side-path where I stood. That done he had taken a ticket at the booking office, and had then made an unobtrusive way back to the villa.

Just then I heard the sound of an incoming train, so I made a cautious way out to the walk and towards the station. The train was in when I reached the platform.

"What about a cup of coffee?" was the first thing Wharton said to me.

"Plenty of time for that," I said, and told him about Pyramid Porle. His eyes bulged, and then he was breathing out threatenings and slaughter.

"What's amusing you?" he asked me indignantly.

"Only that you don't know him," I said. "But why not walk in on him and have a nice little friendly chat?"

I got him to my way of thinking and then we began to reconnoitre. Again luck was ours. As we came near that villa a woman came out of the back door. She didn't see us, but as we turned back I saw her stoop by the door. We stood with our backs to the villa till she had passed us. A shopping basket was on her arm, and it looked as if she were heading for the lower town.

The next move was for George to go past the villa and cast a quick eye up at the window. He came back in a state of excitement. No face was there, he said, but he thought that so much to the good. So we went through the side gate and up to the back door. Under a brick where the woman had placed it was the key.

The door was quietly unlocked and we stepped into a passage covered with coco-nut matting. In front were the stairs, and they were carpeted. Up them we went, I in the lead and at the top came to a landing. There we stood hardly daring to breathe, till I had spotted the right door! I moved across and nodded back to George. The handle of the door turned and I stepped into the room, George at my heels.

Porle was seated with his back to me, and cleaning his telescope. Some slight sound must have attracted his attention for his look round was only casual. Then he was looking like a sceptic who at last sees a ghost.

"Morning, Mr. Porle," I said. "Sorry to break in on you like this, but I've brought a friend along to see you. Superintendent Wharton of Scotland Yard."

Wharton was staring as if he were some queer freak. Porle had lost all that bland poise of his, and was making fluttering movements with his hands. But only for a minute. There was that little bow from the waist.

"I'm honoured, gentlemen." His head went sideways. "Scotland Yard, you said?"

"Yes," I answered.

"A notable institution, sir," he told Wharton. "A notable institution. You will sit down, gentlemen?"

We sat. George was even more goggle-eyed. For my part I had no disposition to laugh. Porle was just as I had left him. The pontifical phrases, the bland courtesy and the self-appreciation were all there, and the self-assurance would soon be back too.

"You left Cleavesham in rather a hurry," I said, "so I wasn't able to return your book."

"You read it, I trust, with interest and profit?"

"With both," I said unblushingly. "But why did you leave so hurriedly? Was it anything to do with that notice you tacked on Maddon's back door?"

That got him in the wind, but only for a moment.

"The name, sir, is Major Travers?" he asked with that side-ways cock of the head as if he hadn't heard my question.

"Yes," I said.

He nodded once or twice, and came to a decision. "You would not be bored, gentlemen, if I proposed to tell you something of my history? It would be without prejudice?"

"Most certainly it would," I said. "Provided, of course that it's true." Then I was hastily apologising, for a look of pain had come to his face. "What I meant was 'complete.' To include your dealings with Maddon for instance."

"That, sir, is what I intended," he told me with a grave re-proof.

He gently cleared his throat, and again I dared not look at Wharton.

"A quiet spot here," he began, "and suited to my means. You perhaps saw the woman of the house."

"Yes," I said. "And I replaced the key. The back door of the house, of course, is unlocked."

"Of no consequence," he assured me. "The key is for the con-venience of a daily woman who arrives usually at eleven."

"Good," I said. "That means we can have a quiet, friendly chat. But you were saying?"

"I was about to tell you something of my history," he remind-ed me, and was settling himself in his chair. I wish you could have seen the man as he told it. Without his overpowering pres-ence it may read stiltedly, and even to me it sounded like some inset story from *Gil Blas* or *Hadji Baba*.

"My father was a wholesale jeweller, in Clerkenwell, and a man of very wide talents," he began. "We lived at Highbury, a suburb, sir, which you may know. I was the only child of his marriage, and as a young man I was somewhat of a weakling, and as my father was not without means, there was no necessity for me to work for a living. It was just before his untimely death that I began to take an interest in certain studies of which you are aware"—his hand had waved round at the table and its books and magazines—"and thanks to them, and the exercise of faith, I began to improve in health. In fact, sir, I may say that I never looked back."

Some reply seemed requested so I said I was glad to hear it.

"But we wander from the point," he said. "My father died and our affairs were left in the hands of a solicitor. A scoundrel, sir! A thief and a scoundrel!"

As he glared at me he looked the very spit of Micawber denouncing Uriah Heep.

"That man, sir, embezzled the moneys of his too-trusting clients—myself and my mother among them. The widow, sir, and the fatherless. But he was caught, sir. Yes, he was caught, and he was clapped into jail. Four years was the sentence and it should have been more. But the shock had killed my unhappy mother, and instead of being a comparatively wealthy man I was left with only a pittance. It is true that a little more was realised by the sale of the house and furniture, but in comparison, sir, I was a poor man. That was why I accepted the offer of Martha, an old servant of our family, to come here."

"One minute, sir," broke in Wharton, and that "sir" was highly illuminating. "Would you mind telling me the name of that solicitor?"

Porle gave him a shrewd look. "Entirely without prejudice?"

"God dammit, yes!" exploded Wharton.

A quick reproof and Porle was nodding. "The name of the man, sir, was Mortheimer. Mortheimer, of Branch, Mortheimer and Branch."

"My God, I knew it!" said Wharton. "Henry Mortheimer!"

"You were acquainted with him perhaps?" asked Porle, with that crafty little sideways turn of the head.

"I knew him well enough," said Wharton grimly. "I helped to get him his four years."

Porle's chubby face lighted. "Then we are kindred spirits, sir. Kindly permit me to shake you by the hand."

For the first time I had a look at Wharton. On his face were various emotions. A sort of amiable inanity as he took the hand, and in the grin a definite triumph at having at long-last solved Maddon's identity. There was also a kind of impish look as he caught my eye.

"But to resume my story," went on Porle, and now he was speaking to Wharton. "A few weeks ago, sir, I was walking idly in the High Street here when I saw this very Mortheimer. He had grown a beard but I recognised him, and I took immediate steps, sir, to ensure that he did not recognise me. I was with Martha at the time and I induced her to follow him to the bus. Later that day I ascertained from the conductor who the man was and where he lived. Then I made my plans."

Once more he leaned forward. "Everything is still without prejudice?"

"Most certainly," Wharton told him.

Porle let out a breath of relief.

"I assure you, sir, that I am grateful. But I was mentioning my plans. I went to Cleavesham and arranged rooms for myself at that cottage known as Lane End. Then I began what might be called a systematic plan of campaign."

"In other words you blackmailed him."

"My dear sir!" He looked incredibly shocked. Then his eye seemed to flicker and I could almost have sworn he winked. "The man was a scoundrel, sir, and a thief. If he had money, then I was entitled to some return of what he had stolen from me."

"Most decidedly," said Wharton heartily. "And what luck did you have?"

Porle shot him a look, then gave a complacent smirk.

"I induced him, sir, by certain methods of my own devising, to pay me two pounds per week, with a promise of a lump sum

164 | CHRISTOPHER BUSH

in the very near future. That promise, sir, he broke. I decided to apply what is known, I believe as the screw. Hence that notice which Major Travers possibly saw me affix."

"You saw him that night?"

"No, sir. He didn't appear." His face took on a due gravity. "The following morning I heard of his untimely end. There was nothing further to detain me in Cleavesham, and I returned here." He gave a little bow. "That, gentlemen, I think is all."

Wharton got to his feet. "And a very good all, too." Porle looked surprised. "You don't propose to ask me any questions?"

Wharton shook his head.

"And I shall not be troubled by the—er—police?"

"No," Wharton said. "You won't be troubled by anybody. This is a free country, Mr. Porle. Good day to you, sir, and good luck."

Porle grasped his hand, and then mine. "One question, sir. The man Mortheimer left money. There will be a possibility of my participating in the—er—estate?"

"Maybe," said Wharton. "In any case I wish you luck."

"Sir, I thank you," Porle said, as if he were conferring a knighthood at the least. "And permit me, gentlemen, to see you to the door."

"We'll find our own way out," Wharton assured him.

"The key, gentlemen," Porle called to us from the landing. "You will lock the door and replace it?"

Wharton called back that he certainly would. Then, as soon as we were in the passage-way again, he was grasping my arm. Probably the Dickensian atmosphere of that half-hour was at the background of his mind, for he was using an old tag of his that he had taken from Sam Weller.

"Well, if that don't beat cock-fighting!"

"He's a great lad," I said. "And you ought to be pleased."

"Yes," he said, and as if the discovery was due to his own perspicacity. "I knew I'd find out who that Maddon was. Not half-past ten yet," he added, glancing at his watch. "What about that coffee?"

I said there was a nice little place at the end of the short cut.

"That reminds me," he said. "You owe me a drink. Didn't you bet you'd find out who Maddon was inside a week?"

"All right, George, I'll pay," I said. It was far too good a morning for argument.

Over the coffee he was still so cock-a-hoop about Maddon that he forgot to ask me about my discoveries. Perhaps I do him an injustice. My question may have put him off.

"Don't you think, George, that Maddon and Temple were in stir together, and that's how Maddon got to know him?"

"That's it for a fiver," he said, and pursed his lips. "Yes, that'd be it. They served their time from '30 to '34 or thereabouts."

"Extraordinary," I said. "Fancy you having got Maddon that four years."

"I knew him before then," he said. "You might not know it, but he was actually connected with Murphy."

"Murphy the poisoner?"

"Who else?" he said, as if there wasn't any other Murphy. In that context there shouldn't have been. Murphy ranks with Crippen and Armstrong and Brides-in-the-bath Smith, and the rest of the murder top-notchers whose lives are a source of income for the novelist-historians. In case you don't happen to have heard of him, I'll only say that he was a chemist in quite a good way of business in the West End. When he died—and that was in Broadmoor—he left well over ten thousand pounds. His particular ideas were far removed from sordid murder. All he did was experiment with certain poisons of his own mixing and devising, by trying them out on customers. That was only at the very end of his career, but he had deprived the country of at least six citizens before he was caught. "Caught" is hardly the word, for no man could have been more astounded than Murphy was when the police called on him.

"That was the devil of a long while ago, George?" I said. "Getting on for forty years," he said. "I knew all about it from what happened afterwards. Mortheimer was a youngish man then, and his firm handled Murphy's affairs. He was very decent at the time. The wife died from shock and he handled the trust for the two children. Either two or three. They were sent abroad to Australia or somewhere."

"Maddon," I said, and he asked what was biting me. "Nothing," I said. "I was just remembering him as I saw him the night before he was murdered. After what you and Porle have said, it's like seeing him again. The educated way he spoke. That touch of cynicism."

"Never mind him," he said. "He's dead and he doesn't affect anything. What about that business you were talking about last night."

"Oh, that," I said, and ordered more coffees while I collected my thoughts.

"There you are then," I said when I'd told him all I knew. "My God, yes!" he said. "But isn't it going to be a bit difficult to prove?"

"Not if *you* handle it," I said.

He swallowed it at that, even if he did protest. "But you've got everything at your fingers' ends."

"So will you have by half-past two," I said. "I'll have lunch at the Wheatsheaf and we'll rehearse things there."

I watched him think that over and I knew he'd take the job on. I wouldn't have done it in any case. Fancy me holding the stage with George sitting there and announcing in everything but words how much better he'd have done the job himself.

"Well, we'll see," he said. "But if he brazens things out then we're sunk."

"Don't you believe it," I said. "I've got a rather effective entry or two I can make. Something that will take the wind clean out of his sails."

"Oh?" he said, and waited.

"But I'm not telling you," I said. "You've got to be just as much surprised as he is."

He grunted, then was asking what Chevalle had been like that morning.

"I think he hated the thought of reopening things," I said. "Once his wife's buried he hopes everybody will forget everything."

"And why not?"

"No reason at all," I said blandly, but I knew I'd touched him a bit on the raw, for that was what he had been hoping for himself. If not, why hadn't he come down by road?

"In any case, to-day should be the last day," I said. "This time to-morrow you ought to be back in Town."

There was a telephone in the restaurant, so I rang up Helen and said I would be out to lunch. It was Annie who took the call. I'd forgotten it was War Savings' day.

There was a handy bus and we took it. As we passed Bassetts I saw a man clipping the hedge in front of Little Foxes. I guessed it was Dewball, but when we neared I saw it was Santon.

"See you at the Wheatsheaf," I told George hurriedly, and pushed the bell.

"Hallo, Major," Santon said when I strolled up, and his tone lacked its old heartiness.

"Dewball about?" I said. "I don't know if he told you, but I happened to be passing on Saturday and I wondered if you had a *Porthaven Gazette*. Will you tell him from me that I've managed to get one?"

"I will," he said. "But it'll have to be when he gets back."

"Any time will do," I said. "Gone out, has he?"

"He was overdue for his annual holiday," he said, and was idly flicking at the hedge with the shears as he said it. "I thought this would be a good time, so I let him get away yesterday."

"I don't think I'd bother then," I said. "He'll have forgotten all about it by the time he's back. And I shall be gone too."

"You're going?" he asked politely.

"At any time now," I said. "I never intended a long stay."

He didn't say anything about another trip before I went. In fact he didn't seem to know what to say, so I brought the brief talk to an end by saying that I'd have to get along to lunch.

"Might as well go the back way," I said, "if you don't mind my using your path."

"Everybody uses it," he said. "I'm going that way, so I'll see you along."

He went with me as far as his boundary. As I told Wharton later, I didn't know if there was anything from which he wanted to steer me away or if his accompanying me was just politeness. But even when I had left him and was making my way along the path I had the uneasy feeling that he was behind me in the wood, watching me.

"A bit risky, wasn't it, talking to him at all?" George told me accusingly.

"Don't think so," I said. We were in the bar having a quick one, so I daren't talk much above a whisper. But I did tell him about Dewball's sudden holiday, and he raised his eyebrows at that.

"Doesn't want him questioned?"

"That's it," I said. "And I've a pretty good idea about what."

CHAPTER XV
EVERYTHING LOVELY

AT ABOUT TWO O'CLOCK Chevalle rang up. I was all of a flutter when I heard his voice.

"Thought I'd let you know everything's fixed," he said. "Would you like to synchronise watches so that we arrive roughly together?"

We did that and I told him to make sure he got Santon to the summer-house. Then I thought of something else.

"By the way, Chevalle, I ought to warn you that some pretty uncomfortable things have to be said this afternoon."

"Uncomfortable for whom?" he asked after a pause.

"For you," I said. "To be blunt, the possible relationships between Santon and your wife."

I heard him give a little grunt. And I had to wait a moment or two more before he spoke.

"That's all right," he said. "I don't think it's going to be news to me."

When I told George he was relieved about that, but when we set off I was for once the cooler man of the two. He was looking on the black side, and worrying about what would happen if Santon stood his ground. I felt never a tremor. Usually, when a climax is at hand my heart begins to race like a mad thing, but that afternoon it was beating so steadily that I might have been merely bored. Maybe it was because I was looking beyond that coming interview. Looking at my theory; my own theory, and knowing that nothing that Santon would do could change it from the fact it now was back to theory again. There, if only to some small extent, I was to be wrong.

Well, we came through the woods to the summer-house. I put my head inside the door and began: "Is anyone there?" Then I had to change it to an "Oh," for Chevalle and Santon were standing not far from me on the lawn.

"Here we are, then," Wharton began amiably. "Sorry to bother you, Commander, but there're one or two points I'd like to go over with you and Chevalle. Just clearing up an oddment or two about Mrs. Chevalle's death."

Santon had shot the three of us a look, and the look he gave Chevalle was vaguely hostile. Maybe he was guessing that Chevalle's rendezvous had been a trap.

"Let's sit in here," Wharton said. "Devilish hot out there in the sun."

He set out the four chairs, with himself facing Santon, and Chevalle and I on the flanks.

"What's it all about?" Santon asked with an attempt at jocularity. "Looks like a regular mothers' meeting."

"The fact of the matter is," Wharton said, and in the same amiable tone, "I've come here to ask you to make a statement."

"Statement? Statement about what?"

"About the way you killed Mrs. Chevalle."

"What!" He stared, but the smile when it came was feeble. "What is this? A joke?"

"Oh, no," Wharton said. "After all, if we know you killed her we're entitled to get you to tell us how."

"Never heard such damn nonsense in my life! You were at the inquest, weren't you?"

"Oh, yes," Wharton said. "Very interesting it was."

"Look here," Santon said. "This *is* a joke, isn't it. Own up."

Wharton heaved a sigh. "Well, if you won't talk I suppose I'd better. It'll amount to the same thing in the long run." He leaned forward. "But you won't mind admitting that you recently spent a few days with Mrs. Chevalle in Town?"

"Who? I?" His face flushed slightly. "Who told you that goddam lie?"

"Ah, well," said Wharton regretfully. "But what I'm not going to do just yet is tell you how I know. You'll claim, of course, that you were at Southbridge."

"I damn well *was* at Southbridge."

"Then you don't mind telling me in what room Lord Kindersley addressed the delegates."

It was at me that Santon shot the look. He remembered all right.

"In the big concert room, of course. A damn great room with a platform at the far end."

"Exactly," said Wharton and was taking out the two clippings. "All you know about that conference is what you read in your *Telegraph*, and that didn't mention the scene and only gave a resume of the speech. But here's a fuller account from the *Porthaven Gazette*. That meeting wasn't held at the Civic Centre at all. It was held on the Town football ground and the speech was made from the main stand."

He put on his spectacles and was peering at Santon over their tops.

"You see," he said. "Much better for you to tell the truth."

"Even if I wasn't there," Santon told him, "and I don't admit even that—then it's my own business where I was."

His tone had been slightly bellicose. That was the wrong way to handle Wharton.

"Well, you'll soon have to admit it in a Court of Law," he told him grimly. "But let me suggest a few things to you. When you got back here, or before—it's immaterial at the moment—Mrs.

Chevalle told you that for some time she had been blackmailed by Maddon. He'd probably seen you together in Town some time. The next thing she had to tell you was that I was going to arrest her for killing Maddon, unless she could prove an alibi. She was desperate and she threatened to own up she'd been with you."

"Very interesting," Santon said dryly.

"But that wouldn't have suited your book," Wharton told him. "Your wife would have divorced you, and it's she who has the money. And you didn't want to marry the ex-Mrs. Chevalle. All right for a nice week-end, but marriage—Lord bless you, no! But you strung her along. Everything would be all right, you said. You and she would go away. She was to pack her bags and be round here at ten o'clock, shall we say. You'd take her back in the car to the empty house, collect the luggage and there we are. And she swallowed it, hook, line and sinker."

"But—" He broke off with a shrug of the shoulders.

"Never mind. Say what you've got to say."

"All you had to do was set the stage," Wharton said. "You fixed an appointment with Major Travers so as to claim a reason for getting out your car. When she was here you rang Chevalle and laid stress on the fact that the lady had a gun and was threatening to shoot herself. You'd got rid of Dewball, and I think you told the lady that a little something had gone wrong with the car and you'd sent him to the local garage for a spare part. At any rate you and she adjourned to this summer-house."

He gave another peer over his spectacle-tops and went on. "I don't claim absolute truth for every detail, but I think you asked the lady to bring her gun with her—the one you'd given her as a present. Maybe she'd told you at some time or other she might be pestered by her husband. But she'd got rid of that gun. Still, that didn't worry you. You had a pair. Picked them up on your Mediterranean travels probably. Dewball must have seen them in his time. I expect that's why you sent him off on a holiday—so that he couldn't be questioned."

Wharton let out a breath.

"And so to the murder. You two were sitting here, she waiting impatiently for Dewball and the spare part, and you waiting for Chevalle. You had your eye on this window and as soon as you saw him you said, 'Oh my God! There's your husband!'

"She was scared stiff and that was what you wanted. You told her to stay put, and out you went by this back door. From just out there you called to Chevalle. 'That you Chevalle?' Then you said you'd be with him in a minute, and back you nipped in here. The bend in the path had hidden you, even if he'd been looking this way. The lady was still scared. You talked like lightning. 'Here's a gun. If he threatens you, pretend to shoot yourself. Like this. Don't worry. It isn't loaded.' She was scared, mind you, and everything took place within a few seconds. You showed her how to hold the gun to her head—guided the limp hand, if you like—and pressed her finger on the trigger. Then out you nipped. 'My God, Chevalle, what's that?' Then you bolted through the shrubbery towards the house and you managed to get back here at about the same time as Chevalle got here himself."

"Finished?" Santon asked ironically.

"For the moment, yes."

"What a lot of damn nonsense," Santon said, and his lip drooped. "I call out from just outside this door? Why, Chevalle knows perfectly well that I was in the garage. He saw me."

"No he didn't," Wharton said. "What he saw was a dummy of some sort you'd rigged up under the running board. The dummy you chucked in the garage pit when he'd gone in the house, and the one you burnt in that bonfire you started as soon as you were sure we'd all gone."

"Guy Fawkes' stuff, eh?" The lip drooped again. "And I suppose I wasn't *talking* from the garage!"

"You were talking from just outside this door," Wharton said. "A schoolboy could have rigged the contraption up. Probably the same sort of apparatus you used in that treasure hunt at your Wings for Victory week. Just a speaker and amplifier and all worked through the wireless in the back of your car." His tone changed to the grim again. "I say you spoke from here, and your voice sounded to Chevalle as if it came from the garage. And so it did. To Mrs. Chevalle it came from here. To Chevalle it came from the garage, especially when he saw what he took to be you, lying under that running-board."

"Well, it's ingenious," Santon said, and as if mildly bored. "I'll certainly say that for it. What next?"

Wharton was losing. I felt it. He was like an actor who feels the imminence of the bird, and after he has tried every histrionic device in his mental repertoire. Maybe Santon felt it too.

"Well, what next?" he said again.

"Next?" said Wharton lamely. "The next thing is for you to make a statement."

"Perhaps I might say something," I said, and my eyes met Santon's. A new opponent, even if it was myself, didn't look so good.

"You remember, Wharton, how you called for me at Ringlands and I wasn't there that morning?"

"Yes," he said playing up.

"And remember how I came through the hedge and held up your car and you wondered where the devil I'd been?"

"Yes."

"And how I didn't tell you till afterwards, and how we agreed not to say a word, but to give Santon all the rope in the world and let him hang himself?"

"I remember," said Wharton.

"Now you, Santon," I said. "You remember how you were going to call for me at Ringlands one day and how I came here instead?"

"Yes," he said, but my God, he was puzzled!

"The morning Mrs. Chevalle died here I was to go out with you again. Maybe I had that last occasion at the back of my mind. Maybe that's what brought me here along that path just at the right time, instead of waiting for you at Ringlands. You see, I'd forgotten the time too. I thought it was half-past ten instead of eleven."

He was moistening his lips, and I knew I had him.

"You were here?"

"Haven't I told you so?" I said.

He sat without a movement for a long half-minute.

"Well, now I'll show you something," he suddenly said, and was getting to his feet. He did it so unconcernedly that we merely watched him, wondering what it was that we were to see. Then with an "Excuse me," he was opening the door.

I told you how natural it was. It was only the slamming of the door that made our mouths gape. Then Wharton got to his feet with a bellow.

"My God, he's gone!"

Through the door went Wharton and Chevalle at his heels. I made a poor third and when I was out on the path there was no sign of any of them. Wharton was shouting orders to Chevalle to head Santon off at the garage. He himself was making for the back door, through which I gathered Santon had gone. Then he was hollering to me to go to the front door.

From there I heard him calling to Chevalle. Chevalle called back that the garage was locked and he wasn't inside.

"Come here and cover this door then," Wharton told him.

Another couple of minutes and he was round with me.

"Inside the house, that's where he is," he said, and drew back and hurled his full weight at the front door. It budged never a bit and he was swearing as he rubbed his shoulder. Then something caught his eye and he was pulling a stake from the zinnia bed. A slash each way and the window was broken. In went his hand and up went the sash. Then he kicked out the broken glass and hoisted himself into the room.

I waited a good five minutes and there was never a sound. Then at last I heard his feet on the stairs and then the front door opened and he was motioning me inside.

"Upstairs!" he whispered. "I know the room. Let Chevalle in."

I made my way to the back door and whispered to Chevalle what Wharton had told me. As we came through the hall, Wharton was beckoning to us both.

"He's in the front room with the door locked. You watch from here Chevalle, in case he tries jumping from a window."

He motioned for me to follow him up the stairs, and at that very moment there was a thud, as if something had fallen from a wall. Wharton turned and his eyes met mine and for a second or two we stared at each other, listening.

Then he was bolting up the stairs and we two at his heels. On the wide landing he turned left.

"Both together," he told Chevalle, and drew himself back.

Best part of thirty stone of body weight hurled itself at that door, and it gave. A second crash and it stove in at the lock and Chevalle crashed into the room with it. Wharton kicked the hole clear and we went through.

Santon was there all right. The heavy Webley was so tight in his hand that it would have taken some prising away. He'd made a nasty mess of his skull.

Chevalle stood silently looking down at him. It was when his eyes rose that he saw the something on the bed—a grey against the scarlet of the bedspread. It was the back of a calendar, and pencil writing.

I killed Maddon. Mrs. Chevalle was being black-mailed. Then she threatened to give me away if I didn't go away with her. I killed her, just as you said.

A.F.S.

I read it over Chevalle's shoulder and I felt his body tremble as if he'd suddenly gone down with fever. Then he was handing it to Wharton, and turning away. When we came at last down the stairs we found him in the lounge.

Chevalle got up when we came in and he seemed his normal self again. Wharton was wiping his brow with that large hand-kerchief of his.

"My God, it's hot. What about finding some water while I get Chevalle to 'phone that damn doctor again."

I found a jug and glasses in the pantry and the water was cold in the tap. Wharton was at the 'phone with Chevalle when I got back, and when he came in again he drank two glasses straight off. Chevalle drank a glass too, and the sweat was in little beads on his forehead.

"Well, that's that," Wharton said. "What about making ourselves comfortable and taking the statements down here."

"It'll suit me," Chevalle said quietly.

"No point in wasting the tax-payers money," Wharton said. "Get everything cleared up and I can get back to Town to-night." I changed the cynical look on my face as he caught my eye. "Major Travers it doesn't matter about. He's got all the time in the world."

"You didn't tell me you were here and saw everything that happened that morning," Chevalle said to me.

"I wasn't," I told him.

"You weren't!" He stared. "You mean it was a bluff."

"That's it," I said.

"Suppose it hadn't come off?"

"Then I had another up my sleeve," I told him. "I'd have said your wife left behind a statement." I pulled out a wad of paper I had ready. "A statement backing up what Wharton said."

Wharton let out a guffaw. "And they call me a liar! My God, I'm not even a beginner."

He was still chuckling as he rifled Santon's desk for paper and he also found ink and a couple of pens.

"What about it?" he said. "Like me to make my statement first?"

"I think so," Chevalle said.

"Well, before I begin, just a question on general principles. Everything's over and settled. You agree?"

"I agree."

"Then we're all satisfied," Wharton said, "and thank God it's ended as well as it has."

He felt for his spectacle case, adjusted his antiquated spectacles and picked up a pen.

It was only a quarter to four when we began those statements. At half-past the doctor came, and Wharton was in such good humour that he cracked a joke about the frequency of visits, and taking a room for him at the Wheatsheaf. Then on we went again and it was after six o'clock when everything was signed and in order.

"What time's there a train?" Wharton asked.

"You might as well wait till the eight," Chevalle said. "That will give you time for a meal. I'll fetch you in my car at soon after half-past seven."

"Suits me down to the ground," said Wharton, and stretched his legs.

"If you like to wait a minute or two I'll run you down to the Wheatsheaf now," Chevalle said.

Wharton wouldn't hear of it. The walk back, he said, would do him good. And me too.

"Much obliged to you, Travers, for all you've done," Chevalle said, and held out his hand.

"I told you he was a warm proposition," chuckled Wharton.

"A bit too warm," I said, for I was sweating like a bull in the heat of that room. "See you again some time, Chevalle." I made George take the path through the woods, and as we neared Ringlands tried to get him to come in. He said he was too busy, and would I make his farewells to Helen. Maybe he'd just pop down again some time to see that everything was cleared up. Then, of course, he had to start pulling my leg.

"Can't forget that chap Porle," he said. "Extraordinary cove. Which reminds me. Don't forget you owe me a drink."

"Do I?" I said.

"Any time will do," he said. "I'm bound to be seeing you in Town." Then he was giving me a look. "I don't know that you haven't earned a drink yourself. You covered a lot of ground in this case."

"Thanks a lot, George," I told him ironically.

"Not that you didn't make a few bloomers," he was going on.

"To err is human," I said. "But bloomers such as what?"

"Well," he said, and pursed his lips while he hastily thought. "Take that photograph and that Orlando business. The damn photograph hadn't anything to do with the case."

"And the next?" I said.

"Oh, heaps," he said, and then was giving me a nudge. "But you did pretty well. Tell you what. Here's a little tip I'll present you with. You can pass it on to Chevalle."

"Thanks very much," I said.

"That's all right," he told me generously. "It's about Temple. I didn't tell you, but he was suspected of doing a little house-breaking. A charge wasn't brought because he was had well enough on the other. Now he's a bloke who had the entry to all the big houses here-—including the very five that were burgled. See the point?"

"I do, George," I said, "and thanks very much. Now you can do something for me."

"What's that?" he said, on his guard at once.

"I like collecting souvenirs of crimes," I said. "I even like souvenirs that reminds me of my bloomers, so why not give me that photograph?"

"Yes, and twenty like it," he said. "It's at the Wheatsheaf. What'll I do—drop it in at Ringlands on my way past?"

"I don't trust your memory," I said. "I'll fetch it myself."

"What, now?"

"Why not?" I said. "I might as well have as much of your company as I can. Besides, I've got a throat on me like the Libyan Desert."

"Not a bad idea," he said. "That'll give you the chance to stand me that drink."

CHAPTER XVI
THE OTHER ANSWER

TWO LETTERS CAME for me the following morning. One was a purely business one which gave me an excuse to make my announcement to Helen, and the other was from my wife. In a month's time she could have a clear eight days' leave. She also said she had heard from Wharton who'd told her how fit I'd begun to look. Just like Wharton that. Irritating as blazes one minute, and then going out of his way to do a kindly turn.

It was those two letters that finally made me make up my mind. When Helen heard I was going back to Town immediately after the next day's inquest, she was very surprised. I gave her various reasons, including the flippant one that as there'd been three deaths since my arrival, I was proposing to decamp before the village was decimated. But I did induce her to promise to come to Town and spend a long week-end with Bernice and myself.

It had been agreed that I should give more or less formal evidence at the inquest on Santon, to save Wharton coming down at seven that evening I rang Chevalle at Bassetts and said I wasn't too sure about a point or two, and would he do me the favour of slipping along to Ringlands after dinner. It seemed to me essential that I should see him, and that was the brightest excuse I could make.

"My legs are much older than your car," I added as an effort at humour.

"Glad to come," he said. "Eight o'clock suit you?"

I said it would suit me fine. Then I told Helen, and added that we'd be talking about the inquest, which was a hint that we wouldn't wish to be disturbed. A few minutes before eight I was in her little summer-house, listening for the sound of Chevalle's car, and wondering for the hundredth time how to induce him to bring the ultimate conversation to the one vital point.

"Sorry to be such a nuisance," I said, as I opened the gate for him.

"A pleasure, my dear fellow," he said, and indeed he seemed genuinely pleased to be seeing me. Or was it relief that at last everything looked like being really over?

Well, I asked a plausible question or two and received due instruction and advice. Then I told him I was going to Town immediately after the inquest, and I shouldn't have time for a word once it was over. The one-fifteen bus was what I had in mind.

"But I thought you were staying much longer!" he said, apparently enormously surprised.

"I don't know," I said off-handedly. "Just a change of plans. I'm likely to have a job of work on my hands for another thing. A rather trying job too."

"Didn't know you had to work," he said.

"Just discipline," I said airily. "I take doses at regular periods. Spiritual Epsom salts."

He pulled out his pipe and began stoking it. I sat still, eyes across the garden, waiting for him to give me that opening.

"You're a queer fellow, Travers," he suddenly said.

"Of course I am," I said.

"There you are," he said, and with a humorous exasperation.

"There I am what?"

"Damned if I know," he said.

I smiled. "Two things you can't do to me, Chevalle. You can't pull my leg, for that was pulled out straight years ago. And you can't give me inside information about myself. I know the cantankerous kind of cuss I am."

"But you're not—exactly," he said. Then he was shrugging his shoulders. "Ah, what the hell!"

"Do carry on," I told him amusedly. "There's nothing so salutary as home truths. What's your own particular grouse about me?"

"It isn't a grouse. It's just that you're so damnably un-get-at-able."

"Sphinx-like?" I said. "Or just damn superior?"

"No, not quite that. It's just that—well, you sometimes look as if you didn't give a damn what everybody else thinks. You have a sort of cynical look as much as to say that if you cared to open your mouth you could put us all wise."

"Fine!" I had to laugh. "That's what my wife sometimes tells me. But to be serious. Give me a particular instance of this deplorably bad-mannered conceit of mine."

"I didn't call it that," he said. "And I don't know that I *can* give you a particular instance. I do know that that was how you often struck me during the whole of this case."

"And why not?" I said, and realised that he had played clean into my hands. "It's true we're no longer a democracy, but as far as the Government allows me, I'm entitled to have my own views. Even when everybody's against me." I smiled. "George Wharton once said about me that the fact that there are two sides to every question means for me that it's necessary to find a third. Take this case, for instance. Why shouldn't I have ideas of my own. Provided, of course, I don't thrust them on others."

"Contrary to undeniable facts? And everybody else's considered opinion?"

"Are you a crossword fan?" I asked him.

"Occasionally," he said. "Why?"

"Ever try one of those super ones which *The Times* used to have occasionally? Two frames in which to put your solutions, but only one set of clues? In other words, each clue has two totally different answers."

"Too hot for me," he said.

"Well, you mentioned this case," I said. "There's a perfectly good and accepted answer to it. It's solved. But that's no reason why a cross-word brain like mine shouldn't have tried another solution."

"And have you?"

"I have," I said airily. "And I'm a damn sight more pleased with my own than with other people's."

He caught my eye for only a moment, and then looked away.

"Like to hear it?" I challenged him. "It won't take all that long. And it's entirely without prejudice."

"What do you mean by that?"

"Well," I said, "if I've found a new solution, then a new somebody has to be implicated. So what I mean—and I say it only too seriously—is that the solution's at present my private property, and it's without any immediate risk for the person implicated."

"Perhaps I *would* like to hear it," he said. "It ought to be interesting."

"It is," I said. "And how would you like it told? Hypothetically? Or as a fact?"

"Just as you wish," he said.

"Then we'll have it told as if it were fact," I said. "Mind if I consult a note or two I've made? And then we'll be off."

"Two solutions," I began, "and to two murders. One solution we have already, and it may be the only one that's ever made public. Maddon murdered, and your wife dead. Santon killed both. He admitted it and it's a cast-iron solution.

"Now for my own ideas, and they involve a discarding of that accepted solution. My solution is that Santon really killed neither. *It was you who killed both.*"

His eyes narrowed and his whole body was suddenly rigid. Then at last he forced a laugh.

"I'm to take this seriously?"

"But certainly!"

"Then pardon one little objection. What about Santon's confession?"

"Pure poppycock," I said. "Heroics, my dear fellow. What the hell did Santon care? He was taking a header into eternity, and he wanted to do it like a little gentleman. He cleared your wife's name of Maddon's murder and made himself out the teeniest bit of a martyr."

"But why should he take the header if he wasn't guilty!"

"Because he shot your wife."

"But you said *I* shot her!"

"Oh, no," I said. "What I said was that you killed her."

"It's beyond me," he said, and threw up his hands.

"Then let me get on with my story," I said. "Maybe I can make it a bit more clear. And I'll begin with your wife.

"With regard to her, you were in a dilemma. If you gave her reasons for divorce, then you were in a jam, for public scandal might force you to resign. And she wouldn't give you good reasons, for that would have given you the custody of the child. You could have got over the difficulty by having her watched, but you couldn't bring yourself to do that. You told me a home truth or two about myself, and now here's one about you. You're stiff-necked with pride about your job and your personal honour. You wouldn't descend to anything so low as having a man on your wife's tail when she took her so-called holidays, even if you suspected her and Santon—which you admitted you did. Then at last you found a solution which satisfied those damn silly scruples. You strained at a gnat, but in the end you were prepared to swallow a camel.

"This was your brain-wave. You had to kill Maddon, and we'll go into that more fully later. Then you saw you could kill two birds with the one shot. You knew your wife would be away on a holiday. Why not kill Maddon then, and implicate her? Put her in a position where she'd have to prove an alibi or be arrested. You knew she'd weaken and prove the alibi. In short, she'd make a confession of adultery. You could divorce her, pose as the injured party, and have the custody of the child. Then you could marry Mary. All that without in the least imperilling your public position.

"And that's what you did—at least according to my solution. And now another home truth. You may be a damn good Chief Constable, but you're the hell of a bad conspirator. Look at the mistakes you made. You went out that morning on your bicycle. You'd begun that habit earlier, and after you'd planned to kill Maddon. Don't tell me you cycle up these blasted precipices in Sussex just to save Government petrol! And, of course, a bicycle has no number plate. Even Galley, by the way, seemed surprised your going to Bycliffe on your bicycle.

"But about that morning. You came to Five Oaks, ostensibly from Bycliffe. But you'd never been there. There wasn't a drop of rain near Bycliffe that morning. You'd been in the wood all the time—except when you slipped out along the lane to the farm to 'phone Porthaven—and watching the house. I rather think you knew Temple came regularly at that day and time, and you knew he'd raise the hue and cry, and you could contrive to be on the spot. After he'd gone you did the 'phoning, and no wonder you were puzzled about Miss Smith.

"That was one slip. The next was putting scent on that chair and too much of it. Scent doesn't linger heavily like that and it doesn't communicate itself even to a chair on which a person has sat. Good enough to convince Galley, of course. You couldn't make it too strong for him. It didn't matter about me at first, and when you'd read Wharton's letter of introduction, it was too late. That is if you believed his adulations. You probably didn't.

"But the worst slip up was when you said there were *three* cigarette stubs with lipstick on them. You'd put them there and so you knew there were three. You didn't know I'd pocketed one. When you suspected that later, it was all to the good. You knew I was an amateur detective, after all, and that if I could meet your wife I'd identify that stub. And another slip in the same context. When you put the stubs in the ash-tray you forgot to put in a corresponding amount of ash.

"You were too pat at finding clues. You were on the hairs like a shot. You found the hair-pin, and you thought of the back way out and found the heel marks. Lecoq wasn't in it with you. You left an amateur like me simply staggered.

"But after reading Wharton's letter you found me a god-send. You knew your wife was coming home that evening, though you pretended she wasn't, so with a courtesy that was so overwhelming you asked me to come to supper. How exasperated you were when she came back! How artistically you were startled when I sniffed at the way she was scented! In fact, my dear Chevalle, and if I'd been the world's prize jackass, I was shown the very woman who'd murdered Maddon. Then, later that evening, you asked me a question about her cigarette. Just to make sure I hadn't missed the point. You knew, of course, she'd be in no real danger. Still, there we are, and if I hadn't entered the case at all, you'd have done precisely the same things with Galley, till even he couldn't miss the fact that it was your wife who had been in Maddon's room."

I was expecting him to cut in there, and he did.

"How do you reconcile that with what you said about my killing her?" Then he gave a little laugh. "I'm taking you seriously, you see."

"Reconcile it? Easily enough. You didn't know that you were going to drive your wife into a position where she'd be, not just desperate, but too desperate. Or where Santon would be too desperate, and have to kill her. But you killed her really. You laid a mine which you thought wouldn't go off. Santon wasn't to know that."

"Very ingenious," he said. "But carry on."

"But your biggest slip," I said, "was the way you handled the Maddon murder while it was in your hands. You took good care he should be buried before you called in the Yard. That was so that they wouldn't get his prints. Oh, yes," I said, as he started to speak, "I know you sent his prints to the Yard. Or rather, you didn't. I don't know whose you sent, but they weren't Maddon's."

"What do you mean?"

"This, and it's something of which you yourself apparently were aware. Maddon did four years for embezzlement. Therefore the Yard had his prints. You see," I said, "I happen to know who Maddon was. We'll call him Mortheimer if you like. Wharton knows too, but he doesn't see any connection between Mortheimer and you. I just tell you that to relieve any later anxiety."

"And what connection is there?"

"All in good time," I said. "Let's finish with the prints. Wharton didn't rumble that bit about the prints, when he found out who Maddon was. It was on Monday morning and we were rather rushed. But if you want further reassuring, I'll tell you this. If Wharton does ask himself why the Yard hadn't Maddon's prints—and if he does that then he'll know the answer—then my idea is that he'll do nothing. He wants this case left just as it is—as you do. Perhaps as I do too. He'll keep his mouth shut, and if only because his failure to grasp things earlier would be a reflection on his own competence."

"All this, of course, being pure assumption?"

"Exactly," I said. "A hypothetical solution, if it were fact. But let's get to Maddon.

"You knew your wife had a gun. You had a key to her room and you gave that away when you unlocked it for Wharton. You took that gun. You made an appointment with Maddon for some very convincing reason, for the early hour of five-thirty. Nobody would be about then even in the woods. Maybe you told him you and he were going somewhere. It's immaterial in any case. But you shot him, and you spread clues all over the place. You hunted the house for the material which he'd used for blackmailing purposes and probably you found it. One bit you didn't find, and I'll show you that later. Then you went home and had breakfast and then set out on your bicycle ostensibly for Bycliffe. Before your wife returned you put the gun back, and probably the very moment before breakfast. When Wharton had her scared, she threw the gun in the pond by the roadside just past your house. So much for the gun. And one thing I'll give you credit for. That outburst to me and Wharton about her not having killed Maddon was perfectly genuine. You knew your wife didn't kill Maddon. And another thing. Since you knew who Skilled Maddon, you had the shock of your life when you read Santon's confession. You shook like a man who's just gone down with fever."

"Well, that's mighty interesting," he said. "I wish to God I had your brains."

"You mean you'd use them to better purpose?"

"Maybe yes," he said. "But to go back to where you left off. I think I can throw a spanner into the works. Why should a man like Maddon be blackmailing *me*?"

Then I knew I had come to what might be the biggest bluff of my highly bogus career. Frankly I'd expected him to cave in long before, but he had the nerve or the devil, and he wasn't dying game. He wasn't looking like dying at all.

"Blackmail was a strong word, perhaps," I said, and to gain time while I brought up my mobile artillery. "He didn't milk you for much, at least so I think. He had at least two other customers beside yourself, and he just asked you all for a nice little regular subscription. He didn't over-do things. That was part of his ironical makeup.

"But about reasons," I said, and took that photograph from my inside pocket. It was in a special envelope, and I could show the actual picture without revealing that the bottom had been cut off. "Mortheimer happened to know that your real name was Murphy."

That hit him where it hurt. He was staggering, so to speak, even if he was still far from out.

"Afraid I don't follow you."

"Son of Murphy the celebrated poisoner," I said. "Mortheimer was responsible for sending you and your sister to Canada. It was only yesterday, by the way, that I spotted the resemblance between her and your daughter. Maybe the sister's dead. I don't know. In Canada your name was legally changed, but he was one of the few people who knew. Probably the only one in England. This photograph of you and your sister was sent to him later. In gratitude maybe, by the relatives or friends who adopted you. Sent from Windsor. Not Windsor, England, but Windsor, Ontario."

I took a quick look at him. Now he was on his way out, but, by God! he was not without a last flicker of fight.

"Most ingenious. Wharton has seen it?—that photograph?"

"He has," I said, "and he saw no possible connection between it and you. Set your mind at rest about that. The boy might have been anybody. Just a grim little fellow looking for the bird to pop out of the camera. I didn't see any resemblance to you either, even when the facts demanded it. Then I saw you on the tennis court that morning. Your face was set and hard. You were looking for a bird to pop out of the devil's camera and you wondered what bird it would be.

"Mind you," I said, when I'd waited a moment for him to speak. "I'm not blaming you for killing Maddon. Blackmailers are like black-beetles. The only thing to do is tread on them. Crush 'em flat out. But unhappily the Law doesn't see it that way. It has its own way of dealing with them, and the victim of blackmail knows that way to be dangerous as well as tedious. And Maddon was specially in need of being eliminated. You had come over with the Canadians in the last war, and you fought with them, and fought damn well. You still have traces of the accent, by the way. Then you stayed on here and made a career for yourself. That career would have been smashed if anybody had ever had an inkling you were the son of the notorious Murphy. There was even more to it than that. Murphy died insane, in Broadmoor. Yet you had taken the risk of marrying and having a child. How would the revelation that you were Murphy's son affect that child?"

I didn't look at him, but I could see his face and almost hear his thoughts. I shall always remember that moment and how incredibly lovely that evening was. The air was luminous and still, and full of the intangible beauty of scented dewy flowers.

Incredibly quiet too, with faint rustic sounds that broke no silence, but somehow made a strange accentuation.

"A hundred other things I could say," I went slowly on. "Why you sent Santon to telephone the doctor and Wharton, instead of doing it yourself. Probably you suspected he'd murdered her and you may even have wanted him out of the way so that you could look for the speaker he'd used and the wires connecting it with the car battery. But even if you did find all that out, you kept it to yourself. The last thing you wanted was more inquiry. Lots more I could tell you besides that. Little revelations here and inconsistencies there; looks on people's faces, and gestures. Things that go to make a background."

I was shaking my head as I got to my feet, for there seemed no more to say. He sat on for a moment or two, and he was game to the last.

"And suppose—purely suppose—that there's even the least bit of truth in anything you've said. What are you going to do about it?"

"Nothing—yet. I've got to think. After that I may still do nothing. But don't mistake me, Chevalle," I said, and forced him to meet my eyes. "I'm not posing as a little god on a tinsel Olympus. I'm not directing the Fates. I'm trying to reconcile myself and my conscience. Propitiate that conscience, if you like. If I do feel that I've simply got to make something of it public, then I promise you this. I'll let you know just how much, and at least forty-eight hours beforehand."

"Thanks," he said simply, and it didn't seem to occur to him that at last in that one word he'd given himself completely away.

He got to his feet and stood for a moment with eyes un-seeing across the garden.

"Well, I'd better be getting back home," he said and was smiling gravely. "I promised my small daughter I'd say good-night. A bit late now though. I expect she'll be asleep."

His hand moved towards me, and then he drew it back.

"I'll say good-bye to you too—if you feel like it."

"Why not?" I told him gravely. "It wouldn't be the first time I'd shaken hands with a murderer."

That was cruel and I could have bitten out my tongue for saying it. But he took it well.

"Are you all that sure?" he said.

"Sure," I said. "Dead sure. Dead plumb sure."

EPILOGUE

I HAD BEEN DICTATING from an easy chair, and when I had spoken that last phrase I relaxed. My long legs went out straight, my eyes closed and my head went snugly to the back of the chair.

Miss X., my stenographer, had done a fine job, I thought. Neat work, hitting that machine as fast as I could dictate, and still with time to suggest a word when I was at a loss! I'd had her at intervals for years, and quite a good critic she'd always been. Constructive too. A bit romantic, perhaps, but you can't have everything. I wondered just what she'd think of this particular book.

I opened my eyes to see her watching me. The blunt end of the pencil was tapping her teeth and the look was one of expectancy.

"Well?"

"Ready," she said.

"Ready for what?"

"Ready to go on."

My smile was definitely condescending. "There isn't any going on. The book's finished."

"Oh," she said blankly, and then flushed. Then as if I might have been joking—"You really mean it?"

"I most certainly mean it," I told her with a touch of the frigid. Then I got to my feet to show I meant it. "Any complaints?"

She shrugged her shoulders. "It's your book," she told me.

"Out with it," I said. "What's on your mind?"

"Well, I don't think you ought to leave things like that," she said, and quite definitely. "You ought to let the reader know that you're not proposing to say anything about Major Chevalle. Then he can marry Mary Carter. That's what most readers will want."

"Really?" My smile was even more condescending. "And if I decide to do just the opposite? To blow the gaff about Major Chevalle?"

"But you couldn't," she said. "Why, you told him in so many words that you could have killed a man like Maddon yourself!"

"You listen to me, young lady," I said. "This is a book, not real life."

"Well?"

"Well this. It's a weakness of yours to identify yourself with the characters in a book."

"But they're just not characters in a book. After all, you go to the country for a holiday and you meet people, you like them or dislike them, and you're interested. Typing this book has been like a holiday, in a way. I've got to know everybody. They are real people and I could find my way about that village in the dark."

"Thanks very much," I said, dryly. "But the real test of a book is this. Not a happy ending, but whether when you put a book down you say to yourself, or not: 'That was a damn fine book.' Later on, of course, you may realise all the hocus-pocus, the coincidences and the manipulation, but it'll be too late then. You'll still think of it as a damn good book. Or, of course, the other way round."

"Very well," she said, but still quite unconvinced. "But there *is* something else."

"Yes?"

"I don't think you do yourself justice. You're not superior and supercilious as you make yourself out. In the book, I mean."

"That's all you know," I said. "But let's keep to the book."

"I know!" she suddenly said. "I know what you can do!"

"Well?"

"Didn't Major Chevalle say he could join the Army again? Then why not say you're writing to him to advise him to do it! That would place the onus on something else."

"I don't quite get that part," I said.

"Well, it'd be a toss-up. A man like him would go where there was fighting—"

"Dear old Beau Geste!"

"It's nothing of the sort," she said. "But if he got killed, it would be some sort of expiation. If he didn't, it would be as if he had paid a debt."

"Pretty cute, that," I said. "I don't know that I won't think it over."

"And something else I think you should change."

"What is it this time?"

"Well, not change, but add an emphasis. To that bit about Wharton thinking things over and remembering Maddon's finger-prints. I think he'll be bound to find out."

"I'll think of that too," I said. "But Wharton's going to think of plenty of other things—if I know him. He'll wonder what all those clues of Mrs. Chevalle were doing at Five Oaks. He'll wonder how the devil Santon managed to get an interview with Maddon at the unearthly hour of half-past five in the morning."

"I hadn't thought of those."

"You needn't worry," I told her. "Wharton will keep his mouth shut. Lion don't eat lion."

She almost corrected that to "doesn't." Instead she asked if she might do the corrections and additions for me later.

"No, thanks," I said. "Very good of you, but I'll manage."

I scanned her bill, added a bit for thanks and good luck, wrote the cheque and saw her to the lift.

"You *will* put in that bit about Major Chevalle rejoining the Army?" were her last words.

"Leave it to me," I told her mysteriously.

When I was back in the room I saw that there was still half an hour before lunch. The wireless caught my eye and I switched it on, and lighted a cigarette while it warmed up. It was one of those Workers' Playtime shows and a man was giving imitations. I smiled to myself, thinking I'd like to hear one of old Pyramid Porle. But he was quite good. I thought at first it really was Raymond Gram Swing talking, and then the applause came and he began on Syd Walker.

Syd Walker's brand of humour just doesn't happen to be mine, so I turned back to switch off.

"Lumme! I do have some rare old how-d'you-do's, don't I, chums. And what would you do, chums? Send me a postcard—"

But I had switched off. And I had been thinking. The thinking was continued aloud and I believe I actually made a little protest to Syd Walker.

"I'm not sending you any ruddy postcard," I said. "As for what you'd do, you can do as you damn well please. And as for what I'm going to do, that's nobody s business but my own."

THE END

CPSIA information can be obtained
at www.ICGtesting.com
Printed in the USA
LVHW02s0108050718
582663LV00017B/439/P

9 781912 574216